Totally Bound Publishing books by Desiree Holt

I0680718

Galaxy

SUPERNOVA

DESIREE HOLT

Supernova
ISBN # 978-1-83943-991-9
©Copyright Desiree Holt 2021
Cover Art by Claire Siemaszkiewicz ©Copyright June 2021
Interior text design by Claire Siemaszkiewicz
Totally Bound Publishing

SUPERNOVA

Dedication

To all the SEALs, past and present, who fight so
valiantly for our country. To those who so
graciously let me pester them for information.
And especially to former SEAL sniper Jack Carr,
the embodiment of what the SEALs stand for.
You are my inspiration.

Chapter One

Fuck, it was hot.

John 'Rocket' Hardin thought that in the mountains it should at least be cooler, especially out of the sun in this little cave. But no, the heat invaded the space and made it into a warm, wet towel. He was sweaty and streaked with dirt that had blown against him as they'd climbed the rocky trails. He used the tail of his shirt to wipe as much off his face as he could, but only a shower was going to attack this mess.

He'd been fucking pissed off when his SEAL team had been told they were being sent to rescue a writer from the Taliban. Ten years in the service and he had to waste his time because some wacky writer thought it would be great to hang out with terrorists and interview them. And, oh, yeah, write books. *Stupid idiot.*

But they'd executed the extraction just as night had begun to fall, hoping to take advantage of the cover of darkness. But it hadn't been cloudy or overcast, damn it, the stars bright in the sky and the moon like a big spotlight. The team had done its best to stay concealed, but without help from nature, someone had discovered their captive was gone before the SEALs were fully away. Rocket had broken off with Mallory, radioed Command to let them know and taken off with her in the mountains so their enemies wouldn't find her. She hadn't complained, just followed him, despite what she'd been through already and the harshness of the landscape.

Getting them out of that terrorist camp hadn't been a picnic, for sure, but his team was experienced and it had almost gone off without a hitch. But then things had gotten very hairy. His stated job was to get Mallory to safety above all else. He hated splitting from the rest of his team, but he had his marching orders. Their job was containment so he and Mallory could get the fuck out of there. The orders had come straight from their commanding officer.

She was a trooper, he'd give her that, moving at his direction until they were far enough away from the camp and could find a place to hide. Using his satellite radio, he'd informed Command where they were and had been told to wait for extraction. Once the chopper arrived and landed on the plateau near their cave, they'd be out of there. And he'd probably never see her again.

Damn!

He glanced over at her and saw she was in almost the same condition he was. Her hair was wild, and she'd managed to push it behind her ears. But her skin looked like his, sweaty and streaked with dirt, not to mention the bruises on her wrists from the rope that had tied them.

He'd been shocked at his reaction when he'd first seen her in the hut where she was being held. In jeans and a T-shirt, hair wild and mussed, hands tied behind her back and smears of dirt on her cheeks and arms, she was still the sexiest woman he recalled ever laying eyes on.

But danger, it seemed, was an aphrodisiac, ramping up everything in his system well past the boiling point. This place was certainly as uninviting as any he'd ever been in, as far as sex was concerned. Despite that, he was so horny his dick hurt and his brain was filling with very un-SEAL-like thoughts. Mallory Kane was every man's wet dream, with her lush, toned body, her curly auburn hair and green eyes that blazed like emeralds.

Maybe it was the aftereffect of all that tension. Maybe it was a need to reaffirm life after escaping from a lethal situation. Or maybe he felt that she needed something to erase the after-effects of her captivity.

Whatever it was, he wanted her more than he wanted to breathe. And wasn't that just a damn shock for someone with his discipline? This was no place for sex to intrude. Life was not fucking fair. At all. But maybe after…

Business first, asshole.

Now they sat side by side, leaning against the wall of the cave, Mallory pulling herself together.

"Thank you," she told him when her breathing finally evened out.

Her voice was soft and rich, almost musical, even with the stress she was going through. He thought he could listen to it every day. The only problem was it went straight to his dick, which was doing its best to break the zipper of his camos.

"You're welcome." He slid a glance at her and grinned. "All in a day's work."

"Those must be some days, then."

"It's part of our motto," he said. "The only easy day was yesterday."

She snorted. "If this is an example, then you guys deserve a ton of awards for what you do. I didn't think I would leave there with my head still attached."

"You should try and get a little rest," he told her. "It will be a while until the helo gets here. I radioed that we were secure here."

"Rest?" Her laugh had a tinge of hysteria. "I almost rested permanently. I am just so grateful that you came to rescue me. I know those people were going to kill me. And soon."

Rocket studied her for a moment. "Can I ask you something?"

"Sure." She shrugged. "You saved my life, so I guess you can ask me anything."

"So, just out of curiosity, you had to have known how dangerous this whole thing was. I mean, you might as well have committed suicide. What made you set this up to begin with?"

When she didn't answer at once, he glanced over at her. She was frowning.

"Is that question a problem?" Rocket pushed.

"No. Not a problem. I just..." She swallowed. "I guess I was just focused on getting the story and writing the book. The last one I did was very successful and I have a great contract for this one."

"But that's not all of it, is it?" he asked.

"The main part."

He waited, but when she didn't say any more, his curiosity got the better of him.

"Is it so exciting that you're willing to risk your life for it?" When she didn't answer, he turned sightly and reached over to cup her chin. "Mallory?"

She sighed. "It's a long story that you wouldn't be interested in. But it's a way to prove myself and I really don't want to discuss it now. Okay? Please?"

"Sure." He could understand that, it that didn't kill his curiosity by a long shot.

"But..." She nibbled her lower lip. "I do want you to know I realize that I owe you my life."

She raised her eyes to his, a whirlpool of emotions swirling there. Okay. There was more than just following a story here and writing a book. But how did he find out what it was? She was the first woman to pierce the emotional shell he kept himself locked in and he wanted to know more about her. No, he wanted to know *all* about her.

"And this may be inappropriate, but I'm doing it anyway, because I really want to thank you for what you did." She knelt beside him, cradled his face in her hands and pressed her mouth to his.

Holy shit! His dick tried again to escape the pressure of his fly and he was sure his temperature went up. It shocked him, because he'd sure had enough sex in his life to be able to control his reactions when he needed to.

He was not prepared for this. He was supposed to be rescuing and protecting her, not thinking about sex. He thrust his fingers into her disheveled hair to hold her head in place, pressed his lips against hers and, when they parted slightly, thrust his tongue inside. She tasted like ten kinds of sin. When he licked the inner surfaces of her mouth, she brushed her tongue against his and before he realized what he was doing, he slipped his hands around to the front and cupped her breasts, gently squeezing them. He felt a tear in the fabric of one cup and anger gripped him. *Did the barbaric terrorists molest her?*

"It's okay," she whispered against his lips, as if she knew what he was thinking. "They didn't rape me. I swear. Just tried to demoralize me. Break my spirit. But it didn't work."

"Good. I can see that."

"But I need to get it all out of my mind. You can see that, right?"

Oh, yeah. And it might be against the rules, but he was all on board with this. "I just don't want you to think I expect—"

She moved until she was straddling him, her hot center pressing hard against his aching dick. "I don't just *want* this. I *need* this, to celebrate the fact I'm still alive."

At some point he'd get the details of what happened out of her, but not now. Right now, he could tell what she wanted was to wipe the worst of it out of her mind, and he was glad to help her. They had another hour at least before the helicopter coming to extract them would be here and he intended to make good use of every single minute. He had never done anything like this before. Business was always...all business. But there was such electricity between them. And they'd just come through a harrowing situation and needed reaffirmation of life.

"If you're sure, then, damn it, yes. I want this, too."

He took her mouth in another kiss, moving his hands to lightly pinch her nipples. She moaned, sliding her hands beneath his shirt and dragging her fingernails across his back. Heat filled his body. *Jesus!* Although he sure never had trouble responding to a woman, he didn't ever remember reacting this way before. Or this fast.

Rocket eased her T-shirt up so he could touch the smooth skin of her abdomen. Before he could even think about it, he had unfastened her bra and pushed it up so he could palm her bare breasts. Rubbing his thumbs over the taut nipples made them bead beneath his touch. The temptation was too much for him, so he pushed her top even higher, bent his head just enough and took one of those nipples into his mouth. When he sucked it hard, she moaned and leaned into him.

He didn't know if she'd object or smack him, but he yanked off the shirt and the bra and tossed them to the side. Then he went after her breasts with a vengeance, licking and sucking and squeezing. Mallory threw her head back, more little moans drifting from her mouth, the sound of them heating him up even more. He didn't even stop to think about what he was doing, or the trouble he could get into because of it. He knew he wanted this woman and that hunger was driving him forward.

Mallory arched up to him, her nails scraping his back, the sensation shooting straight to his cock and his balls. He was afraid he'd come just from sucking her breasts and miss the best part of the fun. He lifted his mouth and slid it to the hollow of her throat, where he swirled the tip of his tongue before dusting kisses along her neck.

Realizing at last that they were in a somewhat uncomfortable position, he lifted Mallory and moved her body so she was straddling him. She sat pressing against him so his cock was nestled right at the vee of her thighs, at the heat of her sex. He was sure she could feel how hard and thick his dick had become. He had to restrain himself from ripping her clothes off and plunging into her fast and quick. But that wasn't him. It was bad enough that he was probably breaking a million rules. He needed to treat her with respect. She was a strong woman who had survived an ordeal that would have destroyed a lot of people. He might never see her again — although he pushed that aside — but he wasn't going to go at her like a rutting pig, either, despite how he'd started out. And he wanted to make sure she knew that.

He lifted his head, cradled her face in his palms and looked directly into her eyes.

"Before we go any further, I don't want you to feel you have to do this," he told her. "You've been through an ordeal and I want to respect that. The fact that I want you, bad, shouldn't come into consideration."

She smiled and raked her fingers through her hair, and her disheveled look only made her appear sweeter and sexier.

"I don't do anything I don't want to," she told him, her breathing accelerated. "And I want this, too." Her lips curved in a very sexy smile. "What better way to celebrate the fact that I'm alive and not with my head rolling on the floor in some barbarian's camp? And who better to celebrate with than the man who rescued me?" She gave him a tiny smile. "I do want this, Rocket. And it's not an obligation for saving me. Okay?"

She grabbed his head and pressed her lips to his, sliding her tongue into his mouth.

Holy shit! Even her kisses were off the charts.

"Okay. Good to know." He cupped her chin. "We've got most of an hour before the helo gets here. I think I know a good way to pass the time, right?"

"Yes." She wriggled against his cock. "I want this. With you."

He locked his gaze with hers for a long moment, but he felt a little better about this now. "Good. I want this, too."

The time for talking was over. Rocket set Mallory aside so he could strip off his fatigues and lay them on the floor to give her as much protection from the dirt as possible. He thought about leaving his boxer briefs on, then figured, what for?

When he turned around, Mallory had kicked off her shoes and stripped off her jeans. She looked at him as she eased her bikini panties down her legs, giving a sexy wiggle. Was it possible for him to get any harder? If he did, his dick might just break off. But he couldn't tear his eyes away from her toned legs, her nicely rounded butt and the trimmed patch of auburn hair that covered her sex. His mouth watered as he imagined her sweet taste.

They were lying on the floor, naked bodies pressed together, the heat of her sex scorching him, when his brain kicked into gear.

Shit!

"Mallory?"

"I thought we were done talking." She wriggled beneath him.

"Yeah, well, I have to tell you this."

She frowned up at him. "A confession? Now?"

"Uh-huh. I, uh, don't have any condoms with me."

She burst out laughing. "I already figured that. You're on a mission, not a night out. No sweat. I'm on birth control."

"And I'm clean," he assured her. "I get tested regularly."

He didn't want to tell her it was a leftover from his days as an extreme horndog. He waited for her to say something, but instead she pulled his head down to hers and licked his lips. Her tongue was like a hot flame, scorching him clear to his balls. He held her head in place as he licked every inch of her mouth before trailing his tongue along her chin and down her neck. He pressed the tip of his tongue against the hollow of her throat, feeling the strong beat of her pulse, before moving down the smooth skin between her breasts. He loved the feel of them against his hands as he palmed them and rolled the nipples between thumb and forefinger.

Mallory moaned, a soft, sensuous sound as he trailed his mouth down over the slight curve of her stomach until he reached that gorgeous thatch of auburn hair. He slid his arms beneath her thighs so he could place them over his shoulders and used his thumbs to separate the plump lips of her sex. The pink bud of her clit peeped out at him and he couldn't resist stroking it with his tongue.

Mallory shivered and lifted her hips, raising herself closer to his mouth. Shit, she tasted like the sweetest sin, a flavor that he had a feeling he could become totally addicted to. He traced the delicate skin on either side of her clit with slow licks, stopping to nibble that little bud every few seconds. Each time he did, she made such a delicious sound that his hunger spiked even more, and she tried to lift herself to his mouth. The painful ache in his dick and his balls told him he was closer than he would have liked. He wanted to make sure she got her orgasm before he lost all control.

Nudging her thighs farther apart, he slid two fingers into her soaked channel, humming his satisfaction as her inner walls tightened around them. Her eyes were closed and her face flushed with pleasure, obvious even in the dim light of the cave. The little sounds she made aroused him even more. When he added a third finger, she planted her feet on either side of him and pushed herself into his touch.

"Don't stop," she begged.

He gave a low, throaty chuckle. "Don't worry. I have no intention of stopping."

As he increased the pressure, he curled his fingers slightly so that with each glide, he scraped lightly against her sweet spot. She pushed against his hand harder and harder, riding it, her little moans making him impossibly more aroused.

Her orgasm rolled through her, tightening her body, her inner walls fucking his fingers. He thrust again, pinched her clit…and she came, making those delicious tiny sounds as her liquid coated his hand.

At last the shivers subsided, the groans of pleasure became softer and her body relaxed slightly. But he was almost at the breaking point, drinking in the sight of Mallory lying naked and flushed on the floor. He was so aroused by this time that he had to grit his teeth and reach for control.

Then he was on his knees between her thighs, lifting her legs to rest on his shoulders so her hips were raised. She was open to him and he could not wait another minute. With his fingers wrapped around his throbbing dick, he positioned the head at the opening of her sex, drew in a breath and thrust forward. Her hot, wet flesh gripped him like a vise, the electricity of it shooting straight to his balls.

Oh, sweet Jesus!

He didn't remember the last time he'd fucked where his cock was bare. The sweet feel of her skin and her liquid sent him into overdrive. He closed his eyes for a moment to gather himself. Then, with his palms beneath the cheeks of her incredible ass, he began the familiar rhythm. It didn't matter that they were in this cave, his clothes spread out as a shield on the dirt floor, or that the light was so dim he couldn't see every inch of her the way he wanted to. All that mattered was that this delicious, hot woman was here and he was having the best sex of his life with her.

She grabbed his forearms, digging in her nails as she moved with him. They fell into a rhythm as if they'd been doing this forever, as if their bodies were used to it. Every one of his nerves was on fire. In, out, back, forth...he wanted to make it good for her, but his control was snapping.

"I can't last much longer," he gasped, "although I'm trying, babe. I really am."

"I'm almost—almost—*yes!*"

He felt the surge of her second orgasm and the clenching of her walls just as he exploded. Their bodies throbbed together, spasming, her tight sex pulsing around his shaft. On and on it went, beyond anything he expected, until finally the last tremor faded. He managed to lower her legs to the ground and fell forward, catching himself on his elbows. He studied her face, seeing the satisfied glow and the look in her eyes. His heart was still beating erratically and hers matched the rhythm.

For a long time, they just lay there like that, staring at each other as if exchanging silent conversation. Then he lowered his mouth to hers and indulged in a deep, deep kiss. And when the last of the tension finally left both their bodies, he eased his cock from her grasp and sat back on his heels. Fishing in the pocket of his pants, he pulled out the bandana he used to wipe sweat from his face and cleaned both of them.

"We'll both need a good shower after this." He chuckled, but then his face sobered. "Mallory, I—"

She reached up a hand to touch his lips with her fingers. "Don't. Do not say a word. Don't ruin it. Please."

"But I should—"

"No." She shook her head. "It was special and let's keep it that way."

Rocket had no idea where the conversation would have gone from there, but at that moment his radio squawked. "Rocketman here."

"Helo is four clicks away," came the voice from the command center. "Get ready. How copy?"

"Good copy." He clicked off and looked at Mallory. "Time to get ready."

They dressed in silence, brushing off as much dirt from their bodies and their clothes as they could. Before they left the cave, he pulled her into his arms for one last kiss, as tender as it was erotic.

"Just so you know," he told her when he lifted his mouth from hers, "I'm never going to forget this, Mallory."

"Me neither, Rocket." She brushed her lips against his. "By the way, where did your call sign come from?"

He grinned. "We'll save that for another time. Because I'm sure, no matter how long it takes, there will be one."

"I'll hold you to it."

"And now we'd better get out there so the helo can see us."

He checked the immediate area outside the cave before motioning her forward. Just as she stepped outside, Rocket heard the sound of the rotors and the helo lowered to the plateau just outside the cave. Rocket grabbed Mallory's hand and they ran for the door one of the men inside was just sliding open. Rocket boosted her inside before grabbing for the hands that hauled him up.

Then they were airborne.

As the chopper cut through the night, Rocket quietly studied Mallory. Was she glowing or was that his imagination? Could the others in the helo look at her — or him — and guess what had taken place? As he studied her, as casually as possible, she glanced over at him and their gazes locked. For one moment, heat flashed, then she looked away. He'd broken protocol with her, but he couldn't find it in himself to regret it. *What the hell, anyway.* He'd never see her again, and that actually saddened him.

When they finally reached the field camp and Mallory was helped down out of the helo, two men came running forward to hurry her off. Rocket watched, and at the last minute before being hustled into a car, she turned and waved.

Then she was gone, and for a long moment, Rocket wondered if the whole thing had even happened at all.

Chapter Two

Five years later

"This is Senator Alicia Kane. I believe you know my sister, Mallory. I'd like to book a trip to nowhere."

Rocket listened to the message that had been left on his phone, wondering if he was imagining it. He'd just turned the phone back on after they'd all left the plane and headed home. He never had it on when he was involved in a case because it distracted him from what he was doing. He had only brought it to life after settling in the passenger seat of his partner Blaze Hamilton's truck, and was looking forward to a lunch and a relaxing afternoon. Maybe catching the Tampa Bay Rays on television. But all that had flown right out of his head when he'd seen Mallory Kane's name.

At least until he got Alicia Kane's call.

And that sentence, the one people used when they wanted to meet Galaxy and hire them.

Mallory Kane. He hadn't heard that name in five years, but he couldn't say he hadn't thought about her.

In point of fact, she'd occupied his mind way too much. The image of her warm, naked body flashed in his brain again, and the remembered feel of her slick channel squeezing his cock surged through him. Somehow or other, he could never completely get her out of his brain. To the extent that he'd taken to reading her books, admiring her skill as a writer and researcher while damning that need to jump into dangerous situations.

She was the only woman he'd ever been with whose memory hadn't disappeared with time. Instead, it had grown stronger, sometimes haunting him when he was very tired, and other times driving him to the shower for icy water and his good right hand. Or it popped up in the kind of dreams he hadn't had since he was a horny teenager. He'd done his best to submerge those thoughts. Being a SEAL had been his life then and, as with his partners, there'd been no room for anything except the most casual connections. Long-term relationships were just not in his wheelhouse.

But now, although immersed in Galaxy, two of those partners had found the women they wanted to spend their lives with. Both Blaze and Viper were on schedule to be married in the next few months. And now Mallory might be in his life again, putting her image front and center in his brain. And his dick was shouting *Hooray!* But more than that, maybe if they connected through this, they could explore the thread of something that had been between them, even for such a short time.

Depending on what her crisis is, he reminded himself. And was he even open to that?

Blowing out a breath, he played the rest of the message. He hadn't heard about a situation in Santa Marita before now. For one thing, it wasn't a place that stood out on people's radar. He'd barely even heard of it. For another, Galaxy had been immersed in one high-value, high-tension case right after another, and was now coming up for air, looking for some breathing room.

And now, just hearing Mallory's name, every drop of testosterone in his body began surging through him.

Can it, asshole. This call has to mean she's in trouble, not that she's lying naked on a bed waiting for you. Damn it! You're a professional. Act like it.

The cryptic message left on his cell phone had two questions colliding in Rocket's brain. One, what kind of situation had Mallory Kane gotten herself into now, and two, how had Senator Alicia Kane gotten his number? Of course, a powerful senator like her could probably find out anything she wanted to. Still, it wasn't as if they advertised or were in some kind of directory.

It was late morning, they were all tired from the situation they'd just resolved and he was sure everyone just wanted lunch, a beer and to veg out for twenty-four hours. Of course, Blaze was going home to Peyton just as Viper was headed off to Hannah. They'd no doubt do a different kind of 'vegging out'. He could probably put this off until tomorrow, but he already knew he wouldn't. He hadn't seen Mallory Kane in five years, but just the sound of her name woke up his brain and his body.

He listened to the rest of the message again.

"Mallory is in trouble." Pause. "Again. And she needs your help. Please call me back at this number."

He sat holding the phone for a long moment, letting the message run around in his head.

"Client?"

Scott 'Blaze' Hamilton glanced over at him from behind the wheel of his truck. They were heading home from the hangar where their Gulfstream 550 was kept.

"Maybe. Senator Alicia Kane."

"Whoa. Big-time, right?"

Rocket nodded, although the senator wasn't the first big-name client in Galaxy's portfolio. Their specialized 'We are your last resort' agency, which also included Matt 'Viper' Roman and Vic 'Eagle' Bodine, had just finished a special job for their attorney and very good friend, Tom Hernandez. Rocket had definitely been looking forward to some down time, but he knew there was no way he could turn away if Mallory was in trouble. But what kind? It had to be pretty bad for the senator to find them and reach out to them. He was sure she knew nothing about what had gone on between him and Mallory, so Galaxy's reputation must be spreading.

"Well?" Scott glanced sideways at him. "You going to call her back?"

"We just came off a big case," he reminded his friend and partner. "And lord only knows what trouble this is."

"I think for a senator we can get it together. That's a nice connection to have. Just like the one Peyton has that helped us twice."

"True. Well, at the very least, I'll return her call and arrange to meet with her. Then we can decide."

"It isn't every day we get a call from a United States senator." He pulled off the Interstate and into the neighborhood where Rocket lived. "Good idea to call her back. Wait. Mallory Kane. Wasn't your SEAL Team involved in a mission to rescue her before you got out?" He glanced sideways at Rocket. "Is there something about Mallory we should know? Did something happen on your team's mission to rescue her five years ago that we should know about?"

Yes. We hid in a cave and fucked our brains out while we waited for extraction.

"No, it's fine." He cleared his throat. He sure wasn't about to spill what had happened to his partners. It was ancient history, anyway. He and Mallory had not had any contact in five years, so what was there to tell?

"Well?"

"Yes. I remember Mallory and yes, I'm going to call the senator back. Right now."

He found the number and hit Redial, putting the conversation on speakerphone. It only rang twice before it was answered.

"Who is calling?"

Not hello, just...who is this?

"This is John Hardin. You left a message for me."

"Yes, I did. Sorry, the number is blocked so I didn't know who was calling. This is my personal cell and not too many people have the number. Thank you for calling me back."

He let out a breath. "Okay. Sorry I couldn't call before, but we were in the middle of an op."

"Understood. I'm told you and your partners have an—unusual—company."

"Effective," he corrected. "And we take the jobs no one else can do."

"So I've heard."

He wanted to ask who she'd heard it from, but he wanted to get to the topic at hand more than that.

"Tell me what the deal is with Mallory?"

"I won't beat around the bush," the senator told him. "I worried about calling you because Mallory never gave indication if you two parted as friends or enemies after you rescued her. But I don't believe there is anyone else who can help her. I flew in from Washington early this morning. I figured if I was already in town, you couldn't refuse to see me, but when I didn't hear back from you right away I wondered if it was a useless trip. I am desperate here."

Rocket was beginning to get an idea of what was going on and his gut tightened. *What is it with a woman who chooses to put herself in danger?*

"I was away on business. We just got back a little while ago. Why don't you tell me what's up and we can go from there?"

"I'd rather meet with you in person." She paused. "I'm not playing games or stalling, but even if these phones are secure, I'd feel safer if I could tell you face to face."

He thought for a moment, turning it over in his mind, but in his gut he knew what his answer would be.

"Are you up for a little plane ride?"

"Yes. I heard that's where you hold your meetings and I'm good with that. Tell me where to meet you and how soon we can do it. Every minute counts here."

Now a tiny thread of fear wriggled through him. *Damn it!* Had Mallory gone and got herself into another situation like they'd rescued her from? They'd just finished a tense and difficult hostage negotiation and everyone needed a breather. Still, he could at least hear what the woman had to say.

He glanced at his watch.

"Give me a couple of hours then meet me at the address I'm going to text you."

He could almost feel her relief over the phone. "Thank you. Thank you so much."

"See you soon."

"So I take it we've got a new client?" Blaze said as soon as Rocket cut the connection to the senator.

He texted her the information then speed-dialed Saint. Jed 'Saint' Francis was the fifth partner in Galaxy, whose primary function was flying and handling maintenance for their agency plane.

"Don't tell me," Saint answered. "We've got a new job. Jesus, Rocket, I haven't even changed clothes from the last one."

"I know." Rocket sighed. "But it turns out this one is…important. Can you be at the hangar in two hours?"

"Yeah, I can. But mostly because I can hear the desperation in your voice."

"Desperation?" He looked at his cell. "Let's call it urgency, okay? I'm meeting our new client there in two hours. This is just the first meeting, so hopefully it won't take more than an hour."

Because if it did, it meant things were really, really fucked up.

"Okay. See you when you get there."

Rocket thumbed off the call, closed his eyes and centered himself. Well, that wasn't a big help. The first thing that popped into his mind was an image of Mallory, naked, her face flushed with desire, her rosy nipples wet from his mouth and her legs spread wide to welcome his cock. At once, said cock swelled and pressed hard against the fly of his jeans. He shifted slightly, hoping his movement wasn't catching Blaze's attention.

"So am I turning around?" Blaze asked.

"No, not necessary. We're almost at my place. Just drop me off and I'll head back to the hangar. I'll call everyone after I meet with the senator."

He had no idea if the senator knew what had happened between him and Mallory, but he wasn't taking a chance. If they took the case, at some point he'd have to let his partners know, but first he needed details. *And a decision on what to do.*

"Well, you know we're here and ready if you need us."

"I do, and thanks."

"Okay, here we are." Blaze pulled up to the iron fence surrounding Rocket's South Tampa home. Like all the partners, he was seriously obsessive about security.

Because of the private work they did, they were obvious targets for a lot of people who'd like to get rid of them. But they all had access to each other's homes, so Blaze punched the security code in, the gate swung open and he drove in and up to the front door.

"Thanks for driving." Rocket grabbed his go-bag, which was sitting on the floor at his feet.

"No problem. Call as soon as you know anything."

"Absolutely."

He thought about the call while he showered and changed, all kinds of wild scenarios running through his head. He'd followed Mallory's career for the past five years, both admiring her for the bestsellers she wrote about dangerous events and pissed off that she kept putting herself in those situations. Was she writing a new book and as usual had stepped on the wrong toes? Had she gotten herself mixed up in something, like the Taliban, that she couldn't control? Did he finally have to admit that she had a self-destructive streak and either find a way to fix it or wipe her from his mind completely?

As if that's possible.

By the time he reached the hangar, his questions had questions and he forced himself to shut off his mind until he talked to Senator Kane. Saint was just finishing his preflight check when a black SUV with tinted windows turned into the driveway and pulled onto the concrete apron. The driver's door opened and a tall man in a suit climbed out and began to look around. A man also exited the passenger side and did the same thing. Rocket didn't think they were sightseeing.

As the driver started toward him, the rear passenger door opened and a woman in dark slacks and a sweater exited and headed toward them.

"Senator," the driver said, "I told you to let us check this out first."

"Oh, for heaven's sake, Daniel," Alicia Kane snapped. "I appreciate your concern, but there's no danger here."

"You don't know that," he protested. "It's our job to keep you safe."

"And you do, but Galaxy comes with the highest recommendations. Plus, John Hardin rescued my sister five years ago. I'm fine. Please."

"But—"

She just shook her head and kept walking. Rocket met her halfway to the open hangar.

"Senator Kane?"

"Alicia, please." She held out her hand. "Today I'm not a United States senator. I'm here as Mallory Kane's sister. And I thank you for agreeing to meet me."

He shook her hand then gestured toward the plane. "We're all set for our meeting. Follow me, please."

They started toward the hangar, but the two men from the SUV were right behind them.

"Sorry." Rocket held up a hand. "Only the client is allowed in this meeting."

One of the men, Daniel, stepped up close to Rocket. The expression on his face was a mask, but irritation flashed in his eyes.

"Where the senator goes, we go," he insisted. "She's our responsibility."

"Understood, but that doesn't change things. And I assure you, nothing will happen to her while she's with me."

"But—"

Alicia shook her head. "Daniel, I explained this to you ahead of time. I was explicitly told only the client is allowed in these meetings. I appreciate your dedication to duty, but I'm the only one getting on this plane. You and Jay are perfectly welcome to wait here until we get back." She looked at Rocket. "That's okay, right?"

He nodded. "Yes."

"Then let's do this. We're losing precious time."

He had to swallow a smile at the look on Daniel's face. He got the idea that protecting Senator Alicia Kane wasn't a very easy job.

"This way."

In less than five minutes, they were in the plane's cabin and he ushered her into one of the very comfortable chairs.

"I'll get the coffee ready," he told her, "and we can have some as soon as we reach cruising altitude."

"Fine. Thank you. I want to explain this to you as soon as possible."

"Understood."

Over the intercom, he let Saint know they were ready. The plane's powerful engines turned over and the plane began to move out of the hangar. Rocket knew the pilot was closing the hangar door with a remote and notifying the control tower at Tampa International Airport that he was ready for departure. He watched the senator as they rolled down the private runway, then as they lifted off. She sat rigidly in her seat, hands gripped together in her lap and not saying a word. The tension she was riding was visible in every inch of her body.

Rocket unfastened his seat belt and stood. "How do you take your coffee?"

"Black. Please. And thank you."

In less than five minutes, he was back with two cups of the hot liquid. He handed Alicia's to her then cradled his as he sat on the couch facing her.

"First things first. Just out of curiosity, how did you happen to contact us? And how did you get our number? We don't advertise anywhere."

She huffed a laugh. "No kidding. Well, I contacted you because Mallory never stopped talking about how you rescued her five years ago. I didn't even know Galaxy existed when I started my search for you. All I got from the Navy was that you were no longer on active duty."

"I see."

"Well, anyway, I wasn't getting much of anywhere, but then suddenly Senator Alston Franz, who I sit on the Senate Armed Services Committee with, invited me to lunch. I was curious when we ended up at a very out-of-the-way place. I mean, no one would question us having lunch together, but he said we needed to be somewhere that absolutely no one could overhear us if I was looking for Galaxy. I guess you all are more secret than the CIA."

Rocket allowed himself a smile. "We try to be. Otherwise, we wouldn't be able to do what we do."

"Turns out, when I asked the Secretary of the Navy where I could find you, although he ducked the answer, he passed the question along to Franz. Who of course knew all about you and Galaxy, because his friend Peyton West is engaged to your partner, Scott Hamilton."

"Yes, she is."

"He told me enough about Galaxy to let me know you are the only ones who can help me. So here I am." She studied his face.

"Okay, Senator. What's Mallory jumped into this time? Off on the trail of a hot news story? Writing another blockbuster about places she has no business being? And why me?"

Alicia took a slow sip of her coffee, as if gathering her thoughts.

"Mallory has always been a strong, independent person," she began. "She's had great success because of it, both as a reporter and as an author. But she's also gotten herself into trouble too many times."

He wanted to say *No kidding* but decided keeping his mouth shut was a better decision. "Yes, by diving into dangerous situations and writing bestselling books about them."

Alicia Kane snorted a laugh. "I see you've been following her career. Or checked up on her."

Rocket nodded. "Enough to know she takes chances, which is probably the reason none of her publicity or book jackets feature her photo."

"You're correct. About that and the fact that nothing's changed. She's currently in Santa Marita. Do you know where it is?

"Vaguely." He frowned. "Aren't they having a revolution of some kind?"

"Worse than that." She nodded. "The Barrera cartel has fought its way to power and created a new organization. General Felix Barrera has built his own organization and has taken over the entire country. No one breathes unless he says so. Her friend who lives there told her the situation is really desperate."

"I can't argue with that." He took a swallow of his own coffee. "Especially where drug cartels are concerned. Meddling in elections is right up their alley. It gives them that much more control and they don't care how much blood they shed on the way."

"That's her theory, and she's determined to write a book about this."

Rocket lifted an eyebrow. "So she's still digging into foreign regimes and power struggles? It's a wonder she hasn't gotten herself killed before now."

And that's the fucking truth. Idiot woman.

Alicia huffed a sigh. "I keep trying to tell her that."

"And she's down in Santa Marita now?"

"Yes." Alicia leaned forward, giving him a hard, intense look. "She's being hidden by a friend of hers, an emergency room nurse who reached out to her about researching and writing a book in the situation in Santa Marita."

Rocket snorted. "Some friend."

"This is her homeland and she's worried about it."

Rocket frowned. "Where did Mallory hook up with her?"

"They went to college together and kept in touch. Inez also worked as an emergency room nurse in Houston where Mallory lived for a while. The friendship has obviously lasted. According to what Mal told me, Inez felt she needed to go home to Santa Marita when things went to hell there. Nurses were needed."

"But?" Rocket prompted her.

"But when she discovered what was really going on there," Alicia Kane went on, "she reached out to Mal. The media was basically barred from the country and the whole story wasn't getting out. She figured a book would be the best way to draw attention to the situation."

Rocket studied her. "And she needs a way out." He kept his face expressionless, even though the first thought that came to him was, *Déjà vu all over again.* The second was, *Fucking shit! Why did I let five years go by without contacting her?* Anger surged through him for the time he'd wasted through his own stupidity, for his continued attempt to convince himself that being with a woman like Mallory Kane would be more trouble than she was worth.

How'd that work out for you, asshole?

"Okay, you'd better start from the beginning. What turned her onto this story?"

Alicia sat back with a sigh. "In college, Mallory majored in journalism and political science. A combination brewing trouble, if there ever was one. She saw it as her 'calling' to expose the criminal elements in political regimes everywhere."

"I figured right from the start she had a habit of putting herself in danger," Rocket said. That streak of daring, while risky, was what made her so successful with her books.

"She does. Yes." She took a sip of her coffee. "Her friends and I keep trying to tell her she could write exciting books without taking a chance with her life, but..." She shrugged.

"Okay, I get it. But how did she end up with no exit strategy?"

"When Barrera killed President Alcante, chased all members of that regime out of the country and set himself up as the new president, they did everything they could to institute absolute control. That means they're also in charge of the airport and the marinas. No one can get into the country or leave without them knowing every detail."

He studied Alicia's face. "Then how did she get in?"

"She has a passport and other identification in the name of Melinda Clayton and a fake background in case anyone tries to dig into it. She had a computer nerd friend set it up for her so it's hackproof."

Rocket held up a hand. "Let me interrupt for a moment. Absolutely nothing is completely hackproof, so don't fall into the trap of thinking that it is. People who can access the dark web can find anything. And I mean *anything*."

"But whoever she had create this for her did not enter any information whatsoever about Mallory," Alicia protested, "so how would they connect it?"

"Did she email the person who set it up? Use any of her real information? How did they get a picture of her for documentation?"

Alicia Kane slumped in her chair. "I can't answer those questions. I'm sorry. I should have thought to ask her, but she set this up so long ago."

"I'm guessing her phony credentials were enough to get her into Santa Marita."

"Yes. And Inez picked her up at the airport. To the average observer, they were just two friends getting together. They didn't ring any negative bells."

"That you know of."

"Okay, yes. But you know Mal. She might think she's been keeping a low profile, but I'd bet a year's salary she poked her nose into one too many places one too many times and caught their unwanted attention. They know she's been digging into the elections and corruption in the country and they'd love to get their hands on her. Make an example of her. Now she's left without options."

Rocket lifted an eyebrow. "An example of her?"

Alicia nodded. "The word we have from one of our sources is that when they catch her, they plan to parade her in the central square of the capital, strip her naked and behead her, as a warning to others."

Jesus! Rocket nearly threw up his coffee, and it took a lot to make him that nauseated. "How reliable is your source and does he or she know where Mallory is?"

"Like I said, very reliable. She feels responsible for getting her there and now she's petrified Mal will be killed because of her."

"But she knows where she is?" Rocket persisted.

Alicia nodded. "She has Mallory hidden in the back of the little house she lives in. At great danger to herself, I might add."

"We have a way to contact Mallory, I hope?"

"She has a burner phone with her at all times."

"Smart woman," Rocket mused. He rubbed his forehead. "Okay. Let's start at the beginning and give me every single detail you have. Don't leave out even the smallest one. Give me all the information, like how long she's been in Santa Marita, the number of her cell phone. Everything."

The tension in the senator's body eased slightly. "Of course. Whatever you want to know."

By the time she'd finished, the feelings swirling in Rocket were a cross between fear and rage. He wanted to get his hands on Mallory Kane and shake her until her teeth rattled. But then he wanted to strip off her clothes and fuck her stupid. He took notes on his tablet while Alicia talked, going over every little detail she had again and again until he was sure he had wrung it all from her brain.

"Thank you for doing this," Alicia told him, leaning back in her chair, limp from the exhaustion of dredging up information.

He shrugged. "How could I not? The small amount of time I spent with her, she impressed the hell out of me." *In more ways than one.* "I'll call my partners as soon as we land. Please stay available because as we put this together, I'm sure I will have more questions."

"Not a problem. That number you have for me? It's my private, personal cell and I always have it with me. You can call me day or night. Truly."

"Good. Excellent. One more question. Who else knows about this? Your security team? Mallory's publishers? Anyone else you came into contact with?"

"No one. First, I trust my security people, but Washington leaks like a sieve. Who knows what they might inadvertently say? Second, her publisher has no idea she's there in the middle of a revolution. Her contract is for a book on Mexican politics. She really had to keep her trip way under the radar for her protection…and also not to call down the wrath of the politicians."

"Understood. Complicates the situation, but complication is our middle name." He made some more notes. "It seems this whole operation, starting this minute, has to be under the radar. What did you tell your team about this meeting?"

One corner of her mouth quirked up. "That it was none of their business. That it was personal and private and had nothing to do with my job as a senator, so they needed to keep their noses out of it."

"Which of course will make them ten times as curious," Rocket pointed out.

"Tough. My first concern is my sister and her safety, which is already compromised enough. Now, I am prepared to write you a check today for a retainer or whatever you call it, if you just tell me how much it is."

"No check. Let me discuss it with my partners, but just FYI, we invested the startup funds for Galaxy very wisely, after our initial expenses. That allows us to take cases without charging the client, depending of course on who the client is."

She smiled. "Senator Franz also told me you'd probably say that. I'm also in a very good position financially, and I don't want you to stint on this job."

Rocket held on to his temper. "We never stint, Senator, whether or not we get paid. It's who we are."

"Of course, I'm sorry. I didn't mean to imply —" She stopped herself, shook her head. "My concern and fear for my sister are throwing me off center here. I can't thank you enough for agreeing to take this on. Galaxy is my only hope."

"You're welcome. And we'll get it done."

But more because there's no way I can leave Mallory in danger. And because I want to see her again. Five years has been too long a time.

"All right. Let's go over everything, including how Mallory ended up in Santa Marita and why."

Rocket continued to make notes on his tablet. At last, he thought he'd squeezed every drop of information from the senator that she had to give. He closed his tablet and called Saint on the intercom to tell him they were ready to head back to base. In a moment, the plane made a turn.

And all he could think was that maybe Fate was nudging him to reconnect with Mallory Kane. And letting him know he'd wasted five good years.

Chapter Three

Mallory Kane unwound the bandana from around her neck and used it to blot the sweat from her forehead. There were a lot of uncertain things in Santa Marita, but the heat wasn't one of them. It was constant and steady. She never thought she'd be willing to kill for five minutes of air conditioning, but right now murder for chilled air didn't seem so very wrong.

This roof had become her refuge, ever since General Felix Barrera, cartel head, butcher and president of Santa Marita, had decided she was trouble and come to the house hunting for her. She really should have known better. Santa Marita was no bigger than a tiny drop of spit in the Pacific Ocean…not a place where she could easily blend in. She should have learned her lesson when tracking the Taliban, and Afghanistan was a hell of a lot bigger than this peanut-size country.

But other writers had created hugely successful books out of the turmoil in places even smaller than this. And her other books had had great success. Besides, how could she say no to a friend?

During the day, she hid in the attic that was barely more than a crawl space, with a tiny little electric fan to move the hot, stale air around. No one ever found the room because a painting of the Mayan sun covered the area where the trap door was, the cutout skillfully blending into the painting. Inez had told her the people who had owned the house before them had painted it to keep the evil spirits out.

But at night, she escaped up here to freedom, breathing fresh air and cooling off. The way the house was built, the roof was flat with a short extension of the exterior walls circling it. Enough to prevent her from rolling off and people in the street from seeing her. And Inez had given her an old quilt and a toss pillow, so she'd have something to protect her from the rough surface of the roof.

Happy vacation. Welcome to Santa Marita.

Whoever would have thought that a country barely bigger than the head of a pin would be so full of corruption and crime? She'd expected something, for sure, but maybe just the basis for a series of articles. Since she'd been here, she'd seen people dragged out of cantinas then disappear, others go to work and never come home. Mallory had detected a heavy layer of poverty beneath the colorful surface and the impression of success generated by *El Presidente* himself, Felix Barrera.

There might have been a patina of gaiety and exotic flavor overlaying everything, but beneath it the country was gripped with danger and fear. Not to mention the faltering economy that had eliminated so many jobs. Her friend Inez was right about the disaster that was Santa Marita and the terror that gripped so many of its people.

With the spreading legalization of marijuana, cocaine and opium had become the hot commodities. Acreage that had produced other crops now grew opium poppies and other similar plants. And meth labs had been set up which produced large quantities of the drug they then distributed like a sales organization. Breaking away from the Sinaloa cartel because Felix Barrera wanted to be the big fish in the pond, they'd made their plans and invaded the island, killing those who got in their way. Setting up their drug business. Drawing international criminals because of the lax banking and no extradition.

Inez had told Mallory there were two things she hated about her work in the emergency room — patching up bullet wounds and treating people who'd overdosed on the products of the Barrera cartel. Both had become primary activities. Santa Marita's economy had been booming under a democratically elected government when Barrera and his army had decided they needed the entire country as their headquarters. Soon, they'd controlled everything, blanketing their drug business over the existing economy. The peaceful regime of President Alcante that had been responsible for the prosperous growth of the country had been destroyed by Barrera's criminals. They had simply killed Alcante and taken control, then Barrera had taken a thriving country and turned it into one big criminal enterprise.

On the one hand, they kept people employed.

On the other hand, they also killed anyone who tried to get in their way and eliminated the cultural and educational faces of the country that had made it so successful. What they did gave them control, cachet in the international market and a more powerful position. Killing anyone in the population who disagreed meant nothing to them and only raised their stature in the criminal world.

When Inez had reached out to Mallory, begging her to come down there and see for herself, to research a book like she'd done in other situations, she'd jumped at the chance for a new project. Her other books had shockingly all hit the bestseller list, giving her a feeling of success and the confidence to do more.

She'd done her best to blend into the life of Santa Marita the way she usually did, scoping out shops and restaurants and any fun places that would appeal to tourists. She'd bought touristy things like tee shirts and straw hats and woven bags. She'd tried hanging out in different popular bars and cantinas and sampled drinks. She'd snapped pictures with her cell phone, trying to be casual about it and mixing generic shots with critical ones. And she engaged people in conversation, as someone who was new to a place and wanted to know what was going on would. She'd tried to be friendly, but it wasn't as easy as she'd thought it should be.

Things were different here from other tourist spots. Everyone here was tense. They walked around with strained looks on their faces. There was an element of fear in the air that permeated the entire city, despite the illusion of life going on as usual. People didn't seem to warm up to visitors without 'connections', and after a while she noticed there was always one of Barrera's soldiers hanging around whenever she was trying to talk to someone.

She'd thought she'd blended in the way she'd learned to do in so many other places, but apparently she was giving off the wrong vibes. She guessed she hadn't been as casual in her observing and questions in Santa Marita as she'd thought, because she'd landed in

Barrera's crosshairs. Part of it was the constant air of tension and fear. No one really wanted to chat with strangers, and efforts to be friendly were met with suspicion.

After the little incident at the hospital, his men had come looking for her a couple of nights ago. Now she was relegated to hiding in the small attic. There was no way off the island under the present circumstances. At least no normal way. Barrera controlled all points of entry and exit. Now more than ever, Mallory wanted to get out of here to write the story of Barrera and what he'd done to Santa Marita. Drugs and drug cartels were hot topics, along with crooked military takeovers, and she could feel another blockbuster coming on. But she needed to stay alive to write it, and that possibility was shrinking by the day.

That was when she'd thought of the only person she had confidence in to get her out — John 'Rocket' Hardin. Five years hadn't diminished the memories or the effect he had on her, no matter how hard she tried. There just wasn't room in her life for relationships. Besides, she'd tried it before with disastrous results. Except now her life was again in danger and he was the only person who could help — the reason why she had called Alicia to find him and reach out to him.

Fate had certainly played a trick on her. Still, she had to acknowledge the fact that five years was a long time not to see or hear from someone, or speak to them. For all she knew, he'd totally forgotten about her. Or maybe he'd figure one rescue was enough and that she was just too much of a pain in the ass to bother with this. She prayed she was wrong, because she had no place else to turn.

She lay back on the flat roof and looked up at the stars, as if she could find an answer written there. The view was great. The Albados' home was higher than the ones on either side of it, adobe like the others but a full story taller, because whoever had first built the house had put a garage on the bottom level, adding that much more height. Mallory could look down on others, but they could not look up and see her. It gave her a strange feeling of protection, even though she was trapped here.

The sound of the hidden trap door to the roof sliding open had her lying as flat as possible on the earth bricks that made up the surface. There was no chimney to hide behind — who the hell would have a fireplace in Santa Marita, which was hotter than hell on a good day? — so she tried to make herself as invisible as she could. No one ever came up here except Inez, but in her situation, she couldn't afford to let her guard down. She let out a breath of relief when Inez's head, with its signature ponytail, popped up.

"Mallory." The word was whispered.

"Here," Mallory whispered back, and pushed herself to a sitting position. There was always a chance someone could look up and see her on the roof, but Inez came up here a lot and no one ever questioned it.

"I brought you some iced tea." She handed over a large thermos tumbler.

Mallory took it, slid the little tab to allow her to drink and took two long swallows.

"Wow." She wiped her mouth with the back of her hand. "Thank you, Inez. That was so, so good."

"You're welcome. I figured you'd be sweltering up here."

"I just needed a change from the attic." She held up a hand. "Which, by the way, I'm not complaining about. Have your parents said anything yet?"

"They aren't saying anything about anything." Inez shook her head. "They're torn between wanting Barrera out of their country and keeping their heads on their bodies and not rolling on the ground over some imagined infraction." She reached down and pulled up a brown paper bag that looked as if it contained something heavy.

"Here." She handed it to Mallory.

And it *was* heavy. She looked inside and nearly dropped it.

"A gun? Inez, where the hell did you get a gun?"

"From a friend." She held up a hand. "Don't say anything. He's completely trustworthy and hates Barrera and what he's done to the country. You said you can shoot one, right?"

"Yes. I can." It was the first thing she'd learned to do after she'd been rescued from the Taliban.

"There's two clips in there. That's all he could give me. But at least it will give *you* some protection until your friend comes." She studied Mallory. "Do you know yet if your sister got hold of him? That guy, Rocket?"

Mallory shook her head. "No. I haven't heard a word yet. It's only been a couple of days since I reached out to her, though, and I'm just praying she's made contact with the man." She loaded one clip into the gun, stuck the other in her pocket and placed the gun next to her.

That was what she got for being a bloodhound, she told herself. She'd soon gotten the sense that they were keeping a closer watch on her as she played tourist in Santa Marita. Whatever it was, Barrera's men had begun to look at her with an expression that was a combination of hostility and suspicion. She'd just smiled and nodded whenever one of them had made eye contact, but casual was her middle name. However, she'd been seen enough with Inez for the goons to link them, although when questioned, she and Inez gave their stock answer—she was visiting her friend Inez and soaking in the local culture.

Then she had gone to see Inez at the hospital where she worked in the emergency room. Mallory had been unable to contain her curiosity about the patients there and she'd wanted to get an idea of how many patients had bullet wounds, knife wounds or other damage. To disguise her visit, she'd pretended that she'd hurt her wrist, a *turista* casualty, as an excuse. She'd figured that was innocent enough. She'd thought she'd been very careful, aware that Barrera's soldiers had begun to pay a little more attention to her.

But while Inez had been wrapping her wrist and Mallory had been looking around and whispering questions to Inez—something she had repeatedly kicked herself for—she'd seen one of the guards who'd been standing watch at the emergency room entrance make a call on his cell phone.

Damn. She had known better, but her consuming curiosity had overridden her common sense. When she'd left the area, he'd asked for her identification. She'd given him the fake ones she carried when she was doing this kind of dangerous work, something she'd started right after Afghanistan. She also had no social media pages, no footprints anywhere. She knew in this day and age that might look suspicious, but if questioned she could always say it made her nervous. The last thing she wanted was for someone to pull information on her from the internet.

"Melinda Clayton." He examined the driver's license and passport as if they contained some secret code. "What are you doing here?"

She held up her wrist. "Getting this fixed. I'm so clumsy. I fell on it."

"No, I mean here. In Santa Marita."

"Visiting Inez. My friend. We've known each other since college and kept in touch. She told me what a great place this is. I had some vacation time, so I thought I'd check it out."

"You've been seen spying on places around town. Asking questions."

Oh, shit.

"No, no, no. What kind of spying?" She managed a smile. "I'm just a tourist. I like it here. I've been trying to get a real feel for the place so I can tell my friends what a great spot it is to visit."

The guard was short and as wide as he was tall. He stared at her, a look on his face as if he'd cheerfully break every one of her bones if he could prove she was lying. He blocked her path for another moment, then stepped out of the way. But he headed toward Inez as Mallory walked toward the exit.

When Inez came home at the end of the day, Mallory learned the guard had asked her many, many probing questions.

Inez just sighed. "They wanted to know who you were. I told them someone I was friends with in Houston who wanted to come down and see what Santa Marita was like. I played it real casual and I think I deflected their interest."

But Mallory's feeling that she'd tripped a switch solidified later that night when Barrera's men came to the house looking for her. Inez had heard the slamming of car doors in the street, peeked out of the window and seen them. She immediately sent Mallory up to the attic, sliding the almost invisible access into place.

"There's a sleeping bag in the corner," she told her. "Lie down on that and open the little windows so you get some air. Don't move, though. We don't want them to hear you. I'll let you know when they leave."

"But what about you? Your parents?"

"We're used to stuff like this. We'll handle it." She managed a smile. "Mama will wail and Papa will grumble and they'll leave us alone."

Mallory had no idea how much time passed while Barrera's men searched the house, but eventually Inez joined her in the attic.

"Bastards," she snapped when she joined Mallory in her hiding place. "They said you fit the profile of someone who is against the regime. That you've been too nosy for someone who's just a tourist."

"Well, that's certainly the truth," Mallory agreed. "What did you tell them?"

"That we had no idea where you were. That you'd left the house to check out some nightspots and we hadn't heard from you. That we were very worried and hoped they could help find you. They searched every inch of the house and told us wherever you were, they'd find you. Thank god the access to the attic is so well hidden."

"No kidding."

"But I know they're keeping an eye on the house. Doing drive-bys now and then. Maybe they even paid some of our neighbors. Mallory, you have to find a way out of here. Not for us but for you. God. I'm sorry I ever asked you to get involved here."

"No, no." Mallory grabbed her hand. "I'm glad you did. When I get out of here, I'm going to pitch this to my publisher. He likes books like this, obviously."

That was the situation that had made her call Alicia and ask her to find the only person she knew who could make that happen. Then she'd settled in to wait, always on pins and needles.

Now she and Inez huddled facing each other.

"I shouldn't have asked so many questions," she told her friend. "But this is not your fault. I should have been a little more careful. Inez, I'm so sorry to make trouble for you and your family."

"No, I'm glad you came. Someone has to tell people about this." Inez let out a long sigh. "But now I wish I hadn't gotten you involved in this."

"Stop." Mallory held up a hand. "All you did was tell me what was happening. It was my choice to come here and write a book about it."

"A book that won't be written if you get killed first," Inez pointed out.

"I'm not getting killed. At least, not if my sister makes a connection with the guy whose name I gave her. I'm so sorry I put your family in the crosshairs."

"They'll be fine. But getting you out of here is a priority now. And keeping you hidden. Thank god our attic entrance is so concealed those thugs didn't find it. We'll have to move you there now, even though it's a hot box."

"I'll survive. I've survived worse. Are you still swamped at work?"

"It's busier than ever." Inez smoothed her ponytail back. "Since Barrera and his thugs swept in and took over the government, I can count on at least five shootings every day. And that doesn't even take into account the number of domestic violence injuries. Mix drugs with people and you have no control over what happens." She shook her head. "I thought I'd be doing some good asking you to write about what was going on here. The media doesn't seem to care, and Barrera has managed to destroy those who tried doing something. All I've done is put you in danger. It will take more than a book to wipe out Barrera."

"Not if I can get out of here," Mallory told her. "If my sister can find Rocket Hardin, I know he can get me out of here and I'll bet he can help me get this info to the right people."

Inez tilted her head. "And just who is this guy who could maybe work miracles?"

"When I knew him, he was a Navy SEAL. Alicia said he'd left the SEALs and was doing something super-secret for people who needed him. I'll bet my life he has connections that can take care of this."

"In case you haven't figured it out," Inez pointed out, "you *are* betting your life, hoping for him to get you out of here. What's so special about him, anyway?"

"Because he did it before, rescuing me from the Taliban in the middle of one of their camps. Not an easy task."

"That's the truth," Inez agreed.

"He's not afraid of anything, but he's smart enough to be careful. And..." She shrugged. "I don't know. Like I said, he was a SEAL. In case you haven't heard, they can do just about anything."

Inez grinned. "Is he sexy?"

Mallory did her best to keep her face expressionless, thankful for the darkness and the minimal amount of light on the roof.

"I didn't really notice."

"Ha." She punched Mallory in the arm. "You are such a liar. Every time you mention his name, you get this little flicker in your eyes."

"I do not." At least she hoped not. "I just..." She shrugged again.

"Just what?"

Before Mallory could fudge some kind of answer, several sharp reports rang out from the street below, the unmistakable sound of gunshots. Keeping low, she crawled to the edge of the roof to peer over it. She was stunned at what she saw. A body lay face down on the ground with three men standing over them.

"What is it?" Inez hissed.

"I think someone just got in the way of the Barreras," Mallory said.

"And they shot him, right?" Inez guessed. "In front of our house? Oh, my god, Mallory."

"I think they had a beef with one of your neighbors." Mallory crouched at the edge of the roof.

"Stop," Inez hissed. "Get back here." She flattened herself and elbow-crawled to where Mallory was watching.

"Ssh." Mallory pulled her cell from her pocket, brought up the photo app and shot some pictures before sliding away from the edge. *They might come in handy.*

"You're crazy. You know that?"

"Crazy like a fox. If they don't pay attention to my words, they will to my pictures."

"Which no one will see if Barrera's men catch you. All they'll see is your dead body."

"I'm done. For now." When Inez edged closer, Mallory pulled her back.

"Don't let them see you," Mallory told her. She tried to keep her friend from moving closer.

"Nothing worse than I see every day," Inez said. "I don't know why they shot him here, but thank god they tossed the body in a panel van parked at the curb. Okay, now they both got in and drove away." She sat back. "Oh, god! My mother. I hope she didn't see anything, although she's learned to stay away from the street at night."

"Good thing. But you'd better get back downstairs."

"Yes, I need to. I hope my mother isn't aware of anything or she'll be in shock." She crawled over to the trap door. "Maybe if we work it right, you can hang out in my bedroom for a while."

But would it be safe?

"We'll see. You go check on your mom. I worry that this whole thing will give her a nervous breakdown."

"She's tough." Inez grinned. "She and my dad have both weathered a lot of stuff. They know how to keep their heads down and avoid trouble. Besides, she wants you to write about Barrera and what he's doing."

"I get that, but I still worry." Mallory sighed. "You all don't need the tension of hiding me."

"Mallory, this is not your fault. I just wish we had a way to sneak you out of here unnoticed. I will be forever grateful that the people who owned this house before us built it with that attic and created the invisible access. Someone said they were dope dealers and needed a good hiding place."

Mallory stared at her. "You're kidding."

"It's just a rumor, but it's certainly logical. Anyway, maybe your friend will call soon and tell you he's coming to get you."

"Let's hope. Otherwise, I don't know what to do. We can't even figure out how to get me out of this house."

God, this was such a mess.

"If it's clear downstairs, I'll let you know."

Inez wriggled her way through the opening in the roof to the attic below it. "Keep that gun next to you and loaded. I'll make sure the windows are open for you."

Luckily, the exit from the attic was in Inez's room, so she could manipulate things however she needed to.

"I'll wait until everyone is asleep before I come down from here," Mallory said.

"I will come and let you know. In the meantime, for god's sake don't go to the edge of the roof again."

As soon as Inez had disappeared beneath the trap door, Mallory double-checked that the loaded clip in the gun was ready to fire. Then she flopped onto her back again. The night was crystal clear, the stars vivid pinpoints of light and the moon a silvery globe in the sky. It reminded her of a night five years ago when the sexiest man she'd ever met had snatched her from certain death. She had no idea why he'd affected her the way no other man had before or since, but she couldn't get him out of her mind, even after all this time.

Six foot three of raw, masculine power, he was sex on a stick. His dark hair, almost ebony, hung down just past his chin line, forming a curtain around his dark beard. His eyes were the same ebony, looking out at the world from beneath thick black lashes. He had a lean face with sharp cheekbones, unexpectedly sensuous lips and eyes that were deep-set, giving nothing away. Except of course in moments of the most intense intimacy, when hunger and desire flashed like bonfires in them.

She had never met a man who set her on fire the way Rocket Hardin did. Maybe it had been crazy, having sex in that cave in the middle of a war zone. But they'd been hidden away, protected by the walls of the cave, and the chopper had picked them up on time.

She just prayed he could rescue her from this.

In five years, she hadn't been able to wipe him from her mind. Now she closed her eyes, letting the memory of their one time together wash over her. This wasn't the first time she'd indulged in erotic dreams about Rocket. Too many times in the past five years when she'd been alone at night, she'd fantasized about being with him again. Mallory could still feel his thick, hard cock inside her, experience the pulsing of the orgasm as her body spasmed. She'd never forgotten the touch of his hands, so unexpectedly gentle, or the feel of his mouth on her nipples as he brushed kisses over her breasts, or his tongue as he licked the insides of her thighs and slid between the slick folds of her sex to torment her clit.

He had been fierce and gentle at the same time, driving her to a powerful orgasm then softly easing her down. He had certainly outdone any other lover she'd ever had, before or since. Not that she'd had that many, but she did have a healthy appetite for sex.

But it wasn't just the sex that had stayed with her. He'd had a quiet, commanding presence that had made her feel safe the moment that he'd stepped into the hut where she'd been held. A strength had kept her fears at bay. Even though the vicious Taliban guards had been mere feet away, and ready to kill them in a devastating, excruciating manner, even when she and Rocket had had to split from the rest of his team to avoid just that, she'd had every confidence he would get her to safety.

And he had, hiding her up in that cave until the helo came to extract them.

Then, *boom!* Her brain was back in that very cave, and she was lying beneath a very naked John Hardin — *no, Rocket,* she reminded herself — who drove her to an explosive orgasm.

He'd never left her thoughts since then. *Damn it!* She had an aversion to long-standing relationships. She'd been burned twice, badly, and that had been plenty for her. It was probably the main reason she hadn't tried to find Rocket. So what was going on with her now?

Without even realizing it, she started to slide her hands into her cutoffs, but stopped herself right away. She was hiding in the middle of a war zone, for crying out loud. Why was she suddenly having erotic dreams about this man and considering pleasuring herself on a roof? This was certainly no place for that. She'd have to be satisfied with the memory of that one hot episode with Rocket and hope that even after all this time he wanted to repeat it.

At this point, all she could do was pray that Alicia had found him and he'd said yes. But then what? He probably had a busy exciting life with no room for her in it. No doubt the reason he'd never heard from him again.

Of course, she'd be glad to see him. If anyone could get her out of this, it was him.

Come on, big guy, call me.

* * * *

Alicia Kane's security team was waiting for them when they landed, striding up to the stairway as soon as it was lowered. They all wore the same stern expression on their faces and barely acknowledged Rocket's presence.

"Pay no attention to them," the senator told him. "They get ticked off at me all the time for doing things like this." She looked at the team leader. "See? I told you I'd be fine. I wasn't kidnapped and we weren't shot down. Now we need to get back to Washington. You confirmed the reservations, right?"

The man nodded. "All set. We need to get moving."

"Wait a minute." Rocket hollered to Saint, who had left the plane and was doing his postflight checklist. "Let me look at something."

"I know what you're going to ask and I'm good with it. We've still got plenty of fuel."

"Good. Okay." He walked back to Alicia Kane. "Saint will fly you. No need to hassle commercial if you don't need to."

"Oh, I couldn't impose on you that way."

"No imposition. Saint loves to log airtime anyway."

"Senator." Daniel, her lead security agent, frowned. "I'm not sure—"

"Oh, please." She flapped her hand in the air. "Better than the mess of flying commercial these days."

"What about the vehicle? It has to be returned to the rental agency."

"We'll take care of it," Rocket assured her. "Just give me the keys and leave the rental agreement in the vehicle."

There was a little more grumbling, but finally Saint edged the plane out of the hangar and Alicia Kane and her team boarded.

"You're not coming with?" she asked.

"No. I need to get the team together and get started."

She grabbed his hands. "Thank you so much. I was so afraid you wouldn't be able to do this. Or maybe wouldn't want to. I really had no idea how you felt about her after five years."

I will always want her.

Rocket blinked. *Where the fuck did that come from?*

"I'm glad you brought this to me. And while you're on your way back to DC, I'll be getting my partners together. And I'll probably have more questions."

"Ask away."

"I will."

He watched them mount the stairway into the plane, then Saint retracted it. He waited in the driveway while his pilot filed his flight plan, taxied out to the runway and took off. Rocket parked the rental vehicle in the garage they'd built. They'd needed a place for their vehicles whenever they left on a case and it was empty right now except for Saint's car. Rocket figured he'd arrange for the rental's return the next day. Finally, he climbed into his SUV and cranked the engine, but before he shifted into Drive, he pulled out his cell phone and sent a message to Mallory at the number Alicia Kane had given him.

I'm coming, Mallory. Just hold on.

Then he put a group text together to his partners.

New client. Urgent. My place in thirty.

He waited until the other three men who made up Galaxy checked in, pleased that no one asked questions. But they'd known each other for so long, and had now worked together as partners in Galaxy for almost two years, that when one rang the bell for a meeting, so to speak, there was seldom any pushback.

He had barely reached his house before vehicles began pulling up. Scott 'Blaze' Hamilton had picked up Vic 'Eagle' Bodine, and right behind them came Matt 'Viper' Roman.

"Does this have anything to do with the call you got on the way home?" Blaze wanted to know as he climbed out of his truck.

Rocket nodded. "It has everything to do with."

"It must be pretty damn important for you to call us in before we're barely home from the last gig," Viper told him.

"It is," Rocket assured him. "Let's get inside and I'll lay it out for you. I'm also ordering pizza. I don't know about you guys, but I missed lunch altogether. Pizza good for everyone?"

They all nodded. Even if they'd eaten, these guys, like him, could always eat more. And brain effort used as much energy as the physical kind. In minutes, they were seated in Rocket's living room, each with a mug filled with strong coffee, ready for Rocket's briefing. They also had their laptops ready to search for information as he gave them details.

"In case none of you remember, five years ago my SEAL team was tasked with rescuing a writer who got herself in trouble with the Taliban. She thought it would be great to write a book about the conflict, looking at both sides of the issue."

"A bleeding heart." Eagle's words were edged with disdain and disapproval.

Rocket had to put a lid on the irritation that surged through him. That was the last explanation he'd use to describe Mallory. His fault. He'd stated it wrong.

"Actually, not at all. Just curious and eager to share information with the world. And record history. She was working on a book about the history and current conflict with the Taliban when I met her in Afghanistan. Apparently although her first couple of books did okay, for whatever reason, she didn't achieve the respect she was looking for. That's why she forged ahead with that topic."

"And did you check?" Viper asked. "Was that book a success?"

"From what I gather, it was a huge success. She finally got the recognition and respect she deserved. She's had a couple more books since then, all equally as successful. That was probably her incentive to write more...probably why she got involved in this."

Eagle's eyebrows flew up. "And she got permission to do this? I thought there were rules, so civilians didn't interfere with ongoing operations."

"Or put themselves in harm's way," Blaze added, "so good men have to go in and rescue them. Like you did."

"She had clearance for her other books, but I'm pretty damn sure she's out there on her own with this one," Rocket told them. "She got caught in a bad situation there and my team got her out. Period."

"But I assume," Blaze interjected, "her current project has something to do with why we're all here. And why you took off on a plane ride to nowhere without even taking time to change your underwear after the last case."

"She is exactly why we're all here," he confirmed. "The thing I remember about her was how smart and fearless she was. And she did everything she was told to do, to effect her rescue." He paused and looked around the table. "Now she's in an equally dangerous situation, maybe even more so. Her friend called and asked for help, and she went. That's the kind of person she is."

"Let's have it," Eagle said.

Rocket laid it all out for them just as Alicia Kane had told them, every detail he'd been given.

"Well, damn." This from Viper.

"Damn is right," Blaze echoed.

"I firmly believe we are the only ones who can get her out." Rocket looked at each of them in turn. "I don't think anyone else has the capability or the smarts. And I want to do this."

He waited for someone to say something. When no one did, he nodded.

"Okay, then. Let's move forward here."

They were interrupted by the delivery of the pizza. Then, when everyone had food in front of them, Rocket again went over everything Senator Alicia Kane had told him in detail. As he spoke, they tapped away on their keyboards. He was pretty sure they were looking up everything they could find about the Barrera cartel and Santa Marita as he gave it to them.

"First of all," Blaze began, "I don't even know who the hell would want to go there if they're looking for a story. It's an island about as big as my thumb whose major economy at the moment seems to be drugs and laundering money."

Viper clicked a couple of keys.

"I've got some stuff, and it's not pleasant."

"Well, let's have it," Rocket told him.

"Santa Marita is a decent-size island off the coast of South America, population a little more than a hundred thousand. They grow cotton and coffee as well as teak and mahogany. There are also a couple of thriving tourist resorts that bring in a lot to the economy. The country has a steady, stable economy, and very little conflict. Or that's the way it has been up until now."

"But?" Eagle looked across the table at him with a raised eyebrow.

"But, that same rich, fertile soil is also great for growing coca plants and opium. Apparently, Barrera decided he wanted out of the Sinaloa cartel and to create his own. He was a smart man and planned carefully how to do it without Sinaloa coming after him. He also knew he needed a headquarters to operate from and create his little empire. From the time he and a large group of his thugs landed on the island until the takeover was complete was a little less than three months."

Blaze shook his head. "And with how many dead bodies?"

Anger flashed in Viper's eyes. "More than you want to know. They killed the elected president and many of his people and have terrorized the residents of the country. They're everywhere and growing stronger."

"What happened to the Santa Marita police?" Eagle wanted to know.

"Dead or disappeared." Viper looked at Rocket. "Your girl walked into the situation from hell. Getting her out could be a lot trickier than rescuing her from the Taliban."

Rocket nodded. "Understood. And if any of you —"

"Stop." Blaze almost shouted the word. "We agreed from day one that if any of us are in a case, all of us are. This one's a little different because of your prior connection to the victim, but we're still all in."

"We'd take a client like Senator Kane anyway," Viper reminded him. "Even after we saw these odds." He grinned. "That's our juice, man. We love the impossible."

"Yeah," Eagle echoed, "so shut your face and let's move forward."

"Getting you in there might not be a problem," Blaze said, turning his laptop around so everyone could see it, "but getting the two of you out poses a bunch of problems."

"I agree." Eagle used his digital pen to point at the map on the screen. "Remember. There's only one airport on the island and it's now controlled by Barrera. And ditto for the marina. And take a look at this place."

He again used his pen as a pointer. "Two thirds of the island is taken up by the city itself. Then there's all the rich land which used to be used for growing things like mahogany and teak, produce and other stuff. Now it's used to grow the raw ingredients for drugs. The rest of it is a jungle that goes almost all the way to the water. It ends at very rocky land with a cliff and steep drop-off to the water here."

He tapped the pen on the map. "Getting through the jungle is very tricky. We've done it before and Mallory kept up in Afghanistan, but still. It won't be as easy for her."

"One slip," Viper added, "and we're looking at dead bodies."

"Yeah." Blaze nodded. "No shit. Okay, we can assess it better when we get there."

"I'll pull up everything I can find on Barrera," Viper volunteered. "We need to know how and where they have their guerrillas set up and what their general operating method is."

"Let me see what I can dig up in the cartel pipelines." Blaze looked around the table. "We need to get a feel for how Barrera operates, how erratic he is, what his triggers are. If we're going to retrieve Mallory Kane from right under his nose, we have to be prepared for his reactions."

They went at it hot and heavy over the next couple of hours, until Eagle looked up from his screen. He tapped a couple of keys on his laptop. "I'm sending this map to the big printer in your den. Then I'll lay it out on the table and we can begin to plan." He looked over at Rocket. "All of us."

Rocket had to search for words. He knew about the "All in" pledge, as they'd once called it, but it had never meant more to him than now. He cleared his throat.

"Thanks."

"No thanks yet," Blaze pointed out. "First we have to put a plan together, and for this mission, it's gonna be a son of a bitch. So let's get started. You should call Alicia Kane and tell her we're putting a plan together and will move ASAP. Then you'd better call your woman and tell her we're going to get her out of this."

Rocket grabbed his cell and wandered into his den so he'd have some privacy. Not having had any contact with Mallory for five years could make it a little awkward. He prayed that the situation was critical enough to bridge the five years without contact.

He thought about Blaze's words. His woman? Far from it at the moment, mostly due to his own pigheadedness. But if he had his way, hopefully after this was over, they could look at the future. Together.

Chapter Four

...his educated tongue drawing lines on the inside of her thighs. Flicking the swollen bud of her clit now throbbing with need. Shivers raced up and down her body, making the inner walls of her sex, wet with her juices, spasm in need. His mouth was great but what she really wanted was to feel his thick cock inside her, driving her to orgasm.

"Inside me," she begged in a hot whisper.

"Not yet." His low laugh set fire to her nerve endings. "I want to be sure you're good and ready."

"I'm ready," she insisted. "I'm more than damn ready."

In response he reached his hands up and pinched both of her aching nipples. Electricity darted through her and she arched her body.

"Like that, do you?" His deep, rough voice rolled over her like a current of electricity.

"Please fuck me," she wanted to cry. "Please don't tease me anymore."

Her body was shaking with need, so much that it actually vibrated. It –

Wait, the vibrating was –

Against her hip? Mallory's eyes flew wide open as she was jolted out of her dream. She yanked her hand out of her shorts, where she'd apparently been acting out her insanely erotic dream, on the rooftop of all places. And the heat creeping up her cheeks had nothing to do with the heat generated by her dream. How in the damn hell had she allowed herself to fall asleep up here when she needed to be alert at all times? And how was it that if she was fully awake her hip was still vibrating?

Because it's your phone, you damn idiot.

Wow! She really had been out of it.

It was a burner phone, and besides Inez, only a couple of people had the number. She looked at the screen, relieved to see Alicia's number but nervous about what she might have to say. Had she seen Rocket? Had he said he'd do this? She didn't even have any idea what he was doing now, except her sister had said he'd left the SEALs and had something going with three friends of his, also former SEALs. Would he even be available? Have time for this?

Or even want to?

She pressed Accept.

"Hey!"

"Hey," Alicia answered. "Can you talk? Are you in a safe place?"

"Yes and no. Can you hear me? I have to keep it at a whisper."

"Okay. Then let's keep it short. Your Rocket is on his way."

"He's not mine," she protested. "But he is? Really? Coming for me? He said he'd do it?"

"He did. And without hesitation, I might add."

Relief surged through her. "So he wasn't tied up with whatever it is he's doing now?

"Apparently not. He and his partners should be on their way soon."

She frowned. "Partners? In what?"

"Well. It seems your rescuer lives up to the rumors. He's partnered with three other former SEALs for an unusual rescue/protection agency called Galaxy. Their motto is 'We are your last resort.'"

Mallory was momentarily stunned, but then she realized it suited him so well. He was the icon for every protector and savior anyone could imagine.

"And they'll do this?" she asked again.

"Yes, and you should hear from him shortly that they will. I'm hanging up because he may be trying to call you even now. Mallory, you are so lucky to know him. I'm positive they'll get this done."

Mallory was, too. "Thanks for finding them," she whispered.

"It wasn't easy, but if they get you out of there, it was worth it."

"Okay, I'm hanging up," Mallory told her. "I'll keep in touch as best I can. Thank you again so much. Love you."

"Love you, too. See you soon."

She was about to slide the phone back into her pocket when it vibrated again. She looked and saw a text on the screen.

It's Rocket. I'm calling now. It's okay to answer this number.

She was glad he had sense enough to warn her, knowing she'd be leery of answering an unknown number. It a moment it vibrated again and she pressed Accept.

"Rocket?"

"Hello, Mallory."

The moment she heard his voice, the deep timbre of it so reassuring, her jittery nerves she'd been working so hard to control began to settle, and every muscle in her body tightened. She hadn't heard it for five years, yet it had hung around in her brain all this time, as familiar as if she'd just heard it yesterday. Time disappeared and she was back in that cave, writhing beneath that hard masculine body. And just seconds ago, she'd been immersed in an erotic dream about him, so hot she'd unconsciously been trying to bring herself to orgasm.

She'd been metaphorically holding her breath to see if Alicia had connected with him and if he'd agree to help her. Five years was a long time and anything could have happened. Was he calling to tell her he was sorry he couldn't do this? Maybe he'd even married and his wife wouldn't be too happy about him going off to rescue an old… Friend? Hookup? Mission target? How would she even describe herself? No, apparently not, since he'd taken the assignment from Alicia and was already on his way.

She clutched the cell phone so hard she was afraid she'd crack the case.

"Rocket?" She whispered the word.

"It's me." His voice still had that very sexy, rough edge to it, deep, the kind she felt in every molecule of her body. "Seems like you got yourself in a tight spot again."

Suddenly she knew everything would be okay. Whatever happened between them afterwards, he was going to get her out of here.

She swallowed. "Apparently I have a talent for it."

"Don't worry. We got you out once. We can do it again."

"You really are? Going to come here for me?"

"Could I do anything else?"

"Thank you." She blew out a breath of relief. "Thank you for calling and for agreeing to do this."

God. If he'd said no, she had no other options.

"There's no way I'd say no," he assured her.

"Even after all this time?" She kept her voice at a whisper. "I mean…"

"And that's my fault, not yours. I've kicked myself for it a hundred times. But we can talk about that when we get you out of there. Now listen. I need to ask some things."

"Okay." She relaxed a little, or as much as she could under the circumstances. "But let me just say thank you again."

"Plenty of time for that after we get you out. First. Are you in a safe place where you can stay for a couple more days? Your sister said you're with your friend Inez. Are you okay there?"

"Sort of." She was still lying flat on the roof and she didn't hear anything from the house below her. She had no idea if anyone had discovered her hiding place. She knew nothing. She'd been indulging herself in erotic dreams instead of protecting herself. She had to believe Inez would have found a way to warn her if there was trouble.

"What do you mean?" His voice sharpened.

"Now she's hiding me in the attic since I came to the attention of Barrera's thugs." She lowered her voice until she was nearly whispering. "And Inez told me that Ruben Vidal, Barrera's top lieutenant, has twice this week had a car full of his so-called soldiers actually drag someone out of their house to arrest them. At least they *said* arrest, but who knows."

"Damn. Mallory, I—"

"It's okay. You wouldn't believe how hard it would be to find where I'm hiding. The panels are exceptionally well concealed."

Rocket was silent for a moment. "You can keep your cell charged, right? I promise you my partners and I will have a plan together to get you out of there, but I want to be able to keep in touch with you so you know what's going on."

"So you're really going to try to get me out of this?" she asked again. And didn't she just sound stupid.

"No, we're *actually* going to get you out of this."

Relief surged through her like a tidal wave. "Thank you, I—"

"You can thank me when you're away from Santa Marita. Like I said, find a way to keep your cell charged because that's our only way to contact you."

"I will. I definitely will."

"Text me Inez's address and anything other details you think we need to put this together."

"I'll do that as soon as we hang up."

"Good. Okay, hang tight. I'll get back to you as soon as I have details for you." There was an infinitesimal pause. "That's a promise."

The call ended and Mallory lay there, her mind whirling. First of all, brutal killers were looking for her and she'd just been lying on the roof having an erotic dream and pleasuring herself? She really was losing her mind. And she was still shocked that John 'Rocket' Hardin had actually said yes to Alicia's request.

She went over every word of the conversation in her mind. Had she said the right things? The wrong things? *Damn!* She felt like she was eighteen years old instead of thirty-five. But that interlude in the cave with Rocket had been the most memorable episode of her life, bar none. She should have found a way to find him after she was safely home.

Of course, he could have looked for her, too, she thought. But he'd been an active-duty Navy SEAL, so his time was surely more obligated than hers. And after months had passed, then a year, then more years, she was too afraid that he either wouldn't remember her or would act like she was just another piece of ass. She thought he probably had plenty.

Cut it out!

Even with the hot sex they'd indulged in, he had treated her with the utmost respect. She had no reason to think that had changed, even if in all this time he had never reached out to find her. But none of that mattered. He was coming to help her now. And soon, she hoped. It couldn't be soon enough for her.

What on earth was she doing here in Santa Marita, anyway? People had warned her about the volatile situation in the country when she'd told a very few confidantes what she had planned. This was foolhardy, all because she was hyped about doing another book that exposed how a population was being terrorized and bringing it to the attention of the world at large. Now she was trapped here with a target on her back. How would these guys even get her out of here?

As soon as she disconnected, she texted Rocket Inez's address, a description of the house and that she was spending a lot of time after dark on the roof. She lay there, holding the phone close to her body, letting both conversations chase each other in her mind, until Inez eased up the flap.

"Mallory." The word was whispered.

Mallory rolled onto her side to see Inez's head just emerging from the trap door.

"Yes?" She held her breath, hoping Inez wasn't about to tell her that her brother was home and all hell was about to break loose.

"Come down and go to bed. Take your sleep when you can get it."

"It's nice up here." She managed a smile.

"But you can't spend the night here. Come on. The attic isn't much, but at least you can sleep on something softer than the roof."

"You're right. Thanks."

She eased down the short ladder until she was in the sweltering confines of the attic and made her way to the sleeping bag Inez had fixed her up with. There was a tiny window right up near the ceiling that allowed in enough air so she didn't sweat to death or suffocate. And she gave thanks for the roof, but that was really only safe after dark.

"You know the attic opens to my bedroom," Inez reminded her. "And you can sneak into the shower. Come on. Maybe your friend will get here sooner than you think."

"I hope." Mallory sat up. "I have to get out of here before Barrera comes banging at the door. I shouldn't have asked so many questions."

"But you needed to get the information," Inez reminded her, "if you are going to tell our story. And hopefully that is what your friend is going to make happen. Come on. We need to be quick about this."

When she was finished in the bathroom, with Inez standing guard, she climbed the stepstool to the attic which Inez then hid in her room. *God.* She certainly hoped Rocket and his friends would get here before Barrera and his men got their hands on her.

* * * *

"I've got something." Blaze sat back in his chair, looking at his computer screen.

Viper scowled. "It can't be good, if the look on your face means anything."

"It's Barrera's history, and it's a fucking mess. Not looking good at all." He clicked a key. "It seems he spent ten years working his way up in the Sinaloa cartel, and doing a damn good job. He was a lieutenant in one of the regional groups when the kingpin decided his nephew deserved the honor. Barrera could have made a stink, but he decided success was the best revenge."

He clicked a key again.

"He gathered his closest, most trusted henchmen and they beat feet to Santa Marita. He purchased a mansion the cheap way — killing the owners and taking possession — and from there it just got worse. By the end of a year, he'd built his own army of disgruntled Santa Marita thugs, intimidated businesses that he needed to bend under his thumb. Destroyed the other agricultural activities of the country, of course."

"Damn!"

"Uh-huh. He built his own distribution chain before you could blink and it's just gotten stronger and bolder. He grabbed hundreds of acres of agricultural land to grow his product and processes it with very cheap labor. He already had contacts for buyers and distribution. He's using the same supply chains to distribute his drugs that he worked with as part of Sinaloa."

"And no one stopped him?" Viper asked. "What about the other cartels, bigger ones?"

"By the time he was making significant money, he'd consolidated his power on Santa Marita and created his own army. It wasn't worth the time, effort, energy and expense for the cartels to bother. Although he's accumulated a disgusting amount of wealth and power, it's all confined to the little island of Santa Marita and I'd guess of little significance."

"And now he also controls the government," Blaze added.

"That he does. When the government tried to have him arrested, he killed the president and half the leaders of the country and just took it over himself. He controls every bit of the country, including the tourist business. Which, by the way, is heavy with criminals 'vacationing' from other countries."

"Rocket, do you have any idea why Mallory's friend, Inez, would leave a good job in Houston to go back to Santa Marita and fall into that mess? If she's part of Barrera's group, I'm surprised Mallory is still alive."

Rocket brought up another page on his laptop. "I didn't find any hint of that. Best guess? Lot of people getting shot there and disease is more prevalent. Her mother probably begged her to come back and work at the hospital there. Once she was home and saw what was happening, she must have reached out to her good friend, Mallory Kane."

"Who jumped in with both feet," Eagle pointed out.

Rocket nodded. "That's just who she is. And she's been very successful writing about it."

"Well." Eagle cleared his throat. "She'll only be successful this time if we can get her ass out of there in one piece. So let's get to it."

The table in Rocket's dining room was big enough to spread out the maps Eagle had downloaded, including those he'd refined using the special software he had. Rocket leaned over it, a thick marking pen in his hand.

"In order to land there, we have to come in at this end of the island," he told the others, drawing a tiny arrow. "The only way is through water, and in a way that we're not seen. According to what I've been reading, Barrera's goons are heavy on the airport, plus there's only the one marina in the harbor of Santa Marita, right near the port, and it's heavy with guards."

Rocket circled it on the map. "So underwater approach. Okay. We can swim a long way in our wet suits and with our breathing equipment. Surface near a building—I'll find pictures and print them out—ditch the wet suits and make our way to the Albados' house." He leaned back. "It sounds too simple."

"It's simple, all right," Eagle told him, "except for the ten million complications we have to prepare for. Like where can we surface and not be seen. Are there a lot of people there after midnight? All that shit."

"Not to mention that we'll need transport," Blaze pointed out.

Rocket nodded. "I'm checking the car rental places in Santa Marita. I'll use one of my other IDs to do it. Then we just have to stay unseen until the place opens."

"We could launch from a Zodiac, but we'd need to pick a place to dive and figure out what to do with the boat afterwards," Viper told them. "But first we have to get our hands on a boat if this is the plan. And we don't know how closely Barrera's thugs are checking every arrival. We're just the kind of people they'd be suspicious of."

"You're right," Blaze agreed, nodding. "We just need to figure out where to launch the Zodiac from. Plus, none of us trained as a coxswain to handle the boat, although how hard can it be? And like you said, Viper, what about when we're done with it? Leave it floating out there for Barrera's goons to find it and start a search?"

Eagle held up his hand. "Stop. We're getting ahead of ourselves."

"Yeah?" Rocket asked. "Well, we're on a tight time schedule here, in case you didn't hear me mention it. And we have to be damn fucking careful who knows about this."

"Understood, but we need help down there. We can't just waltz in there and pluck Mallory out from under their noses. We need details, and knowledge and all the shit that goes into something like this. And this might not be the right way to effect her recue."

"What do you mean?" Rocket glared at Eagle, knowing he was losing his control. "What way do you suggest? We don't have any contacts down there to help us or guide us."

"That you know of," Eagle told him.

"What?"

"Contacts. That you know of. But I just realized I do. Have a contact."

Rocket stared at him. "Who in hell would that be?"

"Ed Teagan. We were on the same SEAL Team together. It didn't hit my brain until I looked at a map of the entire area. Santa Marita is just off the coast of Mexico, not far from the little city of Manzanillo."

"And?" Viper prompted. "Did he just not re-up then leave at the end of the next tour the way you did?"

Eagle was silent for a moment, as if choosing his words.

"Ed lost a leg and injured an arm when our vehicle hit an IED, so he was medically discharged with injuries. He has a prosthesis, but he's so damn good with it you'd never know. He's mobile enough for what we want."

"And this is important because?" Blaze asked.

"But it also gave him a thirst for stopping people like Barrera. It's in his blood. We ding each other now and then to make sure we're both alive. So far, the answer continues to be yes. I get little hints of what he might have his fingers in whenever I talk to him."

"Where is he now?" Rocket asked.

"Running a bar and dive shop in Manzanillo, along with a charter fishing service, which I get the feeling works as a cover for whatever stuff he's involved in. You can take a man out of the SEALs, but you can't take the SEAL out of the man. Truthfully, I don't think he's ever really retired from blackwork, no matter what he says. And Manzanillo is a perfect jumping-off spot for us since we can't exactly pop up in Santa Marita and say here we are."

Viper gave him a hard look. "You trust this guy? Because if we read him in, he could hold a lot of lives in his hands."

"With my life."

"Well, then—" Viper began.

Blaze interrupted him. "Can you just go ahead and call him? Get him on the horn?"

"We usually Skype. I can go ahead and see if he's online."

The others looked at Rocket.

"Your call, Rocketman," Viper said.

Rocket nodded. "Go ahead. Do it."

They watched as Eagle activated the Skype app, clicked on Ed Teagan's name and waited while the call ring sounded. In a moment, a face appeared of a man about their age, well-tanned with hair past his collar and a slightly scruffy beard. He wore a ball cap with *Salty Dog Dive Bar* on it.

"Eagle, my friend. You so bored you're calling me in the middle of the day now?"

"Just thought I'd surprise you." He grinned, but it disappeared almost at once. "Listen, this isn't exactly a social call. You got a couple of minutes?"

Ed looked out at him from the screen for a long moment before he nodded. "Yes. Let me get the door." He left the screen for a moment but was back quickly. "You sound serious, my friend. You got troubles?"

"First let me introduce you to my partners in Galaxy."

The others each poked their faces at the screen as Eagle called their names, then stood behind him.

"Okay." Ed narrowed his eyes. "Nice meeting you all. Eagle said his partners are all former SEALs, so I'm guessing we're not having a tea party?"

Eagle thought for a moment how to phrase this. "Let's suppose, for a second, that I knew someone who needed to steal a person out of Santa Marita right under General Barrera's nose."

"Whoa." Ed blinked. "Are you fucking kidding me? Felix Barrera? Is this a fairy tale or a real mission? Because Barrera is a dangerous asshole and Santa Marita is about the size of my shower. What the fuck is this person, whoever it is, doing there?"

"Just say for a minute it's real and we want to extract this person. Is this something you'd spare a few minutes for? Or are you, as you love to say, long out of the business? A retired beach bum?"

Ed was silent for the space of two heartbeats.

"If it was anyone but you asking, I'd act like I had no idea what the fuck you were talking about. But since it's you, want to tell me what's really going on? Because messing with Barrera can be a death wish."

Eagle gave him a brief but complete synopsis of the situation and their mission to retrieve Mallory Kane.

"And we need to do it like yesterday," Rocket added.

"Uh, Mallory's kind of Rocket's project," Eagle explained.

"Uh-huh." Ed stared out of the screen for a moment then nodded. "Okay, before you give me the details and I agree to anything, let me make you aware of the fact that General Barrera has absolutely no morals, no scruples, no honor. And his thugs—oh, excuse me, soldiers—are everywhere. This may be the trickiest thing you've ever done."

"Trickier than snatching a high-value target from a Taliban village right under their noses?" Blaze asked.

"Rescuing a captive in the same situation?" Rocket added.

Ed nodded. "Because once you got outside the village or encampment, you had miles of desert and mountains to hide in before your exfil arrived. Here, you have no place to go because every inch is covered by Barrera's so-called army."

Eagle frowned. "So you're saying it's impossible?"

"No." Ed shook his head. "Just tricky. Barrera is a cold, stupid, arrogant, power-hungry piece of shit. His thugs dressed in their so-called army uniforms are all over Santa Marita. He's got his sycophants who see a chance to suck up to him if they support his drug business, but everyone else, he terrorizes at will. The bloodshed has been beyond belief."

"Damn." Eagle spat out the word.

"Yeah. No shit. You're up against it here," Ed told them. "But if you're really going to do this, then I'm your man. I know every corner of that island country like my back yard."

"Originally, before we got more information, I had thought sneaking in through the marina would be our best bet," Blaze suggested. "Find a car rental place so we'd have transport. But since you tell us it's so heavily guarded, we definitely need another plan."

Ed nodded. "Most definitely. I know we've all done it that way before, blended in with the population without sounding alarm bells."

"But?"

"This is different. Barrera's paranoid about new people coming to the island, even if they turn out to be harmless. I've seen him order soldiers to follow people for three days to be sure they weren't going to cause him trouble. Besides, he uses the marina to ship out his drugs. He's got a whole fleet of boats where the owners are part of his cartel and they move his stuff down the pipeline for a cut of the profits. Works out well for everyone and they aren't in danger of discovery on highways or on planes."

"But don't agencies like the DEA or Interpol have their eye on him?"

"Sure, but he and his friends have set this up so cleverly and have such tight control over the country that getting even a scrap of evidence is next to impossible. And like I said, sneaking someone into Santa Marita is all but impossible."

Eagle frowned. "Who are the people who own the boats?"

"Not the kind normally associated with something like this. As stupid as Barrera is, his chief of operations is smarter than you can imagination. They recruited people you'd never suspect so stop and frisk isn't an option. But every boat that docks at the marina that he doesn't sign off on in advance has to go through his version of customs. Even if I hid you on my boat, getting you off and into town is impossible."

"Shit." Viper spat the word.

"And you can't rent a car anywhere in Santa Marita because Barrera has such a lock on the country that he'd know in five minutes. People are paid to feed him every piece of information about strangers to Santa Marita. His goons would be all over you."

Rocket was getting irritated by the whole wall of obstacles they were facing. Mallory's life was in more danger every minute she was in Santa Marita.

"So do you have any bright ideas to share with us? Because we need to get this woman out *yesterday*."

"As a matter of fact, yes."

"So let's hear it," Eagle prompted.

"You happen to be talking to someone who Barrera thinks of as a friend. He and his so-called inner circle used to hang out at the Grand Hotel here in Manzanillo while they were making their plans to take over Santa

Marita. We're just outside the borders of Sinaloa, close enough that *El Jefe* wouldn't wonder what they were doing but far enough away that they didn't have people hanging over them."

"And that means?" Eagle prompted.

"He and his men like to fish. While they were putting together the invasion of Santa Marita and the creation of the cartel, sometimes they came down to the beach and hung out in front of my place. I also do fishing charters and a few times I took out Barrera and his men. They're obnoxious shitholes, but their money is good. When they took over teeny-tiny Santa Marita, I kept getting calls from Barrera when he wanted to go fishing. Likes to bring his friends and play the big shot. Still does."

"So you're one of the good guys, as far as he's concerned?"

"Yup. I've been to Santa Marita enough times for him that my presence isn't questioned. But like I said, the place is so tiny I can't just pull my boat into the marina and take you on a tourist jaunt through town. Repeating myself, Barrera wants to know who every person is who arrives on 'his' property. He's so paranoid that I've even had his so-called soldiers follow some of my customers from the hotel here who wanted to check out the town as they soaked up the atmosphere."

The Galaxy partners exchanged a glance.

"Well, shit." Rocket stared at the screen. "That doesn't sound good. Where did this guy come from, anyway?

"Barrera was a little cog in a big wheel in the Sinaloa cartel. When he wanted his own kingdom, he deliberately chose a place small enough that he could control it with fear and muscle. And it's so penny ante that Sinaloa won't make an issue of him doing this. What I'm saying is we can't just drive up to the house where your friend is and snatch your target."

Eagle grinned at the screen. "We're always up for a challenge. Right, guys?"

They all nodded.

"And you're really willing to do this? If Barrera gets wind of this, we could all be dead meat, especially you."

"You're not telling me anything I don't know." Ed's voice was flat and uninflected. "Like I said, I'm completely aware of what's going on there. But you should know that lately things haven't been so steady for Barrera. He's not the businessman that the head of Sinaloa is, so a couple of his drug deals have gone bad. He's beginning to lose control of the country and he's reacting in not very good ways. If not for Ruben Vidal, his chief lieutenant and good right hand, things would really have gone to shit."

"Wait." Blaze's voice had a hard edge. "If all that's true, it's not fair of us to drag you into a mess like this. It could damage your situation."

"Let me worry about that," Ed told him. "Eagle saved my life. That's a plain and simple fact. I'm glad to have a chance to repay him."

They all turned their attention to Eagle, who shrugged.

"Nothing any of you wouldn't have done. Anyway, you can trust this guy, or I never would have reached out to him. He wouldn't do this if he didn't want to and besides, he's our only option."

"I get it." Rocket blew out a breath. "Okay. Let's do it. Ed, tell us what you need from us and what we do to get moving on this. I had Mallory text me the address of her friend's house where she's hiding."

He read it off.

"Got it. The first thing I'm going to do is get photos of the house where your girl is hiding out. I'll also pull up the map of the island and see what our escape routes are. Then we'll have some idea of how to get her out of the house and out of the city. Meanwhile you all should do the same thing with the maps so you have a visual of what we'll be discussing."

"Time is short," Rocket reminded him. "When will you have the info for us? When you give us the Go sign, I'm going to have our pilot fly us down there. We'll land at Manzanillo."

"Yes. Barrera keeps a close eye on everyone in and out of the airport on Santa Marita."

Ed frowned and Rocket could almost see the thoughts whirling in his head.

"How about scheduling a call for late tomorrow afternoon? Say four o'clock? It turns out your timing is great."

"Why do you say that?"

"It so happens I'm going to Santa Marita tomorrow anyway. Among other things, I have business with Barrera."

"What kind of business?" Rocket snapped and looked at his friend. "Eagle, are you sure this guy's on the up and up?"

"Yes," Eagle said. "I'm positive."

"Not to worry," Ed said at the same time. "Listen, I understand your reluctance. The man thinks he owns me, which is not a bad situation to have. I can do a lot of things without raising eyebrows or being questioned."

"What kind of things?" Blaze demanded.

"Uh. Sorry these guys are being so rude," Eagle said.

Ed shook his head. "Not rude at all. This is a critical, dangerous situation and they need to be able to trust me. Listen, sometimes I do favors for other people that require me to be able to move around the country without generating a lot of questions."

"I figured you weren't just hanging in the sun, selling drinks and fishing. And good for you."

A sober expression washed over Ed's face. "It was hard finding a reason to get up every morning in the beginning. Then a little project came my way, I was talked into doing it and things began to look up."

"And now you have other projects if you want them," Rocket guessed.

"Let's just say I can stay as busy or not as I want to. But that all means I can get to Santa Marita without causing a stir and get what info we need. But I have to do it in a way that escapes notice, so four o'clock works best."

"We're in a hurry here," Rocket reminded him again. "Mallory could be discovered at any minute, but I want to make sure we've covered all our bases."

"If Ed says they are, then they are." Eagle jumped in.

"Take it easy." Rocket looked at his friend. "Just checking, like I always do."

"I can get it pulled together by then," Ed assured him. "I'll get on it the minute we hang up." He grinned. "I have my secret resources."

Rocket didn't ask what they were. He figured it was better if he didn't know.

"One more thing," Ed added. "I know I don't have to tell you, but I will anyway. If you haven't already, download detailed maps of all of Santa Marita. Study them like it's the key to success, because you have to know every nook and cranny to stay out of sight, especially after we grab Mallory. We'll go over them tomorrow, but you should be very familiar with them first."

"We already went over them once, but we'll look for more detailed ones and memorize every inch of them." Just as they used to do in the SEALs. "We're plotting this just like a mission, and counting on the same level of success."

They set a time to Skype the next day. When the call ended, Rocket leaned back in his chair and took a moment to settle his nerves.

"I have to say," he told Eagle, "your friend seems to know what he's talking about."

Eagle nodded. "I'd trust him with my life. And yours. And anyone else's."

"That's good, because that's exactly what we're doing. Thanks for reaching out to him." He paused. "That must have been some mission you guys ended on."

"It was bad. Okay, let's go over what we know so we have our act together when we Skype with Ed tomorrow. Let's make sure we have the best maps available, download them, print copies for everyone and get to it. Then we'll look at the clips we've got covering Barrera's rise to power."

Once Eagle pointed out which ones were the best, they all grabbed the copies that rolled off Rocket's large printer and spread them out on the table.

"Like Ed said." Blaze ran his finger over the map. "It won't hurt to get some upfront work done. Let's memorize the layout and mark danger spots. Then see if we're in line with what Ed will have for us."

Rocket pushed back from the table.

"First I'm going to text Mallory and tell her we're working on a plan."

He just hoped Mallory had another day left to be safe.

Chapter Five

Rocket ripped off his jeans and T-shirt, tossed them in the laundry basket and crawled into bed in his boxer briefs. He was both mentally exhausted and emotionally psyched. The conversation with Mallory had been brief. He hadn't wanted to risk the chance of a longer one. But he'd be able to tell how close to tears she was when he'd told her they were arranging her escape plan. And for Mallory — who, in the short time he'd known her he remembered as one of the strongest women he'd ever met — that was a clear indication of how desperate her situation was.

Then they'd spent more than an hour poring over the maps, tracing with blue pens what they thought were optimum routes. *Memorizing details.* Eagle also sent the files to all their phones, cell and satellite, so they'd have the information no matter what. For whichever routes Ed suggested, they'd use red. They also found the street where Inez lived and marked her address, memorizing the image. The houses were jammed so close together that in many cases, they touched. There were, however, alleys in the back, although they looked so narrow that he didn't know if a person could actually fit in one. Getting Mallory off the roof and out of the house would be the first critical point. Hopefully Ed, who they had faith was familiar with all of this, would have some suggestions.

Now he wanted nothing more than to catch some sleep so he'd be alert for the Skype call tomorrow. He lay back on the pillow, hoping he was mentally drained enough to fall asleep and not dream. Since Alicia Kane had contacted him, it seemed he could not get erotic images of Mallory out of his head. Even after five years, he was haunted by the picture of her lying naked on his cammies on the floor of that cave. The desperation of the escape, the sense of the danger still surrounding them, the heat and dust that had filled the environment, had all faded as he'd let his gaze roam over her body.

He could still taste her on his tongue, still feel the slick wetness of her sex as he'd fucked her with his fingers. The hot bud of her clit that was like an ignition switch to her body. And when he'd slid his cock inside her tight, wet heat, it had taken every bit of self-control he could dig up to go slow and make sure she enjoyed every minute of it.

As happened so often to him — too often — the image of a naked Mallory burst into his brain.

This time the scene wasn't the cave, but a bedroom, and they were stretched out on silky sheets. *God!* She was so mouthwatering. Her toned body also boasted luscious curves, like the roundness of her breasts with their tempting nipples. His cock hardened just at the sight of them, not that it wasn't already swollen with need. When he pinched those little buds, she gasped and the pulse at the hollow of her throat accelerated. He sucked first one nipple then the other into his mouth, lightly scraping them with his teeth, eliciting a guttural moan from deep in her throat.

Make it good for her, he told himself. *If this is the one and only time, make it one she'll never forget.*

Sucking her sweet nipples until they turned a deep rose, he gave each breast a last squeeze before trailing his lips down between them until he reached her navel. He traced the curled flesh with the tip of his tongue, then licked a path down to the auburn thatch of curls between her thighs that beckoned to the entrance of her sex. He inhaled her rich scent before moving down so he could push her thighs apart.

Sweet Jesus!

He was no stranger to the sight of a woman's sex, but this one? Damn, it rocked him back. He gently spread the lips apart, the pink flesh a sexy contrast with the auburn hair. And wet! So wet. *Damn!* He treated himself to a slow lick on either side of her clit, up and down, gathering her moisture with the tip of his tongue.

If his cock had been hard before, it was swollen almost to the point of pain by this time. He wanted to drive into her right to the hilt and fuck her brains out until they both screamed from the pleasure. Instead, he gritted his teeth and made himself hold back. Mallory Kane was ten cuts above the women he usually grabbed to have a hot night with and he was going to treat her accordingly.

He nipped her clit, teasing it, before running his tongue over every inch of her tender skin. She moaned and shifted beneath him, thrusting herself up to him. When he peeled the pink lips open again and thrust his tongue inside, she wrapped her legs around his neck and pulled herself to him more tightly. The more he worked his tongue inside her, the harder she rode it. He licked and sucked until she tightened around his tongue, her body going rigid. When he curled it to drag the tip against her hot spot, she exploded, screaming with the pleasure, convulsing, digging her heels into him as she locked herself to his mouth.

Then it slowed and subsided, her legs falling away, her body slack. He took one last lick, capturing her essence on his tongue before shifting positions so he could look directly into her eyes.

"You taste so good." He smiled. "Just incredible."

"I want to taste you, too," she insisted, even as she struggled to even out her breathing.

"And I want to be inside you." His lips curved in a sly grin. "But ladies' choice."

She moved so suddenly that she startled him, shifting her position and shoving him over onto his back. Before he could protest or move, she was straddling him, her mound pressing against his balls, the fingers of one hand curled around his very hard cock.

"Watch it," he warned. "I'm pretty close to the edge here."

One corner of her mouth ticked up in a hint of a smile. "So you're saying I should be quick?"

He barely managed a tiny chuckle. "Well, not too quick."

Even as they were talking, she began moving her hand slowly up and down the length of his dick. Every two or three strokes, she bent down and licked the head, teasing at the tiny opening. With each taste of him she took, the orgasm building in him grew stronger and more fierce. He wanted to be inside her, to feel her wet heat clutching at him while he spilled into her, but fucking damn! Her mouth was the stuff dreams were made of.

He thrust the fingers of one hand into her hair, using the grip to guide her head, eyes closed as sensations flooded his body. He wanted her to slow down. No, he wanted her to go faster. Shit, he didn't know what he wanted, because his body was doing its own choosing and it wanted to come right now.

"More," he growled. "Faster."

Even though he wanted it to last forever, he was right at the edge and Mallory seemed to know it. Her sweet, talented tongue and lips were working their magic as her slim fingers stroked him up and down.

Then he was there. Exploding over her hand, body convulsing with each spasm, over and over again.

"Don't let go," he whispered as the release subsided and his body relaxed. He opened his eyes to look at her and…

And like a slap of cold water realized he was in his own bed, alone, and it was his hand wrapped around his dick. *Well, fucking damn shit.* He let his head fall back to the pillow, eyes closed while he tried to recapture the dream, but it was gone. In its place, though, was an image of Mallory, her eyes wide with fear as he'd first seen them on the day of her rescue.

"I'm coming, Mallory," he whispered. "Please just hang on a little while longer."

The night was anything but restful for him. He was plagued by alternate images of Mallory naked beneath him and Mallory held captive by thugs masquerading as soldiers. There seemed to be no rest for him, no matter how much he tossed and turned. At six in the morning, he realized sleep wasn't in the cards for him, threw on shorts and a T-shirt and went for a run. His house was located on a street that ended at Bayshore Boulevard. Rocket liked to run along the water, especially early in the morning. Usually by the time he finished, his brain would be unkinked and he'd be ready to start the day.

Not today, however. The image of Mallory didn't seem to want to leave his brain. Finally, he gave up the ghost and headed home to shower and dress. His partners would be arriving before long to discuss what they'd discovered about General Felix Barrera.

When they all had their laptops open and mugs filled with coffee beside them, Blaze cleared his throat.

"Let me go first," he suggested. "I spent most of the night researching this clown." Blaze had his laptop open in front him, as did the others. "He's a thug, plain and simple. He spent a long time as a *sicario*—those who did the violent work like assassinations, kidnappings, brutal murder. Well, you get the idea. But he got tired of being on the third rung of power, even as he could satisfy his thirst for spilling blood."

"I thought that was common to all of them," Viper interjected. "No matter where in the world they are."

Blaze nodded. "And you can bet others follow this pattern. But Barrera is in a unique position. He was within spitting distance of a peaceful island country with a thriving tourist business and a good economy. Barrera and his men could overwhelm them, kill any objectors and move right in. Once they did, they began recruiting all the lowlifes they could find in the country, and they were off and running."

"Just like in the Third World countries we saw in Africa," Viper put in. "Right? We've seen how it works. The people don't have a chance."

"Right," Blaze agreed. "They're too afraid. The cartel sees they have just enough to get by on and they kill people who don't like it."

He went on to detail everything he'd found, which wasn't any different from anything else they knew about the operation of other cartels.

"I also read a lot about the Sinaloa cartel," Blaze continued, "and how they grew. Barrera has an advantage because the country is small, easy to control and they can distribute from there at will. Not only are they delivering their own product, but because they control both air and water traffic and use their own guerrilla cops to guard it, they've begun handling shipments from other cartels."

"Right." Blaze nodded. "This is what gives them the control they have of it. They're in charge of all entries and exits into the country. They can send shipments anywhere in the world and take a healthy percentage of the profits."

Rocket raked his fingers through his hair in a gesture of frustration. "The more I hear, the more impossible this project seems."

"Then it's right up our alley," Eagle told him. "Wouldn't you say?"

Viper's lips twisted in a semblance of a grin. "Isn't that why we tell people we're their last resort?"

Rocket nodded. "I guess this is our best chance so far to prove we're right."

Their habit was always to talk an op to death, suggesting the myriad ways something could go wrong then figuring out what to do to combat them. They all projected possibilities and dissected them, continuing even through lunch after it was delivered.

At four on the dot, Eagle's laptop signaled an incoming Skype call. He accepted it, motioning for the others to move around him so they could see, too.

"You guys do your homework?" Ed asked as soon as the call was connected.

"More than," Eagle told him. "What have you got for us?"

"Everything we'll need."

Rocket leaned closer to the screen. "How did you manage that?"

"Trade secrets. But it worked out that I could go over to the island without raising suspicions or showing up on their radar as trouble."

"Why do you say that?"

"One of Barrera's men called this morning and said the general wanted to talk to me about a couple of fishing trips. He's got some customers coming to visit him and he wants to give them a good time."

Rocket frowned. "I can't believe people actually come to Santa Marita and pick up their product."

"They don't," Ed told them. "But he likes to wine and dine and show off for new customers so they believe they're buying product from a powerful man who can deliver with no problem. And, by the way, who can offer sanctuary to anyone who needs it. No one's going to set foot in Santa Marita without his permission."

"So what's the best way for us to do it?" Rocket wanted to know.

"First, we go fishing, so if anyone sees me with you guys, they'll remember I had you out on a charter. I mentioned to one of Barrera's lieutenants that I might be taking out some hotel guests so when they scope out the boat, they won't think it's anything out of the ordinary."

"But we're not going onto the island itself?" Blaze asked.

"No. I thought about it, but Barrera's more uptight these days than usual. Scuttlebutt has it that he's pissed because Mallory has disappeared and he can't find her. That means every new face gets extra scrutiny, and we don't want that."

"That's the truth," Rocket agreed.

"However, I'm going to take a trip over there before you all get here. One of Barrera's lieutenants wants some special stuff they can't get on the island and I said I'd pick it up. It's good cover to get a handle on things."

"We'll leave it up to you."

"Good, because I'm not sure how long the Albados have before Barrera gets tired of waiting for Mallory to show her face and raids the house, tearing it apart. Or scoops up the family to wring it out of them. Now here's what we'll do."

They listened carefully as Ed outlined his plan. The trickiest part, of course, was getting Mallory out of the house, but he'd managed to come up with a way to do that which Rocket thought was brilliant. He'd run it past Ed the moment they sat down together.

"And remember," Ed told them. "We have two options, one of which I hope we don't have to use."

"And they are?" Rocket prompted.

"First is get her to the place I'm thinking of using to land you guys. Get a Zodiac close enough to haul ass out of there. Option two, which is dicier, is to hike through the jungle to the water. But if you recall when we were planning this, on the map it shows the jungle ending close to the water. But..." Ed thought for a mment. "One, the ground there is very rocky and two, there's a steep drop to the water and no real place for a Zodiac to pick us up. If it was just us, I'd say we can rappel down, but I don't want to put Mallory at risk that way."

"A helo pick up would be much better," Rocket suggested.

Ed nodded. "I can arrange for that."

"Saint will be with us," Eagle told him. "Our pilot. He's flying us down. Tell me the best place to rent a chopper and we'll have him on standby."

"Tell him when you get to Manzanillo to contact Vacation Rides, ask for Don and use my name."

Eagle burst out laughing. "Same old Ed. You never really left the game at all, did you?"

"Ssh. Don't tell anyone."

"We'll fly down tomorrow," Eagle told him when Ed had finished. "We've got a Gulfstream 550, so we don't need to bother with commercial schedules. We checked and Manzanillo has a good-sized airport, so we won't be conspicuous. At least under normal circumstances. Does Barrera monitor airports in the area outside of Santa Marita?"

"Not on a steady basis. It's too close to Sinaloa territory for him to have his people there on regular assignment. Besides, I think he's convinced no one would dare invade his territory."

"His kind always are."

"You'll need SCUBA gear, but I have plenty, so you don't need to worry about bringing it."

"What are we using it for?" Rocket asked.

"You'll see. I want to make sure I have everything arranged before I lay it out for you."

"We'll take care of the hotel as soon as we're done with this call. I'll text you the name of the corporation we'll use."

One of the first things Tom Hernandez, their friend and attorney, had helped them set up was a list of dummy corporations with credentials and credit cards. They needed something to serve as a cover when they went into strange places where people might question them. Like now. They had four that they rotated, since Tom had said if they used just one, people could catch on to it. They'd learned in the SEALS that it was best not to leave a real-life footprint whatever they were doing. Anyone could be watching and listening and who would put two and two together. In addition, they'd had many successful missions which had also garnered a number of enemies for Galaxy. They weren't leading anyone to their door.

"Good. You can rent a car at the airport," Ed was saying. "There's three rental companies, but even so, Manzanillo is a busy tourist area, so I'd do it in advance. And rather than trying to hide your arrival, you want to be open and aboveboard, blending in with the rest of the tourists."

Eagle snorted. "It's not our first rodeo, Ed."

"Yeah, yeah, I know." Ed paused. "The first thing we'll do is go fishing."

"Fishing?" Blaze snapped the word out. "This is the second time you mentioned it. What for?"

"Out on my boat. The only place we can have a conversation without in-person or electronic eavesdropping. Got it?"

"We do," Eagle bit off. "As I say, we're not exactly novices."

97

"Also, out on the water, I can give you a good look at Santa Marita without actually having to go ashore. You need to get the image of the place fixed in your minds. I'll make sure you get to see everything from the water before we drop anchor for a while."

"Good idea." Eagle nodded. "But we'll have to go ashore eventually if we're going to get Mallory Kane out of there."

"Yes, but not when the sun is shining bright. Barrera has his men watching every new face coming to Santa Marita. If they do anything the least bit suspicious, they're toast. Barrera is such an immense power in Santa Marita, and is suspicious of anyone and anything. He also has a short fuse. And I think that's where your girl got in trouble. She was a little too nosy for her own good."

Viper snapped his fingers. "That's what the SCUBA gear is for."

"It is indeed. I have the perfect landing spot and the perfect place to hit the water from."

Rocket looked around at the others. "Questions? Comments? Before we disconnect?"

They all shook their heads.

"All right, then. If any pop up, we'll save them until we get there and meet with you," he told the other man.

"Good. The first thing you'll do is check into a hotel, the one that refers me for fishing charters, so nothing looks out of place. I'm sure you guys have at least one credit card to use that doesn't come back to any of you, right?"

"We do," Blaze told him. "And you said the Grand Plaza, right?"

"Yes. You can blend in with the crowd easily there, plus they know me. If anyone asks you what you're doing in Manzanillo and you tell them you're going fishing with me, they'll accept it at face value., When you get here, I'll have more information and we'll go over every single detail. Anything else?"

"We're good," Eagle told him.

"Okay. Write down this phone number and text me when you leave and what your arrival time is."

After Eagle closed out the call, they all stared at each other for a long moment.

"Well," Blaze said at last, "I'd better call Saint and let him know what's happening. He'll have to figure flying time from here to Manzanillo so we know when to leave if we're gonna get there about eight-thirty."

Rocket pushed his chair back and stood up. "I'll get one of our backup credit cards out of my safe and make the hotel reservations."

"Four rooms," Viper told him. "I don't think the kind of guys we're supposed to be would share."

"Got it."

Less than thirty minutes later, they were set and Eagle texted the information to Ed.

The answer came back right away.

Getting things set on this end. We are a go.

* * * *

Felix Barrera thought living in the presidential palace was one of the top perks of ruling Santa Marita. His office was filled with expensive furniture and pictures of him with his 'clients' hung on the walls. A handcrafted humidor sat on the corner of the huge mahogany desk and a phone with multiple lines was at his right hand. Across from him were two hand-tooled leather armchairs for special guests. Everyone else stood. There was no computer, no stack of files or pile of notes. And the phone was mostly to reach people assigned to work for him in the building. Most of his calls were made on one of two cell phones and the only paperwork he did was signing important documents placed in front of him.

The bulk of his time spent meeting important 'clients' of his drug trade, being driven through town to spy on people and assess whatever was going on, and screwing the women he had Ruben fetch for him. It was good to be the king. Or, as in his case, *el president*.

Now he sat back in his well-upholstered office chair, picked up one of the specially blended cigars he ordered each month, lit it and took a long, slow draw. A good cigar and fine brandy could always smooth out the bumps in the road. Lately, he was finding there to be more and more, and today there was one he couldn't figure out how to fix. In fact, it seemed that it had all been so easy in the beginning. Get rid of the president and his loyal followers. Take over the government. Grow and sell a lot of drugs. Kill people if they didn't follow orders.

After all, Santa Marita was only a tiny dot in the Pacific, although big enough for his ego. And this way he could control everything. Plus, it was too small for Sinaloa to bother with. So he operated autonomously, controlling everything, building his drug trade, hosting rich criminals from all over the world. It fed his ego and gave him great satisfaction.

But the excessive killing wasn't achieving what he wanted it to and even the new *turistas* he attracted to Santa Marita, drug dealers and international criminals, weren't too happy with blood running in the streets. He drew them here with promises of a relaxed existence where their money could buy them anything, no extradition and a bank he controlled where they could hide their money. He was beginning to get the feeling that they thought he couldn't handle his situation without so much ancillary damage.

Maybe he was a little hasty on the trigger. His men apparently were. He'd figure out a way to fix that without losing control. Ruben would help him. None of this would be possible without Ruben, his unequalled right hand.

He blew smoke circles in the air and looked at his most trusted lieutenant, Ruben Vidal. The man had been with him since the days with Sinaloa and the only one he'd trusted to be his top *teniente* when he'd made the break from that cartel. He'd done something no one else had, planned his coup and executed it. It had been a bold move but had succeeded only because in the end he'd had a sit-down with the *capo*. He'd told him he could develop a raw territory and Sinaloa would get a cut of the profits. It was certainly better than a bloody battle.

Ruben had been a godsend as they'd built their army and set up the structure of the Barrera cartel. It was Ruben who had convinced him that killing the president of Santa Marita and taking over the government would give him the total control of the country. No worries about having to smuggle things out. Ruben who had reminded him that force was the tool to accomplish things. Ruben who helped him recruit and run the army that daily patrolled the streets of the island.

And Ruben who had first brought the *gringa* to his attention and told him she spelled trouble. He couldn't say why, he told Barrera, but he smelled it. Now the woman had disappeared.

"Still no sign of that bitch?"

Ruben shook his head. "Nada. It's as if she vanished in a puff of smoke, which we both know in Santa Marita is next to impossible."

"And nothing to tell us exactly who she is or why she's visiting Inez Albado?"

"Not a sniff. On the surface she seems to be nothing more than what she appears. And she's been doing the usual tourist things since she got here, wandering around Santa Marita, hitting the bars and cantinas, either by herself or with the Albado woman. Still..."

"Still, you get a strange feeling about her," Barrera guessed.

"I do. Mainly because in the short time she's been here, she can't have acquired anyone to help her disappear like this. We've been keeping an eye on her since she started chatting people up in bars and restaurants on a regular basis and absolutely no one pops into mind that would fit that bill. But someone has to be doing this. The question is, who?"

"And a good question it is. Santa Marita is not that big and we have a big enough army. We need to start looking at strangers."

"But not scooping them up right away," Vidal reminded him. "We don't want to send out warning signals, or screw with someone who could turn out to be valuable to us."

"Of course, of course." Barrera nodded. "As usual, you are right. Your instincts are particularly good. That's one of the things that makes you so important to me. If you think something's off, I agree with you. But what? What the fuck could she be doing here? And why?"

"One of my guards texted me when she showed up at the hospital, but I get a hinky feeling for her. He asked for her identification and she showed him her driver's license and her passport, neither of which gave us any information I could use. I took the information and looked up her passport on the dark web, and nada. All I got was the fact that she's a copy editor for an advertising firm and seems to lead a very boring life." He paused. "That is, for a *chica* who looks like her."

Felix lifted an eyebrow. "So, your antennae were quivering."

Ruben nodded. "There's something there. I can't put my finger on it, but…something."

"And she wasn't at the nurse's house when you went there?"

"No. And we searched every inch of the place."

"Well, keep an eye on it." He took another draw on the cigar. "What do the Inez woman's parents do? What is their work?"

"They both work at Santa Marita Public Utilities. The mother is in customer relations and the father is an electrician. Very dull to watch."

"But you're keeping an eye on them."

Ruben nodded. "Although they are truly dull people. Go to work every morning. They share a car, so he carpools, leaving the vehicle for her. When it's her turn, she has a friend pick her up."

"Wait." Barrera held up a hand. "Could they sneak this woman out of the house in the carpool vehicle?"

"I don't see how. We've watched the house for the past couple of days. When the vehicle arrives, it stops in front and waits for Albado to come out."

Barrera frowned. "I don't know. The gringos are very experienced at planting people who look nothing like what they really are. We dealt with that when we were still part of the Sinaloa organization. She gives off that same vibe."

"I'm well aware," Ruben agreed. "How do you want to proceed?"

"I still have the feeling she's somehow stashed away in that house." He stared at his cigar for a moment before tapping the ash into the ashtray next to him. "Keep an eye on the nurse. If anyone will be involved in whatever that woman does, it will be her. Watch everything she does, but check the house on a regular basis, too."

Ruben opened his mouth to say something, then apparently thought better of it and just nodded.

"What?" Barrera asked. "Whatever it is, say it. You don't have to hold back with me. You know that."

Of all the men closest to him, Ruben Vidal was the only one he gave such freedom to, the only one he completely trusted. The man was smart, smarter than most of his high-level men. *Maybe smarter than all of them.* Sometimes he wondered how long the man would continue to be happy playing second fiddle, but Barrera wasn't stupid. He also knew that having that leading position was almost as good as being the top dog if the rewards were worth it. Barrera continued to make sure they were, because having Ruben in that position was key to his continued success.

"Well, I've been thinking. It's almost impossible to completely disappear in Santa Marita. We're an island, and we control every manner of arrival and exit. We run the marina, the airport, the docks. Everything. A person cannot get off this island unless we give them permission. Right? So I think this is not some stupid bitch we are looking for. And I don't think her name is really Melinda Clayton."

Barrera studied him. "So what do you suggest?"

"Keep eyes on the house. I know that bitch is there somewhere and I'm going to figure how to find out. They can only hide so much."

"You can't be obvious about it," Barrera warned. "I'm sure you know that. They're smart. They have to be in order to keep her hidden. Find a way to hide someone who can keep watch."

"That's my plan," Ruben agreed. "It will take some complicated maneuvering on their part if she's there and they want to move her. We can't let that happen. But don't worry. I'll figure it out."

Barrera smiled. "I know you will. You always do." He dropped another collar of ash in the dish. "But we have other business going on that we have to protect and not call attention to."

"We do." Ruben nodded. "We have a large shipment going out this weekend that needs to be packaged for delivery. I'm sending a crew to handle it. We're meeting the customer out on the water about ten miles from here on Sunday."

"Very good." Barrera nodded his approval. "And I understand we're entertaining a possible new customer this weekend?"

Ruben smiled. "Another reason to postpone the raid on the Albado house until tomorrow night. As I hoped, Gerard Moreau and his team are flying in this weekend, to the airport here. We'll be having dinner with them here Friday night, then entertaining them on Saturday before taking them to the warehouses."

"They want to see the fields, also," Barrera reminded him. Moreau was going to be a high-value customer and deserved the full treatment.

"And he'll get it."

"I trust you'll make sure this Melinda Clayton or whatever her name is will be under control by the time Moreau and his men get here?"

"That's my goal. I am putting our best men on it."

"We can't let the nothing little bitch fuck things up. We have too good a thing going here."

"I know," Ruben agreed. "Trust me. I'll take care of it."

He left, and Barrera continued sitting in his chair, thinking. Breaking away from Sinaloa had been a very dangerous, calculated risk. If he hadn't seen others do it, he might never have taken the chance. But now there were successful offshoots who in a way became extensions of Sinaloa. They assisted in the distribution of product, increasing their income as well with a nice percentage of the profits. He realized *El Jefe* could have gone to war with him over this, but the man had a head for business. Killing Barrera and his men wouldn't have accomplished anything except to maybe discourage others from doing the same thing. But that might have impacted him economically. And he'd figured out a way to send the message that if anyone else wanted to try this, they'd better be methodical planners and have their shit together, like Barrera did.

But all of it could come crashing down if that little bitch was more than what she pretended to be.

Chapter Six

They were at the hangar at eleven the next day, loading their gear while Saint did his preflight check. Rocket would have been happier leaving early in the morning, but Ed had told them they'd be better arriving in time for dinner and drinks, hanging out in the bar and talking about their upcoming fishing activities rather than sitting around with nothing to do for part of the day. He wanted them to establish themselves before they hooked up with him in the morning. They could check into the hotel, have dinner, relax in the bar and have a drink or two.

"I know I don't have to tell you this," Ed went on, "but establishing the image is important. And you have to talk about how eager you are to get out on the water early for fishing."

Rocket had been tempted to tell Eagle to remind his SEAL friend that as a frogman who was a veteran of many covert missions, he knew how the hell to act when setting something up. But Ed didn't know him any better than he knew Ed, and the guy was doing them a huge favor, so he kept his mouth shut.

"Mallory's running out of time," Rocket reminded him, "so whatever playacting we're doing has to be fast."

"Understood. But you've done this often enough to know that if you don't set the stage then the play ends too quickly."

Rocket knew that as well as anyone, but the op usually didn't involve someone for whom he had developing feelings. *Change that.* Developed *feelings.*

"I'll just casually drop that I have some fishing charters for the next couple of days and we'll go from there."

"In case I haven't said it," Rocket told him, "thanks for this."

"Glad to do it. Barrera's destroying this area, so anytime I can poke the air out of his balloon makes me happy."

They arrived at the hangar the next morning at eleven o'clock. Once they had their things on board, Rocket pulled out his cell.

"I'm calling Mallory to bring her up to date," he told the others. "I told her I'd let her know when we were leaving."

"Just be sure she knows we won't be going straight from the airport to the house where she is," Eagle reminded him. "Tell her what the plans are, ask her if she can hold on just a little bit longer and we'll get her out."

"I know that," Rocket snapped. "And so does she. She's not stupid, for god's sake."

"Sorry, man." Eagle held up his hands. "I know it, but just touching all bases here."

"Sorry." Rocket blew out a breath. "And I know being personally connected to a case changes a person's perception. I need to get my SEAL on."

"It's always on." Blaze tapped him on the shoulder. "And never fails us. Go ahead and make your call. Eagle's reaching out to Ed to tell him we're about fifteen minutes from liftoff."

Rocket headed toward the back of the plane so he'd have some privacy. He had already confirmed with Mallory that they were on the job and that they'd made a connection that would be a great help. He'd kept names out of it, since no matter how secure he tried to make them, a cell phone could still be hacked. He hit speed dial for Mallory's number. It only rang once before she picked up.

"Rocket?" The word came out in a whisper.

"It's me. You okay?" He shook his head. "Wait. Don't answer that. Stupid question. Of course you aren't okay and won't be until we get you away from Santa Marita."

"I'm better since I know you're on the job," she assured him. "What's happening?"

"We're ready on this end. In fact, that's why I'm calling. We're wheels up in fifteen. Saint, our pilot, tells us it's about a seven-hour flight to Manzanillo."

"And what happens after you get there?"

"Eagle, one of my partners, has a strong connection there who's very familiar with Santa Marita and with Barrera as well. He's been working on this and will be picking us up at the airport. Then we'll be setting up our extraction plan."

"Rocket, listen." The strain in Mallory's voice was evident. "First you'd have to get me away from this house, and I don't see how that's possible. We know

Barrera has eyes on us all the time, even if we can't see them. I'm either hiding in that tiny attic or on the roof and the Albados are going about their business walking on eggshells."

"We're totally aware of that. I promise you. Our contact knows Barrera and is well aware of the person he is. He's also scoped out the situation. And I think I have a suggestion that might work, but I want to work it out with the others to be sure."

"He knows him?"

"Yes, but don't worry. They're not friends, even if Barrera might think they are. Ed was a SEAL, like the rest of us, and he still believes in the SEAL Code of Honor. He's not going to break that. And he wants to screw Barrera as much as we do."

There was a short pause.

"I believe you. I know you wouldn't lie to me. But I still don't know how you'll get me out of here."

"You leave that to us," he assured her. "We'll get it done. I just wanted to give you a heads-up that we're on our way. Are you in danger if you stay in the house?"

"No. At least, I don't think so. Inez has me hiding in the attic and I've got a gun."

"A gun?" He tried not to shout the words. "What kind? Do you know how to handle it?"

"Yes," she assured him. "After Afghanistan I took lessons and I try to go to the range once a week if I'm not away on a story."

"Okay. Just try not to shoot yourself instead of the bad guys." Rocket tried to make it sound like a joke, but he definitely wasn't laughing. He hoped she meant it when she said she had training and practice. "And let's hope sincerely you don't need it."

"I'm with you. Well, fly safely."

"Always."

He hung up, reluctant as he was to break the connection. If—no, *when*—they got her safely out of Santa Marita, he was going to do what he should have done five years ago. Pull out all the stops to make sure they were together.

He thought about the SEAL Code of Honor he'd mentioned to her. It was something they all repeated when they officially became SEALs, and still lived by.

"I voluntarily accept the inherent hazards of my profession, placing the welfare and security of others before my own. I serve with honor on and off the battlefield. The ability to control my emotions and my actions, regardless of circumstance, sets me apart from other men. Uncompromising integrity is my standard."

"Hey, Rocketman," Eagle called out to Rocket. "It's one fifteen. Takeoff time."

"I'm set." He moved forward and buckled himself into one of the plush seats. "Everyone else ready, too?"

The big engines on the plane which had been warming up, roared to life. The plane moved slowly out of the hangar, rolling over the sensor that automatically closed the big door. They paused on the wide apron Galaxy had commissioned along with the runway that the plane now turned and headed down. Gradually, they picked up speed and were airborne, climbing a path to reach their cruising altitude. When the bell dinged to show they were at forty-one thousand feet—regular cruising altitude for private passenger planes—all four men unclicked their seat belts and headed for the galley and the hot coffee that had brewed while they were climbing. Then, instead of returning to their seats, they grabbed their laptops and settled at the polished mahogany piece of built-in furniture that served both as dining table and a conference table. With laptops open and awake and coffee next to them, they were ready to go to work.

"Eagle, you Skyped with Ed again, right?" Blaze asked.

"I did." He clicked the keys on his laptop. "Ed sent me a list of places for us to identify on the island. I just sent them to our shared folder. Pull it up and take a look."

Having an antenna installed in the body of their plane was one of the first things they'd done after purchasing it. As they flew, the antenna linked up with cell towers, connecting to the nearest transmitter on a rolling basis. It was the main thing that had prompted the men of Galaxy to go with their idea of a flying office. Their laptops were state of the art and backed up with additional security in their homes. But meetings with clients were always held on the plane, because for those, Galaxy wanted utmost secrecy and security.

The men opened the list of places, divided them and went to work.

"He's even got a picture of the house Mallory is staying at," Viper commented. "Hmmm. Santa Marita looks like every other similar place we've been in. No surprise there."

"The key is going to be figuring out how we get her out of there," Rocket told him. "She said Barrera's got eyes on the house, somehow, and I'm sure he does. So we have to a workaround there."

"I guarantee you Ed's come up with something for us," Eagle told him. "That was always one of his strengths. Looking for ways to do the seemingly impossible."

"He's also marked off the marina just in case," Blaze said.

"And he wants us to be familiar with the main streets and a couple that lead to the outskirts of the city itself," Viper added. "So let's get to it."

As the plane cut through the clouds and swept along the blue sky, they pulled up the maps Ed had sent, more recent than the one accessible to the public, and began a segment-by-segment search. Rocket focused on the location of Inez Albados' home and its surroundings. The houses were built on a hillside, each street slightly higher than the one below, the buildings crammed close together to use up every inch of space. The only space was the very narrow alleys that ran along the backs of the rows.

But Rocket reminded himself that they'd been in situations like this before. Taliban villages weren't that much different, just not quite as colorful. His SEAL team had snuck in and out of target villages without detection, at least for the most part. They'd been in hostile territory, after all, and the enemy wasn't just sleeping or hanging out. But like all the SEAL teams, his had been trained well and now he was more than grateful for it.

From what he could tell, there weren't a lot of cars. Of course, there wasn't much room to park them, either. Some houses, though, had single-car garages below the first floor. The Albados' house was one of them and Rocket used his electronic pen to mark it. He hoped Ed had closeups so they could see if there was a way in there. *Or a way out.*

They studied the area immediately around the house as well, looking for places where they could be trapped as well as spots where Barrera could have stashed his spies. Rocket thanked god for all the missions they'd done as SEALs that had prepared them for this. In all the clients they'd taken on in the two years since they'd formed Galaxy, this was the first time they'd had to plan a complicated extraction. Even extracting Jim and Nita Rosen from Mexican kidnappers hadn't been that complicated, because they'd been dealing with a small group of criminals...not an army with a leader who had taken over a whole country.

Still, if they looked at this as similar to a mission against the Taliban, it would make it a lot easier to plan. He went back to the map, enlarging certain areas, tracing routes with his digital pen and making notes in his phone to ask Ed about.

As he focused on the various bits and pieces that made up Santa Marita, he spotted something that kicked his brain over. He'd have to see what Ed had to say about it, but an idea was taking root in the back of his mind. They'd only have so many options, but he had a feeling they could make this one work. If, of course, Ed was able to get them the things they needed. If the man was everything Eagle had said and everything he said about himself, they should be able to pull this off.

About three hours into the flight, Eagle, who also had his pilot's license, went forward to the cockpit to relieve Saint and give him a chance to hit the head, stretch his legs and get a bite to eat.

"We on time?" Rocket asked.

"As close as can be," Saint told him, taking a swallow of coffee. "We've had great weather and a tail wind, which also helps. So where are we with the plans?"

Blaze gave him a rough outline of everything so far, including the study to find a way to extract Mallory Kane from the house she was hiding in. While his partner was talking, Rocket leaned back in his chair, closed his eyes and let all the information sift through his brain. Ed would be the one to have the final say on the plan. It was his territory, and from what he'd told them, he knew it better than the back of his hand.

Whatever the situation, he swore to himself he'd get Mallory out of that house, out from under fucking Barrera's nose and out of that fucking country. His ass was sore from kicking himself for the last two days because he'd let five years go by without trying to find her and reach out to her. He'd certainly had enough dreams and sexual fantasies that she'd never been far from his mind. *After I'm out*, he'd kept telling himself. *After the SEALs*, he'd repeated when the urge to look for her hit him.

But he never had. Missions, and assignments and…whatever…had come along and he'd been trapped by his own sense of duty and obligation. Now he wondered, what if they never rescued her from Santa Marita? What if Barrera's men killed her during the rescue process?

What if?

What if?

What if?

"Rocket?" Blaze's voice burst into his thoughts. "Don't you agree?"

"Agree?" He looked at his friend and frowned.

"Uh-huh." Viper dropped down into the chair across from him. "Just as I figured. Did you leave your brain in Tampa or just part of it?"

Rocket wanted to shoot himself. This was no time to be distracted or let his mind wander.

"I'm good. Let's go over again what we've figured so far. And, Eagle? You need to contact Ed and give him our estimated arrival time and tell him what we've picked up in the hours we've been studying those maps."

"Getting right on it." He opened his laptop again, and in a moment the clicking of the keys sounded.

Saint went back to the cockpit to take over the controls again and Rocket poured himself another cup of coffee. In a moment, Eagle slid into a chair at the table across from him.

"I'm getting ready to text Ed. Saint says we'll be landing on time and I want to let him know. Manzanillo does not have an FOB terminal, but there is space for private aircraft to land, to park temporarily, to refuel and to overnight. And they do have rental car counters."

Eagle's computer dinged and he hit a key.

"Okay, Ed says let him know when we land."

The rest of the trip, they were mostly silent. For the moment, they'd said all there was to say until they reached Santa Marita and scoped out the situation themselves, and went over things with Ed in person.

There was fresh coffee in the galley, but Rocket avoided it, knowing he didn't need anything else to jack up his nerves. He was antsy enough as it was. He hadn't been this on edge since his first mission as a SEAL, but they weren't usually this personal. How, he wondered, could he be this twisted up about a woman he'd spent a few hours with at the most and hadn't seen for five years?

Because she made that kind of impact on me. It's my own stupid fucking fault I haven't seen her in all this time. I was so used to passing women off as casual encounters, but after five years I have to accept the realization that there was nothing casual about my time with Mallory Kane.

He moved to one of the armchair seats, buckled in, tilted the chair back and closed his eyes. Before all his missions as a SEAL, he had learned to shut out everything around him and focus only on the mission itself. That was what he was doing now, mostly to calm an unfamiliar feeling of unease. This was more than just a mission. This was Mallory, and his chance to find what he'd carelessly let drift in the wind for five years. What a stupid shit he was. But he was determined to make up for it now.

* * * *

Playa de Oro International Airport was a large, modern airport with an efficient and visually pleasing terminal and most services that people would require. When Saint landed the plane, they were directed where to taxi and park. Then they had to pass through customs, juggling their luggage and acting like businessmen on a holiday. They'd locked their weapons in the plane, knowing that making arrangements to get them through customs would call unwanted attention to them. Ed had told Eagle he'd have plenty of firepower for them, and they were counting on that.

Then they headed to the rental car counter that Blaze had called before they took off. He'd been assured the vehicle he requested, an SUV, would be waiting for him. The rental company was as good as its word, delivering exactly what he'd requested. Finally they were at the Grand Plaza and checking into their rooms. They made sure to discuss their fishing opportunities while they checked in and tipped the bellboy just enough over the usual amount to maintain their image as wealthy businessmen.

The rooms, as expected, were lavish in every detail, but Rocket knew that for the men of Galaxy, that wasn't important. The place and the trappings were just part of the image, places to park their bodies at night when and if they had the chance. He changed into casual beach clothes, as he knew his partners were, and headed to the bar. The others were already there, having managed to grab a corner table as some people left and ordered drinks.

As soon as he placed his order, Rocket stood up.

"I need to check something outside."

The others all nodded, knowing exactly what he was doing. He headed through the lobby and out of a door that led to the rear of the hotel and the pool. At this hour of the night, there weren't too many people taking advantage of it. He'd had an itch to talk to Mallory since they'd landed, but not knowing who might be at the airport and could overhear him, he'd forced himself to wait. He hadn't even trusted the hotel room, suspicious bastard that he was. Of course, that was how he stayed alive.

He was able to walk over to a corner away from the others, positioning himself against three palm trees in large pots grouped there, and pulled out his cell. He'd already added Mallory's number to his speed dial list, so he punched it. Two rings and she answered.

"Rocket?" She was whispering, as usual. Just the sound of her voice, even low like this, somehow settled him. Stupid, he knew, since she was still in so much danger.

"It's me. We're here. Well, almost."

"What does that mean? Exactly where are you?"

"Manzanillo. Just a short boat trip from Santa Marita. Tomorrow we're meeting with our contact and I'll know more after that. How are things there? Are you good for at least another twenty-four hours?"

"Maybe." There was a pause, as if she was thinking. "I'll make it work. Barrera's men haven't been back, although I think Inez's parents expect them to bang on the door any moment. But I get the feeling they're waiting for something."

Rocket frowned. "For what?"

"Maybe for me to try and escape this house so they can grab me. Or worse, grab Inez and use her to get to me."

"They don't actually have proof you're there," Rocket reminded her. "They didn't find you when they searched the house. Thank god."

"No kidding. But how long do you think they'll wait before they come back again? Barrera isn't someone to just let this go by the boards."

"We'll have you out of there before then." Rocket hoped he was telling the truth. They had a very small window of time. He looked around, relieved to see that no one was paying much attention to him. And he'd been speaking in a very low voice.

"I'm counting on it."

He disconnected and returned to the bar, sliding into his chair.

"Everything okay?" Blaze asked.

"As good as can be under the circumstances." He glanced over at Eagle. "I sure wish we didn't have to wait until morning to hook up with Ed."

"You know there's a good reason," Eagle told him. "Anyway, he just texted me for us to meet him at his dive shack at seven in the morning. He says he has an idea to go over with us."

"Good." Rocket nodded. "Because I have one, too, and I want to run it past you and see if you think I'm off the rails here."

Eagle thought for a moment. "I think I should contact Vacation Rentals, talk to Ed's friend and arrange for the chopper. But not in here where anyone can overhear us."

"Then maybe we should get the hell out of here and discuss it someplace we won't be overheard." Rocket looked around the table. "Okay to put off dinner for a little while?"

"Sure," Viper told him. "No problem."

Everyone nodded.

"Then let's go for a walk on the beach. Better take our drinks so we don't look out of place."

The pathway to the beach was just past the pool. There were other people out there, as well, just enjoying the evening and being on vacation.

When we get her out of here, I'm going to take Mallory on a vacation, someplace where she can relax and we can really get to know each other.

But first he had to get her ass out of there before Barrera decided to take drastic measures.

He walked down the beach with the others until they were pretty far away from anyone who could overhear them. Large palm trees dotted the interior edge of the beach and they gathered next to one of them.

Rocket tilted his head toward Eagle. "So, let's hear your idea."

"Remember when we had to get that ambassador out of a village where people were watching the building he was hiding in?"

"I do."

"Remember what we did? The rebels were only focused on the front of the building. We had him climb down from the roof using a ladder and grappling hooks. Then we rolled him in a rug and carried him down an alley to a vehicle we had waiting. Well, I checked online and many of the houses in Santa Marita have that same kind of thing, a flat roof with a lip around it. If the one Mallory is at does, we could do the same with her."

"Is she in physical shape to do that?" Viper wanted to know. "Climbing down two stories isn't for people out of condition."

"I'm sure she can handle it. She was in great shape when I knew her before." *Well, that didn't come out right.* "I mean, I think she works at it. Anyway, I'll ask her. But what's your plan after we get her off the roof?" Rocket asked.

"There are tiny alleys behind the houses," Eagle went on. "We need to scope it out or ask Ed the best way to sneak someone in there. Or both."

"If we do that," Blaze began, "we need to have transport to get her out of there and someplace to take her unseen afterwards. And in a way that doesn't attract attention."

"Someplace we can move her to," Viper put in. "Also unseen. And we'll only have a split second to do it all."

"Ed needs to find a way to let us have eyes on the area," Rocket told them, "and work with us on extraction."

"He will," Eagle assured them. "He said he knows Santa Marita and I believe him. I guarantee you he worked to set up his 'relationship' with Barrera because he's got black ops things going on the side, official and otherwise. And on our team, he was the best at this kind of stuff."

"We believe you." Blaze drained his drink and turned to Rocket. "Meanwhile, let's hear your idea, Rocketman."

Rocket had listened closely to Eagle's idea and wondered if maybe that was the better one, but he figured he'd put his out there anyway.

"Well, mine's a little more dramatic, but we should at least have two options."

"Then drop yours on us and we'll pick it over."

"Okay. Everyone's on pins and needles that Barrera's gonna show up—or his men will—and just tear the house apart until he finds Mallory, then drag her out of there. She told me his right-hand man, a guy named Ruben Vidal, just in the last few days has barged into a house with his thugs and dragged out whoever they were looking for. She says she's very well hidden, but who knows how long that will last."

He watched the others' reactions. "If Ed can get his hands on what we need, like some uniforms and a car like they run around in, we could stage the arrest ourselves and haul her off under everyone's noses." He looked at Blaze. "Just like you did in Iraq when you had to get that nurse that was being held. The one you told me about one night, remember?"

"I do." Blaze nodded. "But that way might call more attention to us than we want. Then we were dealing with a tribal chieftain who was power hungry, much, as I'm gathering, Barrera is, except he didn't control a whole country. We managed to pull it off, I'll grant you that. Scared the shit out of the people around the house, but we were gone before anyone could discover what we'd done. But we did it, we succeeded, and that's what gave me this idea." He raked his fingers through his hair. "Only you're right. This is a different situation here."

Rocket looked at everyone. "What's the common thought here?"

"We can run both of them past Ed, but I think I know which one he'll go for," Blaze said at last. "Let's lay it out and figure out what could go wrong, and go from there."

"And, Saint?" Blaze turned to the pilot. "You'll need to man home base here in case we need air support of any kind. Or anything else that can't be done from Santa Marita."

Saint nodded. "Got it."

"I say right now we need to talk to Ed," Viper told them, "and get his feedback. Right away. He'll know which one is the most difficult to accomplish, plus he's obviously already made some plans of his own. Eagle, what time are we meeting him?"

"Seven o'clock." His mouth curved in a hint of a grin. "Fishing starts early. He says he'll have breakfast for us."

"And where will he be waiting for us to meet him?"

"Down at the marina not far from his dive shack. I have directions."

"Then I have two suggestions," Blaze told them. "The first is for you, Eagle, to call Ed again and lay out our two options for him. Then we should get a quick bite to eat and grab some sleep. Tomorrow is probably going to be a long day."

"Good idea." Eagle pulled out his cell and hit speed dial.

"I'll be there in a second," Rocket told them as they headed back toward the hotel. "I want to touch base with Mallory."

He turned away before they could make any comments and speed dialed the number.

"It's me," he told her when she answered, breathing a little easier when he actually heard her voice. He kept thinking every time he called her that either he'd get no answer or someone from Barrera's army would answer.

"Hi, me."

Her soft voice settled his nerves just a little. "We've discussed a couple of different options and we're waiting for final feedback from Eagle's friend. We'll finalize the plan in the morning, so hang on, kiddo. It won't be long now."

"I have faith," she told him, although there was a tremor in her voice. "I keep telling myself if you did it once, you can do it again."

"And I will," he promised. "*We* will. Stay strong. I know you can." He lowered his voice even more. "For me."

There was a nanosecond of a pause.

"Okay. For you."

"Call you tomorrow. Keep that phone handy."

"Like it's attached to my body."

He disconnected, the sound of her voice still lingering in his ears. He'd been a SEAL for a long time, completed a lot of missions successfully. Now he was going to use everything he'd learned to make this one succeed.

Failure was not an option.

Chapter Seven

Mallory clutched the phone to her body, holding it against her after Rocket had disconnected, as if she were feeling his touch on her skin. Just the sound of his voice seemed to be enough to soothe her, which she badly needed in the middle of this crisis. Inez's parents, according to her, were being very closemouthed, although they were walking around on tiptoe, as if expecting Barrera's men to burst through the front door at any time. Mallory knew it had to be very stressful for her friend, and she was worried about the safety of her family, but no one suggested she leave or tried to throw her out of the house.

In fact, Mrs. Albado had suggested she come down to Inez's room for a couple of hours each day to get out of the attic. And she made sure to send up plenty of food, although appetite was the last thing Mallory worried about.

She was definitely glad for the rooftop. Now she stretched out on the old quilt, the toss pillow beneath her head, and stared at the stars. The sky was very clear, so they were sharp and bright. If only she was in a different place, where her life wasn't endangered and she didn't have to hold her breath at every sound. Some place where she and Rocket could be together and finally see if the chemistry between them that had exploded in Afghanistan was just a result of the danger they'd faced or was real and maybe the foundation of something.

She'd been asking herself every day since she'd spoken to him why she'd never looked for him in all this time. Telling herself he could just as easily have found her didn't cut it. He was a SEAL, who was off on missions to undisclosed places or stationed who knew where. She had connections, and Alicia had even better ones — she could have made the effort, but she was so used to casual relationships that had no lasting memories, or attachments that she'd tried to write it off. She'd told herself he had a busy life as a SEAL and probably had no room for her.

But the past couple of nights since reconnecting with Rocket and hiding out here on the roof had made her long for something she wasn't sure was even available. She knew next to nothing about Rocket and his partners except for what Alicia had told her, but she trusted her sister, and trusted her memory of Rocket.

She made her head more comfortable on the pillow she was using and closed her eyes. As usual, the first image that floated into her mind was Rocket, with his lean, muscular body, his dark hair and scruff beard, and intense blue eyes. She saw him again, as he'd been that day in the cave, sweat glistening on his muscles from the heat of the day. The damp scent of the cave mingled with the musky odor of their bodies had only enhanced the electric sexual desire sparking between them.

There had been very little discussion, because their hunger for each other had overriden anything else. Despite her desperate situation, when he'd eased into the place where she'd been held, slithering in like a ghost then sliding back out with her, her body had reacted as if she hadn't had sex in forever. Which hadn't been that far from the truth.

Lying here now, just like so many other times, she could feel his hot body pressing hers, the swollen length of his cock imprinting itself on her, one hand squeezing a breast while he tasted every inch of her mouth with his tongue. Just thinking about it now brought back that hunger, that need, that sense of desperation for him to take her, and her body responded.

She slid one hand beneath her shorts and panties, over her mound until she could ease two fingers between the hot, wet lips of her sex. She rubbed them slowly up and down, making sure to abrade her throbbing clit with each movement. She had an urge to hurry, a craving to thrust her fingers into her clenching sex, but she wanted to prolong it, imagine again that it was Rocket's hand stroking her, pinching that hot little nub of flesh between his fingers and tugging on it. She imagined Rocket's hard, lean fingers there instead of her own, his tongue scorching her mouth before sliding across her cheek to taste her neck. His lips pressed against her ear, whispering hot, filthy things to her that made her want him even more.

She increased the pressure of her fingers as the need in her sex increased. Muscles rippled with light spasms, begging for penetration, but she didn't want to hurry.

Trapped here, her world at the moment confined to an attic and a roof, her life in danger, she wasn't going to rush this. Instead, she stroked slowly, imagining Rocket's hand there, his fingers on her slick skin.

Move faster, a voice in her head whispered. *More, more, more.*

Now her fingers moved faster. She could only prolong it for so long before her hunger and need got the best of her. Planting her feet flat on the roof and bending her knees, she reached down and thrust her fingers inside her slick, hungry channel.

Faster, faster, faster.

Then she was...*there!*

Oh, god.

Her walls convulsed around her fingers, squeezing them while she rode her hand, biting her lip to keep from crying out.

Finally, at last, the tremors subsided and she slid her hand out of her panties. Her heart was racing and her breathing was choppy, her pulse still pounding. She forced herself to take deep breaths until she could bring her body next to normal. Her legs splayed out, her muscles weak from the tension, and her heart thundered in her chest as if she'd had real sex. God, how pathetic was that? She was just damn lucky Inez hadn't decided to come up on the roof during her little self-gratification session.

She lay there, letting her heart rate settle, and wondering just how much longer her luck would hold. The vibrating of her cell phone in her pocket startled her. She drew it out and looked at the screen, relieved to see the familiar number there, but wondering why he'd called again so soon. Had something bad happened in just the past few minutes?

"Just had to hear your voice one more time before I close it down for the night," he said as soon as she answered. "I just—" There was a short pause. "Just had to hear your voice again. We're in Manzanillo and tomorrow Ed's setting us up to get to Santa Marita."

"Be very careful," she urged. "Barrera's no idiot. He's a power-hungry, bloodthirsty animal who was smart enough to break off from the Sinaloa cartel and still maintain a relationship. He controls everything. What he can't control, he eliminates."

"Understood. Been there, seen that before."

Of course he had. He'd been a SEAL for twelve years and she was sure he had been in situations worse than this one.

"I'm just…concerned."

"I know." His voice softened. "We're playing it smart, Mallory. And the connection Eagle has down here is going to even the playing field."

"I believe you. And trust you. It's just…"

"I know. It's hard when you wonder if any minute you'll be found and dragged away. I promise we aren't going to let that happen. Can you go up on the roof early in the morning?"

"As soon as the Albados leave for work. After that, the neighborhood settles down a lot. People are gone to work. Kids are off to school. Only mamas with babies are left and they couldn't care less about anything outside their immediate circles."

"Good. We're meeting Eagle's friend at what I think is the buttcrack of dawn. I'll call or text as soon as I can." There was a second of silence. "We're doing this, Mallory. I promise, and I don't give my word lightly."

"I know. And I'm counting on it."

After he hung up, Mallory lay there for a long time, staring at the sky without really seeing anything, Rocket's voice still echoing in her head. *Tomorrow*, she kept whispering to herself, and hoping tomorrow would get here very soon. In the meantime, she wrapped her fingers around the gun Inez had given her, the one always next to her. She would not let Barrera and his men have her. She'd kill herself first.

* * * *

Ed had suggested they meet him at the Salty Dog Dive Shack in the morning. It was on the beach almost directly in front of the hotel and he'd told them that was the usual procedure. He had an arrangement with the Grand Plaza that they would just send anyone interested to see him and he'd take it from there. The beach was already dotted with a decent-size crowd of early sunbathers, but a narrow, paved walk to Ed's place allowed them to avoid the oiled and tanned bodies.

The Salty Dog was open on three sides, although, as they approached, they saw wooden shutters rolled up and fastened beneath the thatched roof. The back end of the place was enclosed and stools ringed the front of the open bar. Ed looked up and saw them coming, and immediately poured four large glasses of orange juice.

"Morning." He pointed to the glasses. "Drink up. That's how we start the day here. I've got breakfast waiting on the boat."

Eagle stared at him. "How fucking early do you get up here? You sounded like you sleep half the day away."

"Only part of it," Ed joked. "Come on. The boat's waiting."

The marina, about a mile away, was a busy place when they arrived. The parking lot was already more than half full of vehicles, and the docks with berths on either side of them were bustling with activity. People were preparing for day sails or longer cruises or fishing expeditions or whatever. Boats were already backing out of their slips and heading for deeper water. And down the beach to the right of the marina, more vehicles were parked at the edge of the sand, with people lugging surfboards out to where the waves rolled up to the sand.

They had all dressed the way Ed had told them to, as businessmen down here for a fishing holiday, wearing the usual attire of loud printed shirts, khaki shorts and hats people would remember because of the color of the insignia, rather than their faces.

"Let's get on the boat before we discuss anything," Ed told them. "Big ears and all that."

Ed led them through a gate and down one of the docks, waving to a man who sat in a little shack at the edge of the parking lot. Rocket watched Ed as they followed him along one of the piers, the slight hitch in his gait caused by the prothesis barely noticeable. He gave the man a lot of credit for not letting the severity of the injury defeat him.

They walked past several other boats until they came to a sleek, white flybridge fishing boat, with the name *Cyclone* painted on the bow.

"Hope that name isn't an indication of the way you drive this thing," Blaze joked.

"It was his code name in the SEALs," Eagle told them. "He could destroy an enemy stronghold and scoop up prisoners faster than any windstorm."

"Good to know." Blaze grinned. "We may need it."

There was a man already on the boat, tanned and lean, with hair almost to his shoulders, and a moustache. He was dressed in bleached denim shorts and a T-shirt with *Ed's Adventures* printed on the front.

Ed waved to him. "Meet Elias. He rescued my ass when I first got here and was a drunken mess. Without him, I'd be dead. I trust him with my life, and yours, too. Believe it."

Rocket figured they had nothing to lose. Eagle trusted Ed implicitly, and the man hadn't gotten them all the way here to screw them over. He stepped forward first to shake Elias' hand, and the others followed.

They all boarded, stuffed their things below in the cabin then joined Ed on deck while he piloted the boat out into deep water.

"You can see how close Santa Marita is." Ed waved his hand at a very large landmass that looked almost as if they could swim to it.

"You weren't kidding," Viper acknowledged.

"We'll skirt part of it before hitting the open water."

Ed skillfully wove the boat between the coast of Mexico and that of Santa Marita before heading out away from shore. Rocket memorized every detail, much as he'd always done on missions. He had no idea how Ed planned to get him onto a land mass that was quite literally Barrera's back yard, and more than that, to get Mallory out of there once they retrieved her.

They were moving slowly, as if looking for a good fishing spot, when a sleek, white cruiser with a raised control cabin pulled close to them. Along the side was painted *Santa Marita Marine Patrol*. The pilot shifted the controls into neutral to hover close to them.

"*Hola!*" A tanned man in a white uniform waved at Ed.

"*Hola, mi amigo.*"

Ed put his own controls into neutral to hold the boat in place.

"Out here to do some fishing?" the man asked.

"*Absolutamente!* The hotel called and told me they had some rich guests with money to spend. I told them to send them my way."

"Excellent. We are always happy when you bring *turistas* to spend their money here."

Although the captain was smiling, Rocket thought the stretching of his lips looked more like a grimace. And his right hand rested firmly on the gun at his hip. This was hardly the warm welcome he'd seen in other countries where he'd vacationed.

"Doing my best," Ed assured him.

"Good. Good. Well, welcome to Santa Marita. Enjoy your stay."

Rocket dipped his head. "Thanks. We expect to. That is if we get some fishing done. Hey, Ed. We gonna set up the rods or not?"

"Right away."

"I won't keep you." The captain looked at Ed. "Bring them to Santa Marita later to enjoy our fine food and drink."

Ed nodded. "Might do that. We'll see."

The patrol boat pilot shifted into gear and the boat roared away.

"Okay, he's gotten a look at you, which satisfies his curiosity. So let's get out of here and get down to business."

When they were a good thirty minutes from the marina, Ed turned control of the boat over to Elias and led them all back down to the cabin.

"Just so you know, Elias is key in tonight's fun and games," Ed explained. "He lives in Santa Marita. In fact, he was born there. Barrera thinks of him as a native who works for the good guy with the fishing boat."

Rocket allowed himself a small grin. "Good cover you've set up."

Ed feigned surprise. "Cover? Whatever do you mean? Why would I need cover?" Then he grinned. "Now. First things first."

Unlocking a cupboard, he slid a panel out of the way and pulled out a large lockbox. He placed it on the table and opened it, exposing a display of .45 caliber pistols which included both Glocks and H&Ks.

"Choose your poison," he told them. "I have plenty of ammo for all of them."

"Jesus, Ed." Eagle let out a slow whistle. "You going to war here?"

Ed shrugged. "Never hurts to be prepared."

They each selected their weapon, placing it and a supply of ammo in the gym bags they had brought on board. While they did that, Ed heated breakfast, and as soon as the remaining guns and ammo were locked away, he placed it on the table. They dug into plates filled with generous helpings of huevos rancheros, tortillas and spiced beans. From a pot sitting on a warmer, Ed poured rich, black coffee into heavy ceramic mugs. Then, after plunking sugar, cream and salsa on the table, he joined the others. Taking a long sip of coffee, he leaned back in his seat and looked around the table.

"Okay, I'm pretty sure you've come up with ideas, but so have I. I spent some time yesterday scoping out the whole situation in Santa Marita, so I've got one, too. But let's hear yours first. Maybe we can blend all of our ideas."

"We based ours on the map we downloaded and the photos you sent us of the area," Eagle told him, "so I'm sure they need fine tuning."

He laid out his idea about the grappling hooks and the rug, then Rocket detailed his fake arrest plot. They waited while Ed digested the information and rolled it around in his head.

"Well?" Eagle prompted when his friend still said nothing.

"Okay." Ed took another swallow of coffee. "Yesterday, while I was here talking to Barrera, scheduling the fishing charter for his friends, I told him I was in the market for a motorcycle. I happen to know one of his men has one for sale because he posted a notice online about it. As I knew he would, Barrera said I should take it for a spin, test it out. So I was able to get a close-up view of Inez Albado's neighborhood and her house."

"And?" Rocket nudged. "What did you find?"

"Rocket, I like the fake arrest, but you guys are right. It's too noisy and calls too much attention to it. Plus it tells Barrera that Mallory Kane really was in the house, which could make trouble for the Albados, and they've already got enough. But we can use part of the one I like."

"What do you mean?"

"Lucky for us, I discovered that a guy who has a burning hate for Barrera and helps me when he can, lives in the house right behind the Albados. Some coincidence, right?"

Rocket wasn't sure he wanted to know what had caused that burning, so he just nodded, but he was grateful for the connection.

"I was looking at ways to utilize that and figure out the best time to do so when I happened to overhear a conversation Barrera had with Ruben Vidal, his right-hand man and chief lieutenant. Barrera's really pissed off that your girl has disappeared right from under his nose. He still thinks the Albados are hiding her somehow and they're planning to raid the house again."

"Fuck." Rocket shook his head. "Do you know when?"

"No, but I'm trying to find out. I just hope it isn't while we're getting Mallory Kane out of there."

"No shit."

"I hear he's got a lot going on Friday night," Ed reported. "So I'd say Saturday. I'll let you know. Besides, he thinks as long as she's on the island he can control where and what she does."

"Then we have a small window of opportunity to do this. Like Friday night. Tonight. So what's your big idea, and is your friend ready to go right now?"

"He is. I talked to him last night. He's just waiting to hear from me."

"And you trust him?" Eagle asked.

Rocket was glad it was Eagle asking, since Ed was his friend and he could smell bullshit if there was any. He was also in the best position to ask those questions.

"With my life."

The way he said it, Rocket had a feeling that wasn't just an expression.

"Then how about showing us your idea and letting us know how it's supposed to work."

"Okay. Let me diagram it out for you."

He pushed his plate aside, grabbed a notebook and a pen and began drawing lines. "And here are the photos I shot while taking my motorcycle ride." He laid them out so everyone could get a good look at them. "Here's the Albado house, and here is the home of my guy, Mateo."

They spent more than an hour going over the details, memorizing everything so they had it all squared away. On paper it seemed relatively simple, but Rocket, like the others, knew that things could go to shit at the last moment.

"Pretty crowded neighborhood," Blaze commented.

"That it is," Ed agreed. "But in a way that makes this easier. It's busy day and night. Lots of people who work night shifts, so hardly any kind of activity will seem unusual."

Blaze looked at the diagrams and photos, then at Ed.

"What kind of work does Mateo do when he's not, uh, being your friend?"

Ed's mouth curved in what Rocket could only describe as an evil grin.

"That's the beauty of my whole arrangement with him. He's a grunt in Barrera's army."

"What?" Rocket pushed up from the tale so fast his coffee cup tipped over, spilling liquid across the table. "What the fuck?"

"Hold on." Eagle clamped a hand on Rocket's arm. "Before you throw a fit, let's hear why Ed uses him."

"We've done it before," Blaze reminded him. "Found someone who played for the other team, but under duress and would cheerfully have killed our target if it didn't mean they'd get killed themselves. But can you really trust this guy?"

"Mateo has a long-burning hate for Barrera," Ed told him. "His sister was in a bar out for a night of fun with some girlfriends when some of Barrera's soldiers sat down with them. Angela, one of the other girls, didn't like the sound of things, excused herself to the ladies' room and managed to get the hell out of there. But Lucia, Mateo's sister, and the two others were stupid enough to stay."

He paused, and Rocket could see him struggling to keep his shit together.

"It's okay," Eagle told him. "We get the drift."

"No. Let me finish. Lucia didn't show up back at the apartment she shared with two friends until late the next day. One of the roommates had already called Mateo, who was searching for her. He came right over and…" He swallowed. "Suffice it to say she'd been drugged and raped. He tried to tell Barrera about it, but he's pretty low on the totem pole, and the general pretty much lets his men do what they want. So any chance he has to stick it to him, he takes it."

No one said a for a long moment.

"Tell him we appreciate his help," Blaze said at last.

"I will. But that's the main reason he's willing to do anything he can get away with to help me. Anything at all. And using his house this way should not bring any problems." Ed sat back. "But we have to do this carefully. Because Barrera's got a bug up his ass about Inez, we may not be able to get Mallory out right away. The trick will be, if we run into a glitch, stashing you somewhere while we work out a new extraction plan. But I've got a place to tuck both of you away where they'll be safe."

"Where's that?" Viper wanted to know.

"A jungle hut I have access to on the far side of Santa Marita. I keep it stocked for emergencies and no one even knows it's there."

"And after that you can get us out without being seen?" Rocket asked.

"We can, barring exigent circumstances." Ed nodded. "I've made arrangements to get a Zodiac to pick you up. As soon as we have your woman, I plan to get you all into it and out to my other boat we use. A faster one I use for diving. Elias will have anchored in deep water. We have to time it just right or our plans are up in smoke." He looked at each of them. "You brought your satellite phones, right?"

They all nodded.

Viper grinned. "Told customs we'd be deep sea fishing and needed to be able to contact our offices."

"How are you going to get us to the Albados' house?" Viper asked.

"In fact," Blaze added, "how are you going to get us to Santa Marita? Like you said, we can't exactly pull up to the marina and stroll the streets."

"Right. Barrera's men report everyone and everything. So I came up with an idea." He looked around at everyone. "You'll be damn glad for the hell that was BUD/S."

Rocket frowned. SEAL training was known everywhere as the most demanding and ferocious training of all Special Ops. *What the hell is going on here, anyway?*

"What's your brilliant idea?" he asked.

But once Ed explained the steps they'd be taking and the arrangements he'd made, Rocket understood. More than that, he was impressed. While somewhat complicated, they looked like they would work. Apparently, Ed did a lot more than run his dive shop and fishing charter business. He was obviously deep into doing the kind of shit they did as SEALs, only without the government looking over his shoulder. Rocket was developing a new respect for him.

"One more thing," he told them. "Once a month there's a big open-air market in Santa Marita, usually held down by the waterfront. Takes up most of the parking lot. They keep it there because people also arrive by boats, both as shoppers and vendors. This isn't the weekend for it, but a little birdie told me they might be having an impromptu one. If so, we'll be able to use it in some way. Something we can figure out once we know for sure, although it could be very last-minute."

When Ed finished laying everything out for them, he looked around the table. "Of course, there's a million things that can go wrong, so I've put together some contingencies. Let's go over them before we hit the deck."

At last, they were all satisfied they'd gone over every detail as much as they possibly could. As they always said, the unknown was the unknown.

Ed leaned back in his seat. "You'll be going ashore in a very isolated area that Barrera never pays attention to. No need to. He's in charge so he doesn't have any reason to sneak. Good thing it's on a Friday night. The city will be filled with people celebrating the weekend, both in town and the marina. Every place will be noisy and busy and Barrera's men will be occupied with sticking their noses in everyone's business. There will be less chance that anyone will pay attention to us once we get into the city itself."

"And how do we get to this very isolated area?" Blaze wanted to know.

"Got it covered," Ed told him. "You'll see when I lay it out for you. We'll head back to Manzanillo early evening and one of my crew will take you to your dive spot well after dark. There won't be any one around, but still, we'll all need to be alert at all times."

Eagle nodded. "Agreed."

"Then I guess we're done until this evening. Let's head up to the deck and do some fishing."

Rocket stared at him. "Fishing? What the hell?"

"We can't do anything until dark," Blaze pointed out to him. "And we have to establish ourselves as just guys here for some good fishing. Just in case."

"Blaze is right," Ed agreed. "And like I told you on Skype, Barrera has patrol boats that he uses to police the waters around the marina and they're not above heading out this far to check on any they see. They might even pull up next to us for a so-called chat. Just concentrate on working the rods and do your best to ignore them. Before I sneak you into Santa Marita, you'll change and no one will recognize you."

Eagle nodded. "Sounds good to me."

Ed turned to Rocket. "Before you head up on deck, you should call your woman and prepare her. Tell her to be up on the roof the moment it's full dark. Give her the basics and let her know to follow instructions to the letter."

His woman. How crazy was it that he was beginning to think of her that way more and more?

"She will," he told the man. "She's smart and savvy and she also wants to get the fuck out of there. Not just for her own self but to keep the Albados safe."

"We'll get her out okay. See you up on deck."

Only when Ed climbed the stairs did Rocket notice a real difference in how he moved. Again, he felt true admiration for the man.

As soon as he was alone, he pulled out his cell phone and hit the speed dial for Mallory.

"Are you in Santa Marita now?" she asked the moment she answered.

"Close, but we will be soon. Are you in a place where you can talk?"

"Oh, sure. Lying on my soft mattress in my luxurious bedroom." She cleared her throat. "Sorry. I think I'm getting a little nuts."

"Very understandable."

"I'm in what I call the crawl space, although Inez keeps referring to it as an attic." Her soft laugh had a tiny hysterical edge to it. "Anyway, no one's home right now so there's no one to hear me, but I whisper anyway. I never know if one of Barrera's men is going to sneak in when everyone else has gone to work."

"Yeah, I worry about that, too. But we're getting close to the finish line. At least to get you out of the immediate area."

He went on to tell her what they'd outlined to get her away from the house, going over it twice so she had all the details.

"Can you climb down and across to the other roof on that rope ladder?" he asked.

"I've done much riskier things," she assured him. "I can handle it. It's getting out of the immediate area that worries me. Barrera's got eyes everywhere."

143

"Agreed, but I think Ed's plan is as good as we're going to get. He says Friday and Saturday nights are wild in Santa Marita so people don't pay much attention to what others are doing."

"Let's hope."

"He also has some contingencies if we need them."

"What if tonight is the night Barrera decides to have his thugs storm this house to arrest the Albados?"

"The word we got is he's doing it tomorrow night," he told her, "but just in case, are they home? I wanted to get them out of there first, but there wasn't any way to do it in the time we had without calling attention to it."

"It's okay. Inez's parents went to a late dinner with friends and Inez is spending the night with the guy she's been seeing forever. I think his name is Diego Flores. No one's here. Except for me, that is."

"My guess is he knows they're gone and wants to wait until he can do another search with them there. It's much more intimidating." He bit back a curse word. "Anyway, once we get you out of there, I'm going to ask my friends to see about getting them to safety."

She was silent for a moment and he wondered if she'd just hung up.

"Thank you, Rocket," she said at last in a soft voice. "For everything. You don't know how much this means to me."

"If you keep doing this, I'll get a lot of practice," he teased.

Her sigh hissed over the connection. "I'm sorry. I try to be better about this stuff, but..."

"But it's in your DNA," he finished.

"Yeah, I guess so. But I swear, if you really get me out of here..."

"Don't make promises you can't keep, sweetheart. Let's just take care of this, first. Remember. Be up on the roof as soon as it's full dark. Just be careful in case Barrera decides to send one of his men tonight to check things out."

"And I have my gun," she reminded him.

He let out a slow breath. "Okay. Good. And you're clear on what you need to do?"

"Got it. See you tonight." There was a tiny pause. "And thank you again."

After the call disconnected, Rocket stood there for several moments, just reliving the conversation and calling up his memories of Mallory Kane, even if they were five years old. Tonight couldn't come soon enough for him.

Chapter Eight

Felix Barrera took one of his specially blended cigars out of the humidor in his den, inhaled it for a moment then lit it with his sold gold lighter. He took a moment to blow perfect smoke rings while he waited for Ruben Vidal to arrive. Lately his specially ordered, hand-rolled cigars seemed to be the only thing that calmed him down.

There was still no trace of Melinda Clayton, which royally pissed him off. He'd had men following every member of the Albado family and that had led nowhere, which pissed him off even more. He was sure the bitch was in that house somewhere, but the question was, where? His men had gone through it top to bottom, but there hadn't been a trace of her. How the hell had the Albados managed that?

His men should have done it tonight. *A good way to start the weekend.* Except everyone in the Albado family had been out. He didn't want to raid an empty house. It was important to him that the people who lived there, who had committed the sin of protecting an enemy, should witness the search and be punished for it. The fact that the house was empty frustrated the fucking hell out of him.

"Still nothing?" he asked as Ruben walked into the room.

Vidal shook his head. "Not even a sniff. And let me tell you, I've had people looking everywhere."

"The checkpoints are still up?"

"*Sí*! And I just did an all-points check and they are now all in place. We've pretty much locked down the city as far as they're concerned, although where the hell would they go, anyway?"

Barrera shrugged. "The marina. The airport, maybe trying to sneak onto a private plane. Depends on how stupid they are."

"Okay, I'll change the teams at eight in the morning. How long do you want to keep them going?"

"Until I find that stupid bitch. Whatever it takes."

"Well." Ruben shrugged. "There's no way she can get to the water without us knowing it. Every single road out of town, even the narrow ones, has a checkpoint."

"The airport is out. She can't get on a commercial flight without my being notified and I have men watching every private plane leaving here, even checking the inside before clearing them for takeoff. I keep telling myself we've got her, but then why don't I have my hands on her? How has this bitch made herself so invisible?"

Ruben frowned. "I'm still not so sure why you have such a hard-on for this female. I didn't see anything about her that stands out."

"It's my instincts, Ruben. Instincts I've developed over all these years. There's something about her that smells like trouble, and I'm going to find out what it is. Then I'm going to find her and peel her skin off one layer at a time. We have to find that Clayton woman." He bit down on the cigar. "I can't believe she got off the island without any of us knowing. We keep a tight rein on every place a boat can land at Santa Marita and control every aircraft in and out of the airport. We're missing something here. You need to take another crack at digging around the internet."

"I was pretty thorough the first time, but there really was nothing to find. On the surface, she looks like the most boring person in the world."

"On the surface." Barrera pounced on the words. "I know you hit all the usual places, but dig deeper. There's got to be something there. My senses tell me she's not just some nosy tourist, and my senses never let me down. I reached out to my connection on the dark web but he hasn't gotten back to me yet." A situation that pissed him the hell off. "I can't just sit on my ass waiting around. Especially since I have this itchy feeling that who she really is could spell big trouble for us. What about handing it off to Marta? She's smart and keeps her mouth shut. Can she dig into the dark web, too?"

"Yes. I will get her on it right now. She's the best tech we've got. I don't know why you go outside for someone to do this."

"I don't trust women," Barrera snapped. "Just remember. If she fucks up, it's your head, too."

"No worries. I like my head just where it is."

He pulled out his cell and selected a preset number. Barrera listened while he explained to the woman on the other end exactly what he wanted. Then he disconnected.

"She'll be on it right away, *jefe*. If there is anything to find, she's the one to discover it."

"And you set up the checkpoints?"

Ruben glanced at his watch. "It's getting late. I'd think if she was trying to sneak out of the city, she'd want to do it in the dark. We'll keep doing all-points checks. In fact, maybe I'll tell all the guards whoever finds and stops the woman gets a bonus."

"*Bueno. Bueno.* I cannot let that bitch slip through my fingers. If she tries to leave town, I want her to be in for an unpleasant surprise."

"Okay. We'll make it happen. And the whole Albado family is out of the house tonight? That's why you scheduled the raid for tomorrow?"

"Yes. They are. The parents are having dinner with friends at Casa Valentina and the daughter is spending the weekend with her boyfriend. I want them there when I do it, so if I find even the least little trace of that bitch, I can spell out for them exactly how they will be punished. To their faces."

"All right. But, Felix, if this Clayton woman was still in the house, would they go off and leave her? With no lights on and none of the window air conditioners running? She'd fry in there."

"I know. I know."

Barrera blew another smoke ring. He was holding on to his self-control only with the greatest effort. He was not used to being thwarted in anything or short-stopped or in any other way prevented from getting what he wanted. If he didn't find that bitch soon, he was going to start killing people out of frustration.

Ruben looked at his watch. "Meanwhile, Gerard Moreau and his people will be here in thirty minutes. I suggested they land at your private dock and we can move along from there."

"Good, good. Let's get ready to meet them. I just hope that fucking bitch doesn't end up doing something that blows this all up."

"What can she do? She's one person, an insignificant female. Worst case, you can make an example of her if you find her. It will be a lesson for others, including Moreau, that you don't fuck with us."

"True. Yes, true."

"And keep in mind, Moreau may want a lower price if they're buying more product."

"No." Barrera flicked a collar of ash into the glass dish with a sharp movement. "No discounts. Does Sinaloa give discounts? Juarez? Tijuana? Los Zetas?" Irritation rose. "Are we a discount operation? We give them good product at a fair market price. And we are already pricing it just a hair below the others. Tell them no deal."

"I figured, but I had to run it by you."

"Go ahead and check with the blockades. Then we need to get down to the dock."

* * * *

They swam through the water in familiar silence, clad in full SCUBA gear. Elias had ferried them out to the dive spot in a smaller powerboat that Ed had told them he used for taking out his diving customers. Ed dove with them, prosthesis and all. He didn't mind blending in with the crowd after he was there, but he didn't want to do the whole arrival scene with his boat.

The distance from where the five former SEALs slipped into the water to the very isolated little cove where they'd surface was two miles. They'd done more than five miles in BUD/S, so this was a snap. And Ed had assured him he'd practiced a lot with the prosthesis. He'd never do anything to hold them back.

They surfaced in a tiny cove surrounded by very large boulders. Between that and the road was a long thick stand of trees that stretched at least half a mile in each direction. Rocket thought Ed was right when he said Santa Marita had a lot of hiding places that Barrera's men never paid attention to. From what they had learned about him, he probably wasn't smart enough to think of them as danger spots.

And that was good for them.

Now, if they could just get Mallory out of the Albados' house and here to this little cove, they could execute the rest of the plan and get the fuck out of here with their asses still intact. Ed had gone over the process with them at least a dozen times. Rocket just hoped it worked. In a setup like Santa Marita, with a dumb, power-hungry, bloodthirsty man at the helm, anything could go wrong. *Been there, done that.*

Emerging from the water, they divested themselves of the SCUBA gear, leaving them dressed in jeans and T-shirts. Then they retrieved their handguns and sat phones from the waterproof bags attached to their dive suits. Rocket checked to make sure the little baggie he'd stashed in there before donning their gear was still safe. To him, it was almost as important as his gun.

They carried everything to a car that sat waiting for them in the trees. Ed dumped all the gear into two large waterproof bags and stored it in a compartment in the floor in the back. He dug the keys from beneath the front floor mat and they all climbed in. Looking like regular tourists—or as regular as they were in Santa Marita—they drove slowly through the trees to a crappy dirt road and finally to a narrow badly paved side road.

"Do I even want to know whose car this is?" Blaze asked. "I thought you were low key here?"

Ed shook his head but grinned. "Not really. It belongs to another guy who does odd jobs now and then for me. Lets me borrow it when I need to."

Blaze chuckled. "Why do I get the feeling these odd jobs you have people doing aren't the kind you want to discuss?"

Ed glanced over his shoulder. "Rocket, text Mallory and tell her to be ready."

"I guarantee you she is, but I'll do it anyway."

"Tell her to get up on the roof," he added. "Mateo's home, waiting for us. I stopped by there to scope out the streets and the area and checked in with him."

"Who else in in the house?" Rocket wanted to know.

"Just Mateo's sister, Lucia. Not a problem there. His parents are at the home of friends. But no matter. The streets are so busy no one will pay attention to us. And Barrera's men are either watching trouble spots or partying themselves."

"Okay, then let's do this."

They rode silently after that, no one saying a word as they made their way into town and the residential area where the Albados and Mateo lived. Rocket noticed that Ed had been right. People were strolling the streets, or sitting on doorsteps with their drinks. Cars drove slowly with celebrants inside, saluting with beer bottles. Ed had made sure the Galaxy men had their props so they could blend into the environment. Now they just needed a little luck.

When they pulled up in front of Mateo's house, he was waiting for them on the stoop, his party face on. Ed had told them it would look better if they all went in, since little groups of people were going in and out of other houses up and down the street. They all greeted Mateo as if he were a long-lost friend and followed him into his house. But once they were inside, it was all business.

"This way," Mateo told them, led them up to the roof and pointed. "That's the Albado house, right there. Across from us."

Rocket guesstimated the distance then turned to Mateo.

"Ed says you have the grappling hooks?"

The man nodded. "I got them from him earlier today as a grocery delivery." He walked to the edge of the roof and grabbed a large plastic sack sitting there. "Ready when you are."

While Ed and Blaze unpacked the grappling hook and the machinery to shoot it across the alley, Rocket texted Mallory.

We're here and ready to rock and roll.

The answer came back at once.

Me, too. Take a look.

He looked across the alley and up and saw her kneeling at the lip on the edge of the roof. She raised a hand to him. He raised his back.

You can do this.

Yes. I can. In fact, I did it once before.

What????? Mallory?

But she wasn't answering him. *Damn woman*, he thought, even as he forced back his fear for her.

"Okay." He nodded at the others. "Let's do it."

Blaze took the grappling hook pistol from the bag and locked all the pieces into place. While he did that, Viper took the trailing ends of the rope ladder and he and Eagle each wrapped one around their waist. Then they sat down, making the ladder taut and reducing the chances it would swing free with Mallory on it. Blaze shot the hooks across the alley and they landed perfectly on the raised edge of the Albado roof.

Mallory tested to make sure the hooks were set then climbed over the lip and onto the rope ladder. He had to admit, even as he watched with his heart in his mouth, that she seemed to know what she was doing. Still, he didn't draw a full breath until she made it to the bottom of the ladder and Ed and Mateo helped her onto Mateo's roof. Ignoring everyone else around them, he pulled her against his body and wrapped his arms around her as tightly as he could. He was dying to kiss her, but he didn't want to do it with an audience.

"I've got you," he whispered.

"Thank you," she whispered back.

"You're amazing."

"So are you."

"Did you bring your gun?"

"Gun?" Ed whipped around and stared at them. "What gun?"

Mallory pulled it out from beneath her T-shirt. "This one. Inez gave it to me. Bullets are in my pockets."

"I hope to Christ you know how to use it. Let's get going. We're not out of the woods yet. Mateo just got a call from his commander that Barrera is setting up checkpoints around the city. The guy told him to boot out any company and get his ass to work."

"What do these checkpoints consist of?" Blaze wanted to know. "Do they have barricades up, stopping every vehicle?"

"I've only seen them do this a couple of times. They usually park a cop car — or a private one if they use up their fleet — and have a couple of patrol guys standing there. Vehicles have to slow down to pass them and give the police a chance to get a good look at them. They'll only stop someone who looks suspicious. Mallory had to show her phony ID to one of the idiots who approached, so my guess is it's available on the internet, they pulled it down and everyone has her picture."

"Shit." Rocket scowled. "That sucks."

"We may get lucky and find a way out they haven't set up yet."

"Then let's move," Blaze agreed.

Ed and Blaze yanked on the rope ends of the ladder, freeing them from the grappling hooks, and rolling up the ladder. Inez would have to get up there and dispose of the hooks. They left the house as a noisy group of partiers, waving goodbye to Mateo, holding beer bottles, scrunching Mallory in the middle of their group, and laughing as they climbed into Ed's vehicle. They stuffed her into the middle seat, Rocket and Blaze each putting an arm around her and Rocket leaning forward to kiss her. He wasn't about to let anyone else do it, and for a moment the taste of her, after all this time, almost made him forget what this was all about.

"You can save that for later," Blaze told him. "We need to get the fuck away from here and back to the cove. You said Elias would be meeting us with a Zodiac."

"He is. We didn't bring you in on one because we didn't want to give any warning of your arrival. Leaving's different. We'll be gone and away before anyone can do anything."

"You're right about moving out of here," Rocket agreed. Then he whispered in Mallory's ear, "We'll have plenty of time when we're out of here."

She didn't say anything, but she pressed closer to him.

They did okay for a few blocks, heading away from the residential area they were in. But then they ran into a roadblock on a street which they backed away from.

"Checkpoint," Ed murmured.

"Uh-uh," Eagle agreed. "Let me see if there's another way to get to our launching point."

But after they'd run into two more checkpoints and backed away from them, Ed drove them away from the area and out toward what he told them was La Jungla — the jungle.

"Very thick and overgrown. It's on the edge of town, past the fields where Barrera grows his dope, and no one ever goes there. The entrance isn't even visible — there won't be a checkpoint, though, and no one can find you in there. Barrera's men are not going to want to try hacking through miles of it to find you. If he thinks you're in there, it's more likely he'll decide you'll die there and save him the trouble."

"And we're supposed to — what — sleep in the bushes?" Rocket asked.

Mallory was quiet, letting him take the lead.

"Got it covered. Remember I mentioned the cabin on stilts — a jungle hut of sorts — that I, uh, have access to on the far side of the island? I set it up some time ago for a sort of op I was involved in."

"A sort of op?" Eagle glanced over at his friend. "Jesus, Ed. Exactly how many things do you do besides dive tours and fishing expeditions?"

"Just enough to keep my hand in. As I said, I keep it stocked in case of emergency, which I think you'll all agree that this is."

Again, there was a long moment of silence.

Rocket shook his head. "I guess we don't have a choice. Any idea how long this will be for?"

"My guess," Ed answered, "is no more than a couple of days, while Barrera tears up the town since he won't find you at the Albados'. When he doesn't find you, he'll move on to someone or something else."

"Yeah, right," Blaze snorted. "I know his type."

"And I know Barrera," Ed insisted. "He has a short attention span. Something else will come along to piss him off. Some unsuspecting tourist will do something, or one of his men will mouth off. If it doesn't happen by itself, I'll make it so."

"I'm not sure I even want to know what all you do," Viper said. "Just as long as you can get all of us out of here safely."

"You can count on it. Now let's get you to your jungle hideaway."

They had driven for about fifteen minutes past acres of rich green fields before the narrow, paved street changed to a short dirt road barely large enough for a single vehicle. It was almost invisible, thickly overgrown as it was. Ed had the headlights on dim as he moved through the dense flora and fauna that concealed what was obviously a little-used entrance.

Blaze leaned over from the back seat. "Won't Barrera send his men to search this area?"

"No." Ed shook his head. "No one goes in here because it's so easy to get lost. Besides, there are a lot of stories about La Jungla and Barrera's men are very superstitious. They won't even look for you here. That's why I set up the hut here."

He drove them slowly into the thickness of the jungle, maneuvering around trees and immense bushes. No one said a word for the next ten minutes, until the lights landed on a wood hut with a thatched roof. It sat on stilts in the middle of a miniscule clearing surrounded by giant, thick-leaved trees. A ladder led up to what passed for the door.

"And you have this why?" Eagle asked.

"I had, um, a friend who needed a place with some privacy for a little while here on Santa Marita. Until he could be, uh, extracted. I had a friend who had a friend who did a deal with us, and when the crisis was over, they decided I should keep this in case I had to help someone again. And so here you are."

Eagle shook his head. "I'm not sure I even want to know what all you do besides your touristy stuff, but thank you."

"Come on. Rocket, let's get you and Mallory settled."

Rocket climbed the ladder first, glad to discover that it was a lot sturdier than he expected. The hut was basically one room, with a large pallet on the floor with pillows and two thick quilts, a couple of sling chairs, and a small counter against one wall that held a camp stove.

Mallory was right behind him, followed by Ed. The others waited below.

"There should be enough here to take care of you for a couple of days," Ed told them, opening cupboard doors to show them the supplies. "Sorry there's no indoor plumbing, but there is an efficient outhouse right behind us."

"Wow," Rocket snorted. "Thanks."

"Also, not far from the hut is a waterfall that beats any shower you've ever used."

Rocket lifted an eyebrow. "All the comforts of home, right?"

"It's fine," Mallory assured Ed. "From everything I learned about Barrera, I don't want to cross paths with him."

"No, you don't," Ed agreed. "Okay, be right back."

He hustled down the ladder and over to the vehicle, opening the rear door and rooting around. Then he was back with a canvas gym bag. When he opened it, Rocket saw a Glock .42 nestled among boxes of bullets. He handed it to Mallory.

"There's ammo in here for both of you. Mallory, I had no idea about your skills with a handgun or how big a piece you could handle, but this little sweetheart packs quite a wallop."

She smiled for the first time that night.

"I actually took firearms training and try to hit the range once a week. Thank you. This will be great."

"Not that I expect you'll need it, but I always believe in being prepared."

Rocket shook his friend's hand, doing his best to convey his thanks.

"I owe you big-time for this," he told the other man. "I'll forever be grateful."

"Save your gratitude until we get you all safely out of here."

"I've got my sat phone." Rocket pointed to his pocket. "It was in the waterproof bag with my gun. You have the number?"

Ed nodded. "And I know your partners do, too. All right, we're gonna get going. I want to scope out Santa Marita and see what Barrera's got going on tonight. See if I can find out how long he'll have checkpoints at all the streets leaving each town."

Rocket climbed down the ladder so he could shake hands with each of his partners. No words were said, but they exchanged silent messages.

We've got your back.

We'll get you out of this.

I trust you with my life. Our lives.

Then they climbed back into the vehicle and Ed drove it slowly out of the jungle.

Now it was just the two of them. Rocket looked at the woman standing in front of him. It was the first chance he'd had to take a good look at her. She hadn't changed much in five years. Not much at all. Her hair was a richer auburn and probably still as wild, but now it was restrained by a ponytail holder. Her body was just as toned. He wondered if she kept it that way through exercise or running from bad guys when she got herself into impossible situations. The T-shirt she wore clung to breasts that his hands itched to cup, and worn jeans hugged a body that still made his mouth water.

Okay, he'd better get them up into the hut before he stripped off her clothes and took her right there on the jungle floor. Besides, he had no idea what her memories of that night were, if they were pleasant or if she regretted every single moment. Right now, her safety was primary.

"Let's get back up into our hotel room," he joked. "No telling what's roaming around out here."

Mallory frowned. "You mean like apes and tigers and things like that?"

"No." His mouth quirked in a tiny grin. "None of those. But they do have jaguars. Will that do?"

She gave a tiny shiver. "What else?"

"Spider monkeys. And snakes. Lots of snakes. Oh, and bats. They seem to thrive in jungles like this."

"Damn, Rocket. I hope you're a crack shot in case one of them decides to come after us."

"Not to worry. I've got it. But let's get up there before we have to deal with any of them."

Mallory climbed the ladder ahead of him, and keeping his shit together was one of the hardest things he'd ever done, what with her very appealing ass practically smack in his face. But at last, they were in the hut, standing there, looking around.

"Let's see what Ed means by keeping this place stocked."

He wandered around the small room, opening cupboards to reveal canned goods, boxes of dry snacks and one cupboard filled with bottled water. There was also one with towels and toiletries like toothpaste and mouthwash.

"Glad to see he thought of our personal hygiene," Rocket joked.

"I hope we won't be here long enough to drink up all that water." Mallory looked around the room. "Although we could be hiding away in worse places."

"Like the cave in Afghanistan?" He tried to inject a little humor into his voice.

One corner of her mouth turned up in a hint of a grin. "It had its advantages. You agree?"

More than he could express. He closed the distance between them in three long strides until a sheet of paper would have barely fit between them.

"I have great memories of that cave." He stared into her eyes, the color in them darkening almost to a forest green. "Can I assume you do, too?"

She drew in a breath and let it out slowly. "Memories I haven't been able to wipe out of my mind."

Rocket took a moment before replying. "Same goes."

"But you never tried to get in touch with me," she pointed out.

"No, I didn't." He chose his words carefully. "I know this probably makes me sound like an asshole, but that was my usual method of operation. The SEALs came first for me in everything. And all the time. I had convinced myself that a relationship—*any* relationship—would distract me and diminish my ability to operate fully."

"How very macho and patriotic of you." She shook her head. "I wasn't expecting a proposal, Rocket, just something that told me you recognized the hot connection between us. Plus…" She shrugged. "Plus I wanted to thank you again for saving my life."

"I'm guessing you didn't try to locate me, either."

"Do you have any idea how hard it is to locate one of your guys? Even after you're out of the military? The government guards that information like it's the secret to world domination."

Rocket chuckled. He couldn't help himself. Then his smile disappeared.

"You'd be surprised how many people think they have a grudge against one of us. Or want revenge for something."

"Alicia said she used every bit of influence she had to learn how to contact you."

"Okay. So now here we are. Once again, some asshole wants to eliminate you and once again, I'm going to be your way out of here. But we're all alone here in the jungle. No one except Ed and my partners even knows we're here. From what Ed told us, I don't think more than a few people even know this hut exists. What do you say we put all that aside and concentrate on the here and now, and see if what happened five years ago was more than just physical attraction incited by the danger?"

She nibbled on her lower lip, a tiny gesture that made his semi-dormant cock instantly spring to life and push hard against his fly.

Jesus, Rocket, keep it in your pants at least until you find out how she feels.

"I can't believe I'm saying this when I could be killed in the next twenty-four hours. Barrera will chop off my head, literally, if he locates me. I'm worried about Inez and her family and wondering why he didn't execute the raid on their house tonight. And the chances of my getting out of here alive are fifty-fifty at best. Right?"

He couldn't help himself. He just had to touch her, so he cradled her face in his palms.

"One. You will definitely be getting out of here alive, because you have men arranging it who don't make mistakes and who successfully complete their missions. Two. I personally am not going to let anything happen to you, even if I have to do this all myself. Which, by the way I won't. Have to, that is."

"I hope you're right."

"Three. We're all alone here in the middle of noplace and I am dying to get just one taste of you."

She didn't say anything for a moment, so long that Rocket wondered if he'd be spending time with his good right hand. Then she leaned closer, just enough that he could touch his mouth to hers, feeling her soft lips beneath his firm ones. *And damn!* She tasted just as good as he remembered, a flavor that was distinctly Mallory. He ran the tip of his tongue over her lower lip. A slow swipe over the velvety flesh sent heat coursing straight through his body.

Jesus!

He hoped he had enough discipline not to get to the finish line before she did, because he wanted them both to enjoy every minute.

When he thrust his tongue into her mouth, sliding it over her tongue, a soft moan rolled from her throat and she pressed her body against his. She lifted both hands to run her fingers through his hair before cupping his head to hold it in place. He drank from her mouth, slipping his tongue everywhere, tasting, licking.

She gave as good as she got, using her own tongue to duel with his, the slide of the soft flesh so erotic he thought his cock would explode. He sucked her tongue slowly into his own mouth, letting his teeth graze gently against the surface. The delicious noises she made set his nerves on fire. He broke the kiss only with great reluctance, then released the ponytail holder so her hair cascaded wildly to her shoulders. He thrust his fingers through it, holding her head in place so he could kiss her again. But then he pulled back.

"W—What's wrong?"

"Nothing." He shook his head. "Well, something. I want to do this right. While fucking you against the wall appeals to me at this moment, it's not what I want after five years apart."

A tiny laugh bubbled from her mouth.

"Me neither," she told him, "although I must confess that the moment I saw you again, I wanted you the same way I did five years ago."

The tiny knot of tension in Rocket's insides eased. *Okay, then.* He wasn't going to have to convince her, because she had the same feelings he did. If possible, his cock swelled even more.

"We have no place to be," he told Mallory, "and no one waiting for us, at least right now. I don't want to rush this, Mal."

"Neither do I."

He wasn't sure whose hands were shaking more, his or hers, as he slowly unbuttoned her blouse and drew it down her arms. His breath caught at the swell of her breasts above the line of her bra, and the dark nipples visible through the lace fabric. He pushed the blouse down her arms, tossing it to the side, and swiped a tongue across the rounded flesh. Then he placed his lips around one of the nipples and sucked it into his mouth, fabric and all.

Mallory gripped his upper arms, holding herself in place, head thrown back as she arched into his mouth. Another moan slipped from between her lips, the sound so erotic it made him clamp his teeth down on her flesh. When he'd teased the little button until it was swollen and hard, he moved to the other one, finally unfastening the bra and tossing it to the side with her blouse.

Holding tight to his control, he dropped to his knees, unzipped her jeans and slid them down her long, toned legs. The lacy bikini panties came next, leaving every bit of her exposed to his sight and his touch. Pressing his face between her thighs, he inhaled her scent, one that had stayed with him all these years.

Then he rose to his feet, yanked off his shirt and dropped it on the pile of clothing. Next came his jeans

The last thing to go were his boxer briefs, which he had to remove carefully since his dick was sticking almost straight out. Then he lifted Mallory in his arms and carried her to the pallet, stretching her out on the thickly padded fabric. He couldn't believe his hands were actually shaking. He'd thought about the possibility of this moment for so long that he could hardly deal with the fact that it had arrived. He stretched out next to her, loving the feel of her naked skin against his.

He didn't know where to start first, which part of her to taste, to touch. He started with her mouth again, stringing kisses along the line of her chin to her neck, aroused even more by the sexy sounds she was making. Palming one breast, he turned his mouth again to the other one, scraping his teeth over the nipple, giving it gentle little bites. It was already aroused from his previous attention, so it didn't take long until he had it swollen and dark, and turned his attention to the other one.

Mallory writhed and moaned, the sexy sounds urging him on. When he moved his mouth down over the soft swell of her stomach, pausing to tease at her navel, the little sounds grew even louder. Weaving her fingers into his hair, she pressed his head harder against her body, urging him on to more and more.

He was ravenous for her by the time he slid down to the tempting mound of her sex, opening her with his thumbs so he could taste the slick pink skin he exposed. He didn't have to nudge her thighs apart. She let them fall wide open on her own, thrusting herself up to his mouth. He traced the flesh on either side of her opening with long swipes of his tongue before taking gentle bites of her clit.

"Oh! Oh! Oh!"

Mallory thrust her heels into the pallet to lift herself closer to his mouth. And when he slid two fingers inside her, she pushed hard against them, riding them, crying out in obvious pleasure as he added a third finger and beginning the delicious glide toward orgasm.

When he eased his fingers out, she gave a small cry of disappointment. "Don't stop. Please."

"Not stopping," he assured her. "Just marking my territory." With that, he slipped his slick fingers down the cleft of her ass, teasing her hot, tight opening. "One of these days," he murmured, "I'm going to fuck you here and it will be the best thing you ever had." Then he pushed them back into her hot, wet slit.

"Oh, god." Her inner walls clamped down on his hand, squeezing his fingers.

He was torn between bringing her to orgasm with his hand and letting her slick walls squeeze his demanding cock, and the cock won out. He grabbed the little plastic baggie, pulled out a condom and rolled it on, his hand actually shaking with need and desire. Then, kneeling between her thighs, he spread her legs wide, pushed them back so she was completely open and exposed to him, and drove into her with one hard thrust.

"Look at me, Mallory." He hardly recognized his own voice. "Open your eyes and look at me."

When she did, he saw the same heat and hunger flaming there, and something indefinable speared through him. Then he could think of nothing except the feel of Mallory and her heat.

They were both so close to the tipping point, so ready for each other, that it took only a few hard pumps of his hips to drive them both over the edge. The moment he felt her inner walls spasm, he fell over the edge, taking her with him. Nothing existed except him and this woman. She had wound her legs around him and now she dug her heels into the small of his back, locking his body to hers while the intense orgasms shook them both.

He had no idea how long it went on, only that he'd never felt such pleasure. And when at last it subsided and Mallory's legs fell limp to the side, he cupped her head in his palms and gave her a long, slow kiss, sliding his tongue over hers in a lazy motion. At last, he forced himself to withdraw from her body, easing away from her and rising slowly to his feet.

"Don't move," he told her. "Just give me a second here."

He disposed of the condom in a wastebasket stuck in a corner, then lay back down again next to Mallory. They were both sweaty, and the lack of air conditioning didn't help the situation, but he didn't care. He was mentally cursing himself for not making time to find her in the past five years.

Stupid schmuck.

"I have to tell you this." He brushed damp strands of hair from her forehead, looking hard into her eyes. "I never thought I'd say this, but I'll be kicking myself for a long time for being so stupid and self-focused that I let the past five years go by without looking for you."

Her lips, slightly puffy from kissing, curved in a little smile.

"But maybe we weren't ready for each other. I'm not sure that I was, so obsessed with hitting all the danger spots and writing these books."

"Which I discovered have all hit the bestseller lists. Congratulations."

"Thanks. I wasn't sure I'd get out of here to write the next one until Alicia told me you'd agreed to come and get me out of here."

He couldn't help smiling. "Just as long as we don't make a real habit of this."

She sighed. "I promise to try, okay?" A small grin teased at her mouth. "Maybe someone could point me in a different direction if they were around enough."

He quirked an eyebrow. "Are you offering me a job?"

She frowned. "I thought you already had one."

"I might be persuaded to handle two." All traces of humor disappeared. "I definitely want to talk about it when I get your ass out of here."

"Okay, then." She studied his face. "We *are* getting out of here, right?"

He nodded. "That's a promise. Now, we need water so we don't get dehydrated, and we should get some sleep because we don't know what tomorrow will bring."

Mallory nodded, but she was pretty sure she wouldn't be sleeping much tonight. Not with the danger to the Albado family hanging over her head and Barrera determined to find her. Only Rocket's steady presence settled her at all. The fact that not only had he come to get her out of this mess but also that the chemistry between them was still there and he wasn't fighting it gave her a bright ray of hope.

But they couldn't stay isolated in this hut forever. She'd just have to trust that his friends would make this happen.

Chapter Nine

Blaze took a swallow of his coffee and set the cup down on the scarred table. After having cruised the streets carefully for almost two hours, they'd decided they needed to get out of sight of the checkpoints, of which there were a shitload. All the soldiers had communications devices and he was pretty damn sure that if they showed up on too many radars too many times, they'd have a problem. They especially didn't want the so-called soldiers seeing the faces of the Galaxy men over and over again.

Deciding they needed to get off the road, Ed had taken them to an old coffee bar that stayed open very late and wasn't really on the tourist scene. But, he told them, it did serve the best coffee on the island. Even at that very late hour, the place was crowded, but they'd managed to find a table in a corner, which was ideal for them. Plus no one seemed to be paying attention, a welcome change from the soldiers at the checkpoints who were scrutinizing the people in every vehicle and even questioning some of them. Smartly, they'd backed away from each station before the guards could lay eyes on them.

Once they were seated, Blaze looked at the man who was taking all these chances helping them.

"What if Barrera's men see you driving around with three strangers in this car?" he asked. "You'll be in a shitpile of trouble."

Ed shook his head. "Maybe if it was a night when there wasn't something else happening. Something that drew his focus. Plus, neither he nor his asshole-sucking lieutenant, Ruben Vidal, are anywhere to be seen. That means something else is going on, something very important, that's taking them away from this."

Viper lifted an eyebrow. "What do you think it might be?"

Ed shrugged. "If I had to guess, it's either one of their major customers or a new one with a big order." He took a sip of his coffee. "Anyway, I've gone out of my way to present myself as unremarkable to the general. I play the role he expects — a possible alcoholic bum who runs a little bar and takes people fishing. I never give him a problem, he always gets a decent catch when I take him out and I don't do anything to annoy him. I even take his customers out for daytrips. I'm so unexceptional they treat me like a part of the boat. And his men sitting at checkpoints look at me the same way, I'm sure. However..."

He let the word trail off.

"Right. However." Eagle gave a soft laugh. "If he only knew that invisibility and the ability to blend into your surroundings were what made you so very valuable to our SEAL team. These guys have absolutely no idea how effective you can be and how much information you can obtain that way."

"And lucky for us." Viper touched his beer glass to Ed's. "Thanks seems too small a word for what you're doing."

"Wait until we get Mallory Kane out of here safely along with all of you. Then you can give me a big thank you and I won't even object."

Blaze leaned forward. "So what do we do now?"

"Now we need to figure out a way to sneak the Albados out of their house before Barrera can pull his big show tomorrow. And that won't be easy."

"Is there a way we can reach them tonight and get them into hiding, at least for the time being?"

"Let's make sure they're where we think they are," Ed told him, "then figure out what to do."

He pulled out his cell phone and punched in a number.

Blaze glanced over at Eagle. "Does he have the whole country on speed dial?"

Eagle snorted. "Seems like, it, doesn't it?"

They waited while Ed spoke quietly into his phone, disconnected and made two more calls before putting the phone back in his pocket.

"Okay. Here's the deal. Inez's parents are still at Casa Valentina, a very homey neighborhood restaurant with a relaxed atmosphere and great food. They met friends for a later dinner and they are now having coffee and dawdling over desert. I'm guessing they're enjoying the change from the stress that's been consuming them since Mallory had to start hiding in their attic."

"We need to get them out of there," Eagle said, "but how and where? Then we have to get them away from Santa Marita under Barrera's nose."

Ed took a swallow of his coffee. "Yes. Okay. First, we need to scope out the restaurant and see if any of Barrera's men are around there. My guess is he knows where the Albados are tonight and thinks they're too stupid or weak to be a problem as long as they're with friends. He's looking forward to squashing them like a bug. Their destruction will be his satisfaction if he can't get his hands on Mallory."

"And where's Inez?" Eagle asked. "Is she out somewhere, too?"

"She's spending the night with her current boyfriend, Diego Flores."

Viper chuckled. "Remind me never to try keeping secrets when you're around."

Eagle nodded. "You know it, man. He could work for the CIA."

Ed gave a fake shudder. "Not in a million years. Government agencies and I don't get along too well."

"And don't ask him why," Eagle added.

"No problem. But what's our first move? We have to get the Albados out of danger before the raid scheduled for tomorrow night."

"We can't do it tonight," Ed pointed out, "or Barrera will think something's up for sure. Using the boat for any of this is out. Barrera's got his thugs checking every single point of egress from all of Santa Marita so he can get his hands on Mallory. So let's look at other options. Our first priority is figuring out how to get Mallory and Rocket off this island unobserved."

"And you're sure people who see us won't wonder who you're driving around with?" Viper asked.

Ed shook his head. "I hang out here sometimes after I fish with one of Barrera's fishing trips, or a little jaunt he has me take some of his friends on. The reason I didn't want to plug you into that same process is that you guys look like you could eliminate a whole country without breaking a sweat. Sorry, but it is what it is. That's not what my usual clientele is, and I didn't want to take a chance. For one night, though, we'll manage. We'll just avoid places where we'd attract attention."

"Can't be good for business if they go after visitors."

"Sometimes I think they just don't care about it," Ed told him. "As long as their drug business is healthy and they control life on the island, what do they have to worry about?"

"Someone else coming in and pulling the same kind of coup Barrera did?" Viper suggested.

Ed's mouth curved in a slow grin. "Good point. If only."

"I hate to say this," Blake put in, "but we may have to do it in order to get all of us out."

Viper frowned.

"What do you mean?"

"It's possible we need to create one extraction plan for Mallory and Rocket and another for the rest of us. Moving a crowd of people might be too complex."

Eagle nodded. "We've had to do that before, so I agree."

"Let's make plans for it but hope we don't have to use them," Ed chimed in. "I'd be a lot happier getting everyone out in one package. Okay, let's finish up here and go someplace where we're alone to figure this out. But first we should do some reconnoitering again." He looked from one to the other. "But carefully."

"Hey." Eagle winked at him. "Careful's our middle name."

* * * *

Bruno Elizondo was a man hardly anyone ever noticed. In some ways, that was bad. He was never on anyone's radar when good stuff happened. After five years, he was still a lowly private in Felix Barrera's army and no one ever brought his name up to *El Jefe* for promotion and special assignment. He was always given the lowest, most menial tasks and he'd had only had one increase in his pay.

But it also meant that his invisibility was an asset. He could observe things and overhear things without anyone even aware he was doing it. Blending into the color of the walls had its distinct advantages.

For one thing, as the inconsequential driver who fetched Barrera's whores, he had collected quite a notebook on *El Jefe*'s sordid sex life. He had even, on occasion, had to dispose of a body or two, someone who had provoked the man's uncontrollable rage.

He washed and maintained the general's vehicles, and it was amazing what kind of things the man left lying around. Money, which Bruno stuffed into his own pockets to subsidize his own meager wages. A couple of times, one of the expensive, made-to-order hand-rolled cigars. Women's panties. Once even a tiny plastic baggie of coke, that he'd sold for what to him was a substantial sum.

And when he was pressed into service as a houseboy, he overheard conversations that he knew people would pay much money for if he ever had the guts to try to sell them.

But tonight, he was sure he had hit the jackpot. Tonight's menial job had him doing coffee runs, one after the other, to what that asshole Barrera called the real soldiers, who were busy mounting checkpoints around the city. Their theory was that the woman they were looking for had not been able to reach any of the outskirts like La Jungla. She had no transportation of her own. Hadn't used any of the public ones available. And finally, could not do it without the help of someone else.

So this asinine exercise tonight was an attempt to spot a stranger — or strangers — who might be the one or ones helping her. Exactly how any of these idiots would know who that was totally escaped Bruno. Did they expect people to wear tags that said *I am helping Melinda Clayton*? For one thing, strangers didn't just wander onto Santa Marita. Barrera and his men vetted every single visitor, and casual tourists didn't come here anymore. For another, how would they even get onto the island without being seen? Barrera had every entry spot well covered.

Still, Bruno had to agree that somehow, someone or many someones had slipped through and were getting ready to sneak the Clayton woman away from Santa Marita. If he could find out who that was, perhaps Barrera would finally see his value. He had stopped into his friend Leo's place, where he knew he could get a richly brewed cup of coffee generously laced with fine brandy.

He happened to be sitting there when four men walked in and sat at a table in the corner. He watched while Leo served them, something tickling his brain. He was sure they weren't regular visitors to Santa

Marita or he would have bumped into them now and then doing one of his many, many menial chores.

But two things made his spidey senses leap to alert. One, he had seen these same men in an old SUV turn away before hitting a few checkpoints. And two, they didn't look like any tourists he had ever seen, or even regular fishermen. They looked like warriors of some kind. He'd seen plenty in his time and they gave him the shivers. This had to be them. He just knew it. The problem was, how did he find out who they were and where to locate them when they left the coffee bar?

He had a cheap cell phone in his pocket that he carried so his wife could get hold of him if she needed to. It didn't have many features, but one thing it did have was a camera. He drained the last of his coffee, nodded to Leo and slipped out through the back door. Positioning himself where he was pretty sure these guys would not see him, he snapped a few pictures of the car he'd seen them driving. When they left the place, he managed to get a couple of shots of them, sliding back inside before they could notice him.

This could be the very break he was looking for.

He was sure they weren't going into hiding anywhere, not if they were planning to get Melinda Clayton out of Santa Marita. He just had to find out where they were going from here and what they were doing. And where they had the Clayton woman stashed. Barrera had already said he was keeping the checkpoints in place through Saturday night. All Bruno had to do was find a way to monitor where the beat-up SUV was going between now and then.

He smiled to himself as he climbed into his innocuous vehicle and pulled out into the roadway.

One thing he had become very good at was ferreting things out.

* * * *

Mallory came awake slowly, blinking as she became aware of the warm, naked male body next to her. At once, everything that had happened in the preceding hours popped back into her mind. The past five years disappeared like a cloud of smoke, the connection hot and strong. And God! The sex had been off the charts. If it weren't for the extreme danger like a third person in the room, it would have been close to perfect. She stroked a hand up and down Rocket's arm, loving the feel of him beneath her touch.

"Morning."

His voice had that early morning huskiness to it.

"Morning to you, too."

He rolled over and cradled her face in his palms.

"I'm never letting you get away from me again," he promised.

"Good. Because I'm all for that, too."

"I just—" He stopped and blew out a breath. "For whatever reason, I had it in my head that if I had a relationship, it would distract me from my work."

"Even though I'm sure you saw other SEALs in long-term situations?"

"Even though. And I saw just as many that didn't last." He traced the line of her jaw with the tip of a finger. "But lately I've seen two of my partners commit to relationships and they seem better than ever. I decided I needed to stop being such an asshole. Your sister calling me gave me the chance to see if I could correct the biggest mistake I'd ever made."

He peeked out through the slats of the shutters covering the windows. "It's beautiful out there. How about a walk to the waterfall and an early morning shower?"

"I'd like that. Then we can scrounge for breakfast."

She grinned. "Works for me."

They dug around through all the displays and found, amazingly enough, toothbrushes, and they shared a bottle of water to handle brushing their teeth.

"We can figure out how to do breakfast when we come back."

In minutes they had climbed down the ladder and headed toward the sound of the cascading water.

The walk to the waterfall was somewhat complicated, since there was no real pathway and all the overgrown bushes and trees presented one obstacle after another. They also had to navigate and avoid the wildlife endemic to La Jungla. The word was that jaguars had long since disappeared, hunted to extinction, but there were red howler monkeys — which made a horrendous screeching sound — squirrel monkeys, anteaters and tapirs. They both brought their weapons with them, just in case.

Nevertheless, Mallory had to admit it was worth it. When they finally broke through into an opening, she could only stand there for a moment and stare. What she saw was like an entrance into a magic world. Directly ahead of them, a thick waterfall cascaded down over a massive wall of rock, the sound of it thundering in the air. The water dropped into a pool it had carved out from the rock at the bottom, and around it grew more tropical plants than she had ever seen. Vibrant colors — red, orange, royal purples, azure blue — were scattered in and among the thick, wild, low border of greenery.

Mallory just stood there for watching a long moment, mesmerized. "It's gorgeous," she breathed.

"It is indeed," Rocket agreed.

"You could almost forget all the bitter viciousness out there when you're standing here." She reached for Rocket's hand, grounded by the touch of it. "Wouldn't it be nice if we could just shut out the rest of the world and stay here?"

He laughed. "Don't tempt me."

"Let's take off our shoes. Look, there's this nice big flat rock here that we can set them on and they won't get wet or knocked into the pool. As if it was made for this. Maybe nature created our own special place for us," she teased.

"Maybe." He grinned. "Anything is possible." He set both pairs of shoes on the rock then pulled her into his arms. "I think we should put our clothes there, too."

"Are we going to take a shower in the waterfall? I've never done that before."

"Good. I want you to have a lot of firsts with me."

She studied the look on his face. "What are we doing, Rocket?"

"We're going to shower in a waterfall, near as I can tell."

"No, I mean, what are we *doing*? We don't see each other for five years, not even a text or phone call. Then life throws us together again and it's like we have this major thing going."

He brushed his mouth over hers. "Major thing, huh? Well, I'll tell you this. The dumbest thing I did was staying away from you all this time. And I can't even give you a really good reason why I did it."

"You were busy being a SEAL," she reminded him. "Then getting ready to do…whatever it is you do now. I understand. I wasn't much better. When my first couple of books unexpectedly became such hits, I was like an addict with a stash of coke waiting for me."

"Not to mention being an adrenaline junkie," he teased.

"I could say the same for you." She nipped his chin. "You didn't exactly settle for a nine-to-five job when you left the SEALs."

"So we both ignored the possibility that something good might be waiting for us." His eyes burned into hers. "I think most of the blame for that falls on me. Isn't the guy supposed to do the pursuing?"

"Only if you believe in antiquated practices." She brushed her mouth against his. "We have so much to catch up on. Let's not waste any time with regrets."

"I can buy into that. I'm sorry I've been such a stupid shithead and wasted so much time. We have a lot to make up for."

"Then we should probably get started."

She wanted to hear about every one of those five years. Wanted to ask him how he and his friends had come to form Galaxy. Did he like what he was doing? Like living in Tampa? Was he involved with another woman?

No!

No, she could answer that question herself. If he were, he wouldn't be involving himself with her. That was not who he was.

They placed their guns in their holsters on top of their shoes on the flat rock, which was dry and easily accessible. Then Rocket added the satellite phone he'd brought with him, placing it next to his gun. Before

Mallory could think any more, she tugged her T-shirt over her head and dropped it to the side on top of the shoes. No bra. She'd left that in the hut, along with her panties. Next came the shorts, which she tossed onto the pile.

"I think you're overdressed, mister," she teased.

"First let me say one thing." He cradled her head in his palms, the look in his eyes both heated and serious. "I'll be kicking myself forever for letting five years go by because I refused to admit that I'd let the best thing that happened to me walk out of my life."

"But you're admitting it now, and so am I. My crazy streak of getting into dangerous situations worked in my favor for once, because it brought us together again." She searched his eyes, trying to read his expression. "Just tell me we're not going to walk away again and I'm good."

"We're not. Neither of us. Maybe it was good things happened this way, because I got to see two of my partners fall in love and settle into relationships. I saw first-hand that it can work. And as soon as we get you out of here, you and I are going to make some plans. Sound good to you?"

"Yes. It does. But you're still overdressed."

Then he got rid of the jeans he'd tugged on, having left his shirt and shorts in the hut, then pulled her against his body. She could feel every muscle and ridge, including the thick, swollen length of his cock that pressed hard against her stomach.

"Let's get into the waterfall. I've never stood in a waterfall with a naked woman."

She grinned and held out her hand to him. "Lead on."

They picked their way around the heavy curtain of water as it thundered down to the ground until they reached a level spot behind the cascade itself. Mallory felt as if they were enclosed in a glass dome, a private cocoon, with all the world locked out. When Rocket turned and pulled her against him, she tipped up her head, ready for him, and greedily fell into the kiss.

His tongue was wild in her mouth, sweeping everywhere, tasting everything. Licking every surface. She dueled her own tongue with his, loving the slick taste of him, every nerve ending in her body firing. He slid his hand down her back, stroking her spine, and when he came to her ass, he cupped one cheek and pressed her body hard against his. She could feel the long, solid length of his swollen cock against her mound and rubbed herself back and forth against it.

He lifted his head, his breathing uneven.

"I don't have any condoms with me and I…"

"I'm safe," she told him, breathless. "And I haven't been with anyone since—"

She shut her mouth. How could she even tell him that?

He stared at her. "Are you telling me you haven't been with anyone since Afghanistan?"

She looked down at her bare feet, standing on the slick granite with the cool water running over them. Would he look at her differently? Maybe lose his desire at the thought no man had wanted her for five years? But that wasn't the truth. She hadn't wanted *them*. It had been her choice, just as it was now. She rested her head on his shoulder, still looking down at her feet, while she waited for him to say something.

He wound the length of her damp hair around his hand and gently tipped her head back.

"Look at me," he commanded.

She opened her eyes to stare at him and saw so many emotions swimming in his that it stole her breath.

"I am."

"Are you telling me for real you haven't been with *anyone* in the past five years? Not even once?"

She managed a little smile. "Well, there's Henry."

"Henry?" He almost shouted the name. "Who the fuck is Henry?"

She bit her lower lip to keep from smiling.

"Well, he's eight inches long, dark purple and runs on two batteries."

For a moment she thought he was going to step away from her. Then he threw back his head and laughed so hard that his shoulders shook.

"Well," he said at last when he could catch his breath, "my ego has certainly expanded if you're telling me our time together spoiled you for other men."

"It was you that spoiled me," she told him. "Every other man I met seemed so...shallow. And after a while, it hardly seemed worth the trouble."

"Jesus, Mallory." He blew out a breath. "If you'd told me that, I would have made an effort to do much better last night."

"You did just fine. So fine, in fact, that I'd like a repeat performance."

"If you want it here, it's gonna be a lot quicker and with a lot less finesse," he warned her.

"That suits me. In fact, it'll suit me a lot better if you get to it."

He laughed again, but then the laughter was replaced by the heat in his eyes. He skimmed his hand between her thighs and slid two fingers into her hot, waiting sex.

"Jesus, Mallory. You are so ready. Just from touching each other?"

She nodded. "So get to it."

He knelt on the granite between the fall of water and the wall of stone, spread her lips with his fingers and proceeded to lick every inch of her sex. She dug her fingers into his shoulders to steady herself while he ate at her core, the flick of his tongue sending shivers racing through her body. She rocked against the pressure of his mouth, moaning with the pleasure of it. Then—

"Stop." She had trouble getting the word out.

He froze and looked up at her. "What the fuck, Mallory? What's wrong?"

"What's wrong is this is the second time you've given me so much to me and I haven't returned the favor."

She was shivering as pleasure still coursed through her and her body demanded release.

Rocket cupped her face in his palms.

"Listen to me. This isn't a tit-for-tat kind of thing. I get just as much pleasure from using my mouth on you as I do from being on the receiving end. I love that I can make you tremble with pleasure just by using my tongue, not to mention that you taste incredible."

"But…"

"No buts. Plus I'm not shy about asking, But, Mallory? There will be no more walking away from each other. We're going to have a lot of years together, to enjoy every single thing together. Besides, I'm so fucking hard right now that even one sweep of your tongue could finish me off." He grinned. "So shut up and let me enjoy myself."

"Okay. Yes. Okay."

Then get back to it, she wanted to shout.

But it was obvious he needed no urging. He knelt again, thrust two fingers into her slick flesh and began to work her clit with his tongue. As aroused as she was, it took only seconds before an orgasm rushed up through her body. Throwing her head back, she braced herself and gave in to the spasms.

Her body was still quaking when he lifted her, turned so her back was against the wall of rock and thrust his cock deep inside her in one swift, hard movement.

His thickness filling every inch of her—his *naked* thickness—set off her body again, and the orgasm that had never quite finished demanded to be let loose again.

He clutched her ass with both hands, digging his fingers into the soft flesh, and began to pump into her as if his life depended on it. She grabbed his biceps, riding the length of his cock as he drove in and out of her with ferocity, as if he'd never be able to do this again.

"Hope you're ready," he said through gritted teeth, "because I can't hold out much longer.

"I am," she gasped, hardly getting the words out, digging her heels into the small of his back. "Do it."

The words had barely left her mouth before he gave one last thrust into her and the orgasm grabbed both of them. She closed her eyes as his cock spasmed and her inner walls pulsed. She had no idea how long it went on, just let herself fall into the incredible pleasure. Finally it slowed and at last halted. The walls of her sex squeezed his dick, wringing the last drop from it.

Rocket dipped his head and leaned it on her shoulder for a moment. The heavy beat of his heart pounded in time with hers. They stayed in that same position until she lowered her legs and leaned her body into his for support.

Rocket brushed a soft kiss over her mouth.

"Wow. Just wow."

She managed a grin. "Sometimes short is best, you know?"

"After that, how can I argue?"

"Shouldn't we feel guilty doing this while everyone else is out there trying to save our asses?"

"Yeah." But he grinned. "I'll feel guilty as soon as we're done here."

Just as he cupped her cheeks and tilted her head up for another kiss, the sat phone rang. He walked over to where he'd set it in his shoe and picked it up.

"I hope you have good news." He paused. "Uh-huh. Uh-huh." There came another pause. "Okay, we're good for the time being, but we gotta get the fuck out of here. Yeah. Okay. Thanks."

"Well?" She was anxious to hear what was said.

"The team had a couple of options to get us away from here. They're working on it and will keep in touch. Meanwhile, we're to stay put."

"I trust your guys," she told him. "Meanwhile, we can shut out the world for a while."

"How about a nice cool shower?" Rocket asked. "Then a walk back to our deluxe accommodations and some breakfast."

"Sounds good to me."

"And, Mal?"

"Yes?"

"We *will* get out of here and start a life together. I'm not making the same idiotic mistake twice."

She hooked her arm through his.

"If you say so, I believe it."

"Good. Keep believing."

Chapter Ten

Felix Barrera lowered himself into the big chair in his office and leaned back, momentarily closing his eyes. It had been a long night, although a profitable one. Gerard Moreau had been impressed with his operation, including the checkpoints he had set up looking for what he called, "those who would commit crimes against the government."

"*I see you have established tight control,*" Moreau had told him. "*Good, good. That gives me confidence that no one from the outside can come in and disrupt your operation.*"

"*That's why we have so many satisfied customers,*" Barrera had preened. "*We own this island and everyone on it. If a stranger arrives, we make sure they can't be a troublesome force.*"

"*I know many cartels control parts of the country where they are located, but here?*" Moreau had laughed. "*You own the country. I look forward to a long and profitable relationship.*"

The deal they'd struck tonight was even larger than he'd hoped for, with the hint at more customers to come. Visions of the area his cartel could control expanded in his brain. He was glad they had product available to fill the order. But he realized he would need to 'acquire' more land to plant additional crops. Well, no problem there. The people of Santa Marita did exactly as he told them or they disappeared.

Now he would turn his attention back to the Melinda Clayton *puta*. Once she was dead, he'd take a full breath again. He'd tried telling himself she was just an annoying bitch, one of many he'd met. A little fish that he was paying too much attention to. But there was something about her that set off his warning sensors. He secretly admitted he wasn't the smartest of men, but he had good instincts. That was what had helped get him where he was. And his instincts were telling him that there was something off about this woman. That she could be a danger to him.

He glanced at his watch. Marta, the computer whiz, had been working on the project for several hours now. Either there was nothing to find about Melinda Clayton or it was hidden so well it couldn't be found. Neither answer appealed to him. The first one told him he was losing his edge and becoming paranoid. The second said she was fucking smart enough to bury who she really was. And who the hell knew who she was connected to?

Ruben had left after they'd driven Moreau back to his boat and was probably asleep by now. Still, Barrera was tempted to call him and see if his crack computer female had been able to find anything. He reached to pull his cell phone out of his pocket, but before he could punch the speed dial number for his top dog, it gave off Ruben's ring tone.

He hit Accept. "Yes? Tell me you have good news for me."

"*Si*. That is, after a fashion."

"What the fuck does that mean?"

"It means Marta finally dug deep enough to find out who this woman really is. But you won't like it."

Barrera heaved himself out of the chair and, cradling the phone between his chin and his shoulder, he poured a brandy for himself. He took a hefty swallow before sitting down again. He was sure he wasn't going to like what Ruben was about to tell him.

"All right. Let's have it." He took another swallow of brandy.

Slow down, slow down. You don't want to get drunk if there's a bigger problem to deal with.

"To begin with, her real name is Mallory Kane. She used to be a news reporter but now she writes books about places like Afghanistan and Santa Marita and they become bestsellers."

Shit! Fucking shit!

Barrera knew about people like that. Always sticking their nose in where it wasn't wanted and bringing publicity to people who didn't need it.

"*Jefe*?" Ruben's voice penetrated his brain. "Did you hear what I said?"

"I did. Fucking damn. God fucking damn. Why can't people mind their own business?"

"I hear you. But that's not the worst of it. Marta dug around and learned she was rescued five years ago on a secret mission to get her out of Afghanistan."

"If it was so secret, how did anyone find out about it?"

The sound of Ruben's snort was plain. "Nothing is a secret on the dark web. There are people who can dig into the best-kept secrets. And this was one of them. At least until now."

"Let me think." He tossed back the last of the brandy and refrained from pouring another. "How are the checkpoints working? If anyone arrived at Santa Marita that even smelled like a SEAL or other black ops idiots, we'd know about it. The reason I like ruling an island is because we can contain what goes on here. Get rid of people who end up being in the way."

"We're getting ready to change out the checkpoints," Ruben said. "I'll do it myself and personally question every guard being relieved. Someone has to have seen something, even if they don't realize it right now."

"Your instincts are good," Barrera agreed. "Perhaps we need to put vehicles in action cruising the streets, to see what they can find."

"Let's hold off a bit," Ruben cautioned. "As you say, we're on an island. They have no place to go without us seeing them. And the raid we have planned for tonight at the Albados' house may bring them out of hiding if they are here. Then we can kill many birds with few stones. But I want you to tell all the new shifts to be on the lookout. These guys don't work out in the open, but they could be walking around in some kind of disguise. Do you have anyone who can work with you on that?"

He frowned as another thought popped into his head. "You haven't slept, either. If you're drowsy, you'll hardly be on the alert."

"Don't worry about me," Ruben assured him. "I'm used to going without sleep and relying on power naps."

"Be sure to let me know every single thing. Don't leave anything out. And send someone to the warehouses to make sure we're not falling behind on our production schedule."

"Consider it done."

Barrera disconnected the call and leaned back in the chair. Ruben had never failed him yet, so why did he have such an uneasy feeling now? It was the whole situation. Finding out that Melinda Clayton wasn't who she said, and that her reality was worse than he thought. Her disappearance. Everything. He should just go pick up Inez Albado now and put her through the wringer until she told him the truth. That was what he usually did. But something held him back, maybe the thought that if he played this smart, he'd end up catching bigger fish.

He couldn't afford to make a mistake. He'd built his own kingdom here and was enjoying great success. One mistake, one misstep…

No! No, he would not let that happen. He'd planned for too long and worked too hard to get what he had. No one was going to take it away from him, even if he had to kill a bunch of people to save it.

With all that whirling in his mind, he climbed the stairs to his bedroom. Morning was almost here and he needed at least a short nap to be functional.

* * * *

"They still have the damn checkpoints up." Viper shook his head. "Aren't they afraid the tourists will be intimidated by them?"

Ed snorted. "Only because they need enough regular tourists to provide cover for the pieces of shit that usually come here, with their dirty money and their terrorist friends and their—" He flapped his hand in the air. "Never mind. You know what I mean."

It had been a very long, very tense night. They needed to assess the situation at each exit out of the city, but at the same time they couldn't afford to show themselves. They found stores and gas stations and other facilities that they could pull into and pretend to have business there, but they couldn't do that too much, either. The people working there would recognize them and, if they were snitches for Barrera, pass along that they'd been around maybe once too often.

"They've got soldiers everywhere," Viper commented. "It's like being back in Afghanistan or Iraq."

"It is," Eagle agreed. "It's the same atmosphere. Soldiers everywhere and people just going about their business. And if you look closer, you can see there is a strain in the way they move and you don't see a lot of smiles on people."

"I wouldn't be smiling, either." Ed grunted.

They pulled into a deserted warehouse that looked like it had once been something else. Pieces of large machinery lay on the floor, along with other unidentifiable objects.

"No one will bother us here," Ed told them, "and we need to take turns catching a power nap. We're going to need it."

When they were all awake again, they made a run for breakfast tacos and coffee, which they carried back to the warehouse so they could eat without being in the open.

After crumpling up the paper wrapper and stuffing it into the takeout bag, Blaze pulled out his sat phone. "Before we do anything else, I think we should check in with Rocket and Mallory again. We haven't spoken to them since this morning."

"Good idea," Viper agreed.

"Wait a sec." Ed looked at everyone. "Mallory Kane has Inez's cell phone number. And we need to talk to Inez about getting her whole family out of here. I just talked to a friend and I've got a good idea how to do that, but I have to talk to Inez first. And we can't just walk up to her and say, 'Hi, we're here to save you. Come along with us.' She doesn't know us from a concrete wall and her boyfriend might shoot us."

"So what have you got in mind?" Viper wanted to know.

"After you get Rocket on the phone and check in with him, have him put Mallory on. She can reach out to Inez so the woman will talk to us."

"Good idea." Blaze punched numbers into the keypad. "Hey!" Blaze snapped his fingers to get everyone's attention and nodded to indicate a connection. He pressed a button so everyone could hear. "Just checking in with you guys again. Sorry we haven't been able to move this train more today, but we're working on it. How's it going there?"

"Well," Rocket drawled, "it wouldn't be my first choice for a vacation, but it's not all that bad." Then his voice hardened. "But seriously, you guys making any progress on getting us out of here? Barrera still have his checkpoints in place?"

"Working on it, and you have my word for that — and yes, he does. He's a real dog with a bone when he gets fixated on something. Barrera's apparently paranoid about her getting out of here so he's doing his best to contain the island. Got checkpoints at every road leading out of the city to the rest of the island, and there seems to be an increased military presence. Although I'd more likely call them thugs. He wants Mallory and he'll use the Albados to get to her."

"What are the options? Will making our way through the jungle take us to a good exfil point?"

"Maybe, but more likely not. You might have to do some hiking over pretty rough terrain." Blaze paused. "We might have to end up giving Saint the go-ahead signal to execute on his end."

"You think they have any idea we're hiding in the jungle?"

"No." Viper shook his head, even though Rocket couldn't see him. "If they did, he'd have put a large group together and gone after you. I don't think anyone really wants to go digging in there, truth be told. But before we get to that, we need Mallory to do us a favor."

There was a long moment of silence. Then, "What kind of favor? I'm not putting her in any danger."

"What do they want?" he heard her ask. "Whatever it is, if it helps Inez, I'm in. Please."

Blaze handed the phone to Ed.

"Hey, Mallory, this is Ed. I have the name and address of Inez's boyfriend. I think he lives only about ten minutes from where we are. We need to talk to her, but she's not about to open the door to a bunch of strangers. Not with all the shit going on. I'd like to catch her before she leaves to go home or wherever, or if both of them head out for something for the day. Can you call her and vouch for us?"

"No problem. But when you get to her, tell her Mallory wants to know if she's still drinking those gin gimlets?"

Blaze frowned. "Gin gimlets?"

"Uh-huh. We had a wild night with them. No one knows about it but the two of us, so that's your entry word."

"Good, good. Thanks. And we'll be getting you guys out of there before the end of the day if we can."

"Thanks. That'll be good."

"All set?" This was Rocket, who had apparently taken the phone back from her.

"Yes. Thanks. Stand by for an update."

"Okay. Just keep us in the loop."

Blaze disconnected and shoved the phone back into his pocket.

"While we wait for her to call Inez," Ed told them, "let me text Mateo and see what he can tell us about Barrera's plans for today. He might decide to remove the checkpoints since they've come up with nothing and put all his eggs in the basket of tonight's raid."

"I have a hard time understanding why he'd wait until tonight," Eagle said, "when it seems so many people know his plans already. Isn't he afraid they'll disappear?"

"He knows most people are too terrified of him to give help in a situation like this. His thought is, where would they go?"

"We've found ways out of worse situations," Viper reminded him. "Let's get the Albados taken care of first. Then we'll get the rest of us off this fucking island."

"And I have an idea about Inez and her family," Ed told them.

Less than five minutes later, Blaze's sat phone rang.

"All set," Rocket told him when he answered. "Inez is expecting your call."

"Good deal. Okay, we're on it."

Ed dialed the number and put the phone on speaker.

"Hello?" The voice sounded cautious.

"I have a question for you. Mallory wants to know if you're still drinking gin gimlets."

The woman on the other end of the call gave a shaky laugh. "Not if I can help it."

"Smart woman. Okay, this is Ed. Some friends and I are coming to visit you in a few minutes. Please don't shoot us."

"Uh, okay. When you knock on the door, mention the gin again. You have the address?"

"I do."

"I'll be looking for you."

As they drove to the address Ed had, Viper noticed a lot of activity in the streets. Small pickup trucks, some of them as battered as the SUV they were in, were navigating the narrow streets in this part of town. Other vehicles jammed with people and cartons pulled out of driveways and alleyways.

"Does this have to do with that open-air market you told us about?" Eagle asked. "Are you sure it can't screw up what we're doing? Maybe by having too much of Barrera's army around?"

Ed glanced at him, his mouth curved in a sly grin. "Actually, it can be a help. Let's get the Albados taken care of. Then we can work on Mallory and you guys."

Ten minutes later, Ed had pulled their battered SUV into the alley that ran behind the apartment buildings where Inez Albado was. He parked between two huge dumpsters. Putting the car in park, he began texting with someone. No one said a word to interrupt him, knowing it had to be important. Finally, he stuck the phone back in the cupholder.

"Okay, got what I need. I think this only takes two of us, so who wants to do the deed with me?"

"I will." Eagle climbed out of the back seat.

"Okay. Blaze, move your ass over here to the driver's seat and keep it the engine on. No telling what we'll run into."

"Ed?" Eagle leaned forward from the back seat. "You want to share with us what your plan is, because we seem to be winging it a lot here?"

"Have I ever not had a plan?" he demanded in a quiet voice. "Trust me, okay? Let's move it."

Blaze and Viper waited in the SUV, the car in park but the engine running, for what seemed like an hour, but turned out to be no more than ten minutes. They spotted Ed and Eagle returning with a woman in jeans and a pink T-shirt, her long hair pulled back in a ponytail and distress lining her face.

Ed opened the door and ushered her in next to Viper. In seconds, they were pulling out of the alley and moving away from that particular area. Then he made the introductions.

"Gentlemen, say hello to Inez Albado, a very gutsy lady who's been risking her life to hide and protect Mallory."

"Please." She shook her head. "It's my fault she was here in the first place. I'm the one who put her in danger."

"From what I know about Mallory Kane," Viper said, "she does exactly what she wants. You told her about a situation that she could expose to the world. She took it from there. My guess is when she gets back to the States and writes her articles and her book, General Barrera and his penny ante cartel won't be long for this world."

"Don't you mean *if* she gets back?"

"Not at all. That's a given. We don't fail."

"I hope you're right." She blew out a breath. "I can't believe you're actually taking the time to protect my parents and me, too."

"Of course. And this open-air market is just the ticket for it. I'm guessing your parents will be shopping at it, right?"

"Yes. They always do."

"Okay," he told her. "I want you to call them, and here's what you tell them."

She listened carefully, a slightly stunned look on her face, as Ed laid out the details for her.

"I can't believe you're doing this for total strangers."

Viper turned in his seat to face her.

"First of all, you aren't strangers. You and your family went out of your way to protect her and you shouldn't have to suffer for her. Mallory is special to us, so people who take care of her are special."

The smile disappeared from his face. "But it's unfortunate that you and your parents have to leave your home. You must hate this. You've built a life here."

"A life?" She snorted. "What kind of life is it when I spend most of my time in the emergency room treating bullet and knife wounds and other injuries resulting from Barrera's activities? And my parents are so depressed at what has happened to their homeland, at the way Barrera controls everything and has turned the country into one big criminal enterprise, that they can hardly stand it here anymore. They fully supported my inviting Mallory here to do what she does best and will be very grateful for a way out of this. Believe me."

"Okay, then. Go ahead and make the call," Ed told her, "and we'll set things up."

He pulled slowly out of the alley and turned into the narrow street. It was tougher going now, with more vehicles clogging the narrow roadways and more people walking along, many carrying large bags and boxes.

"For a lot of these people," Ed explained to them, "this is a major source of their income. The people who bring their boats to the marina, or keep them berthed there, love to spend money on things from a foreign country."

"And the people here put on a good show," Inez added. "Many residents of Santa Marita spend all their time growing the produce and making the craft items because it's their only source of income."

Blaze frowned. "When I looked it up on the web, I read that you grow a variety of trees and sell the wood for a good price. Also that you have a thriving factory that processes some of the produce and sells it to small grocery chains and restaurants."

Inez gave a derisive but ladylike snort. "That's all out of date. Almost all the fields have been taken over to grow poppies for opium and ephedra for meth. He tells people it's much more profitable. At least it is for him. The cannery has been turned into a meth lab and the lumber mill used to be in this old warehouse. Barrera has destroyed the company so he can have his own cartel and be a drug kingpin. That's why I wanted Mallory to come here and see what was happening. I thought maybe if she wrote about it, someone in power someplace would pay attention and do something about it."

Blaze nodded. "And maybe we can help make that happen."

"But in the meantime," Eagle said, "let's get your parents taken care of."

Chapter Eleven

Barrera was in a foul mood. Everything was going wrong. Every. Fucking. Thing. As if it weren't bad enough that the Clayton woman had disappeared, now he'd learned that wasn't even her name. She wasn't just a nosy tourist but a bestselling author who had made her bones going into places like Afghanistan and Venezuela and writing books about what was really happening there. When Ruben had discovered her real identity, he'd also learned she had a price on her head if she ever went back to any of those countries.

He'd be happy to sell that head to them, especially after he chopped it off her neck.

How was it possible that with every fucking exit from the city watched and guarded, no one had seen a hint of them? He was pretty damn sure no one was lying to him. They knew what he did with liars—it wasn't nice and it wasn't pretty. And the longer it took to find that bitch, the angrier he got.

To add to his misery, there was a problem at one of the farms that grew the poppies and he'd had trouble with two workers at the meth lab. That last one had been easy enough to take care of, but he couldn't keep 'erasing' people. Too much of that and the residents of Santa Marita would get suspicious. They'd also try to figure out a way to get away from here. Too bad for them he had the marina locked down tight, but that didn't mean he wouldn't have to weather an unpleasant hassle.

As if that weren't enough, Ruben had just told him that today there would be one of those impromptu open-air markets down by the marina. He approved two a month, so the people whose jobs he had eliminated could scrounge enough money to feed their families. Ruben had reported to him about disgruntled reactions, but as far as he was concerned, they were lucky he didn't just eliminate the people who displeased him or argued with him, the way many other cartels did.

And now there was another one of these impromptu events that would take up a huge part of the waterfront, occupying a lot of the parking area and even setting up small tables on one side of the docks. He would need extra men there today, because there was no telling if Mallory Kane would try to sneak off the island in the crowd.

He was sitting at his desk in the presidential palace this morning, trying to look at the situation from all angles, when Ruben Vidal rapped on the door jamb.

"Bella said I could just come on in."

Bella was Barrera's secretary and a very tough guardian of the gates. She was actually the one who made the machinery run smoothly. Ten years ago, when he'd still been with the Sinaloa cartel, she had been one of the tempting pieces of ass he'd grabbed off the street one night and brought back to his home. Even today, he had to admit she was one of the best fucks of his life. She was so good, in fact, in both performance and attitude, that when she'd told him her dream of becoming a secretary, he'd paid for her training and gotten her an office job with one of his friends. When he'd taken over Santa Marita, he'd snatched her away and brought her with him, which was one of the best decisions he'd ever made. Without her and Ruben, this whole thing would fall apart.

Now he looked up at his right-hand man.

"Yes. Please. Come in. We need to discuss the situation."

Ruben dropped into one of the chairs opposite the desk and crossed his legs, the ankle of one foot resting on the opposite knee.

"And which situation is that? Finding Mallory Kane? Tracking down the Albados? Making sure word does not get out about tonight's raid?"

Barrera sat forward. "What do you mean, tracking the Albados? This early on a Saturday, they should still be at home."

When suspicions about Inez Albados' guest had first been relayed to him, he'd asked the regular street patrols to keep track of the activities of Inez Albados' parents. They seemed to be creatures of habit, which made them easier to watch.

"One of my men doing a regular drive-by saw them leave about half an hour ago. They may be headed toward today's open-air market. I radioed back and told them to keep a sharp eye out."

Barrera grunted. "Let's hope their eyes are really sharp. I have a very bad feeling about the way things are going."

"We probably should have raided last night as you originally planned."

"But no one but you and I and our key soldiers even knew we were going to do it," Barrera pointed out to him.

Ruben shrugged. "Secrets have a way of leaking out no matter what. You know that."

"But I also know," Barrera said, "that they had no place to go and no one was going to hide them. One of the many advantages of ruling a country that is completely on an island is that people can't get away from you. They do what we want or we kill them. So even if they found out ahead of time, what could they do? Where could they go? Besides, I had already arranged for Moreau to be here on Friday night and there's too much money involved there to have made changes."

Ruben nodded his agreement. "True, true."

Barrera nodded. "And I want to be there myself to see what they find. Fuck it all, anyway." He drew on his cigar and blew a smoke circle. "If we lose them, we're in deep shit, for a lot of reasons."

"Let's hope we can frighten the truth out of them about the Kane woman, because there's still no trace of her, and we've scoured the island."

"Fuck." Barrera spat the word.

"I've tried to think where she could go and keep hitting a blank wall. We know she hasn't left town because of the checkpoints."

Ruben rubbed his jaw, a sign Barrera knew meant he had a new wrinkle to throw into the mix.

"What if she's in La Jungla?"

Barrera's jaw dropped. "What? What the fuck do you mean?"

"I mean, we haven't had any luck locating her in the city and the jungle can be accessed without using exit roads."

"If she's there, the jungle might do its work for us. Although it would deprive me of the pleasure of torturing her myself. It is a very tough environment to make one's way through."

"I'm just offering it as a possibility."

Barrera thought for a moment. Would the bitch be brave enough to traipse though all that overgrown area to find a way out? And what then? There was that rocky stretch bordering the jungle and a steep cliff dropping down to the water. It would be almost impossible for a boat to pick her up there.

"All right. Let's give it until we make the raid tonight. Maybe wherever she's hiding, when we go after her friends, she'll show herself to save them."

"Maybe. She certainly didn't seem the type for that kind of physical exercise, though. What do you think?"

Ruben shrugged. "It's hard to say. I haven't been in La Jungla myself for years. No reason to except to dump bodies. Then I have my men do it. It isn't an easy trek, though."

"Can she get through there and find a path off the island?"

"Again, difficult to answer. One area of the jungle butts up to the rocks, but it's treacherous getting to it. And even though I haven't hiked those rocks since I was a lot younger, I remember at the time it being very difficult and stressful. Besides, where would she go? There aren't any beaches on that part of Santa Marita."

"A boat can't get close enough for her to board," Barrera commented. "She'd have to swim out to it, and with the huge breakers and the wind on that side, it could be a death sentence. There's no way she could be rescued from there."

"So are you saying just leave her and let the island kill her?"

"No." He studied the ash on the end of his cigar. "That would be nice if we knew that definitely would happen. I'm saying we may have to send people into the jungle looking for her if we don't find her anyplace else." Barrera shook his head. "Let's leave all that for a last resort. Meanwhile, put a team together if needed to go in there looking for her, if we can't find her anyplace else. I won't rest unless I can see her body."

Ruben just shrugged. "Your wish, as always, is my command. Let me put more men on the streets and see if we can flush her out from wherever she's hiding."

"And find the Albado family. Call me the moment you locate them and keep an eye on them. If they're at the market, which I assume they are, put a man on them so we don't lose them. We may be able to use them as bait."

"Consider it done. I'm going to the market now myself to see if I can spot anything. I stopped by to ask if there was something particular you wanted me to do. I'll put the Albados at the top of my list."

Barrera leaned back in his chair, frowning.

"I say again. They have no way off the island. The marina is under watchful eyes as always, but that doesn't mean they might not try something. So be sure everyone and everything is checked. I want regular reports."

Ruben nodded. "As you wish."

Barrera sat staring at the opposite wall after Ruben Vidal had left, everything jumbled in his mind. La Jungla was a shitty place to look for someone, what with the thickness of trees and plants, the abundant wildlife and no path to follow. Somehow, he didn't see the woman making it through there. Then what? Traipsing over rocks? To where? To who? She certainly hadn't looked the type for any of that.

Was he overreaching here?

Fuck. How had things gotten so complicated? He couldn't lose control here, not because of some stupid bitch and an insignificant family. Not now, when things were going so well. And if he had to kill a few more people to protect what he'd built? *Well, so be it.*

* * * *

Even though Ed was Eagle's friend and Eagle had been the main contact for this exercise, Blaze had somehow slipped into the position of Galaxy team leader. It would have been Rocket since this was his gig, but of course he was somewhere in the middle of La Jungla waiting for word on their next move. Therefore, Blaze was riding shotgun with Ed as they managed to move the car through the narrow streets. They had spent the better part of an hour getting everyone ready. Eagle, who for whatever reason looked the least threatening, had done what he called 'moseying' along the motley group of display tables set up at the edge of the parking lot and spilling over onto some of the docks.

"Pretty damn big for an unscheduled event," Blaze commented.

Ed snorted. "It's only unscheduled as far as Barrera is concerned. He makes a big deal out of the regular markets as a way for people to earn money and sell products of Santa Marita. But he also knows he's changed the economy so much, focusing on his drug business, that these people need a way to feed themselves and their families. And he can play the big *patron* by quote unquote *letting* them have these extra events."

"What an asshole," Eagle muttered.

"Top of the line," Ed agreed.

More ambitious vendors — and probably those with a bigger cash stash — had set up tents back behind the tables, which made it easier to do some of the switching they needed. It also helped that Inez was a favorite with a lot of people who also loved her parents. And the Galaxy men, blending into the scene with beach clothes they'd scarfed up from one of the vendors, very carefully maneuvered the process, all the while managing to put themselves in positions that would not call attention to any of them.

Ed was standing next to Blaze at a crowded table filled with colorful scarves and shirts, Eagle and Viper nearby. They were holding up shirts that partially concealed them and pretended to be examining them. He nudged Blaze and inclined his head to the left.

"Part one's about done. Steal a glance over there."

The Albados, dressed as tourists, carrying bags from the outdoor market and wearing big straw hats, had made their way one at a time to the end of the middle dock. Inez, who had camouflaged herself well, was window shopping at one of the tables while her parents boarded a fishing boat that had been docked there overnight. The owner, a friend of Ed's — *of course*, Blaze commented silently to himself — was also on the dock, standing beside his boat and drinking beer with three other boat men. Blaze watched as the owner gestured at his boat, lifting a bottle of beer, and when he ushered the other men onto his boat, the Albados moved along with them. Then, in the blink of an eye, the Albados disappeared — and not a second too soon.

Blaze nudged Ed and inclined his head in the direction of the parking lot. Two large vehicles full of Barrera's soldiers had driven up and parked at the edge of the market setup. Ten of them were disgorged from the vehicles and began walking through the market and along the docks.

"Watch, my friend," Ed told him in a very low voice.

Blaze shifted his gaze to the boat the Albados were on and saw the owner standing on the deck with the men he'd been talking to, all of them drinking beer. Apparently, the man had told them a funny, raunchy joke, because they were all laughing boisterously. The man grabbed the empty bottles and carried them below. When he opened the cabin door to jog down the short flight of steps, Blaze strained his eyes to see if the Albados were in there.

"What the hell did he do with them?" he asked Ed.

"Most of these guys carry contraband of some kind along with fishing equipment, so some boats have hidden compartments. They aren't all that spacious, but it's better than a coffin."

As two of the soldiers walked down that dock, eyeing all the boats, Ed's friend climbed back up to the deck, fresh beer bottles in his hands, the door open behind him. He grinned and nodded at the guards as he kicked the door closed and handed out the beer.

The guards glanced at each boat again as they moved along the dock. Blaze kept his gaze focused on the scene until the men reached the end of that dock and made their way to another one. They made no stops along the way, including the boat where the Albados were hiding. When they finally reached the end and headed for the next one, Blaze let out his breath and felt the tension ease a fraction.

Then he glanced at Ed. "How are the plans to connect Inez with her parents coming?"

"Good. Very good. She's a smart woman and knows what she has to do."

"Just curious, but what are you going to do with them when you get them all to Manzanillo? That's still too close. I'm guessing Barrera's men go over there now and then. And I know you don't want to keep them in an expanded kill zone."

Ed shook his head. "They'll be transported to another location far away from this where they can start a new life."

"Here's what I wanted to tell you. I don't know if Eagle communicated it, but if we get Mallory Kane out of this mess — no, *when* we get her out of it — her sister, who hired us, will be very indebted to us. That sister is a very powerful United States senator who I am sure would be very happy to help us with the Albados."

"Good to know. We may take her up on it." Ed glanced at his watch. "In fact, Inez should be on her way right now."

Blaze looked around. "Yeah? Like where?"

"Check the dock on the far end. The little short one."

Blaze looked where Ed was pointing. The last dock was only long enough to accommodate one boat. The one currently tied up looked like it had seen better days. From the activity on deck, Blaze could see it was a fishing boat that was bringing its catch to Santa Marita. Panel vans from two restaurants were parked at the dock and employees were busily unloading carriers of fish. There appeared to be seven people on the boat, all wearing jeans and denim jackets, managing the transfer. Once the fish were all offloaded, the vans pulled away and the remaining workers began cleaning up the deck.

At that moment, the motor on the boat kicked over and it slowly chugged out of the harbor. Some of Barrera's thugs stood nearby, watching it. And Inez Albado was nowhere to be seen.

Blaze hid a tiny grin. Ed knew his damned business all right. They were damn lucky he was helping them.

"Okay, we've got all the Albados to safety," he murmured. "Now we need to get ourselves the hell out of here. Barrera has locked down any exit by water or from the airport, so we only have one real choice."

Eagle nodded in agreement. "And we don't have a very big window. You can bet Barrera's got a picture of Mallory Kane by this time and has sent it to every one of his so-called army. I think when he can't find us anywhere else, Barrera will send his soldiers to the jungle to hunt us. Time to pick up Rocket and Mallory and head for that cliff. And I mean now. When Barrera discovers all his targets are gone, he'll turn this island upside down."

Ed headed away from the marina. "Amen to that. Let's move. Now."

They had planned a method of leaving the market and hooking back up together without drawing attention to themselves. They followed the plan and fifteen minutes later, without any of Barrera's guards noticing, they were back at the battered SUV and driving slowly away from the area of the marina. Ed did his usual, zigzagging through streets and neighborhoods until they were at the very edge of the city limits where the jungle began.

"I just hope we haven't fucked up your situation here." Blaze glanced over at Ed. "You've had to use a lot of resources taking care of our project."

Ed shrugged. "Maybe it was time to move on anyway. But that's for later. Blaze, call Rocket and tell him we're on our way and to watch out for us."

"On it."

"No shit." Viper grunted. "Ed, you did a masterful job getting the Albados out of here, away from Santa Marita, but they're secondary characters to Mallory Kane. And when Barrera executes his raid tonight and finds the Albados in the wind, all hell will break loose. And he'll redouble the search for Mallory."

"Agreed. Call your pilot. He's got that chopper, right? From Vacation Rentals?"

"He does." Eagle leaned forward from the back seat, sat phone in hand. "He rented it right away when we gave him the go ahead. He's done a couple of flyovers so no one will ask why he rented a helicopter and isn't using it. Plus, he wanted to get a visual of Santa Marita."

"Good, good." Ed nodded.

"He also said there were a few other helicopters getting some airtime, so he doesn't stick out like a sore thumb."

"Better yet."

"Besides, when I told him where the exfil would have to be, he wanted to get a good look at it and mark the images in his brain. He's good to go. Let me get hold of him."

* * * *

Bruno Elizondo didn't usually consider himself a lucky man. His life had proven that to him over and over again. He thought it was his usual lot in life when he'd lost track of the men he'd seen and overheard in the coffee bar. But then good fortune had smiled on him. He took a break from his multiple coffee rounds to check out the nonscheduled open market and decided to spend a little of his meager salary to buy a present for his wife. She loved scarves and especially the ones she found here.

He parked his car on the street and made his way to where the market was set up, found the scarf booth he wanted...and there was his reward. Two of the men he'd eavesdropped on, pretending to shop but in reality watching the docks. Bruno found himself a place to be invisible in the crowd and watched the same crowd. He had no idea who he was looking for, but when two of Barrera's men marched down one dock, eyeballed the boats then returned to the market, he knew something was going on. He just didn't know what, but he'd figure it out.

Then he saw them watch a fishing boat making its deliveries at the last dock, the short one. He noted a woman helping with the deliveries and boarding the boat before it chugged out of the harbor. Could that be the female they were looking for? If it was, he needed to get to Barrera right away.

He edged a little closer to the men, standing slightly behind them, and realized it wasn't the woman at all. *Maybe Inez Albado?* He knew there was a raid scheduled for the Albado house that evening, either to find the Kane woman or force the Albados to say where she was. Would Barrera be upset they were gone? Was this Kane woman on one of those boats with them?

No, he decided, when the men regrouped and headed away from the market. They looked like men with a purpose. They hadn't rescued their friend yet. He would need to find a way to follow them without being detected, then he would report back to Barrera. And hopefully earn himself a promotion and a fat raise.

When the car they were in drove slowly away from the area, Elizondo followed at a safe distance. Lucky for him, two cars pulled in between him and the battered SUV. There was enough traffic to swallow him most of the time. It was only when the traffic thinned out that he had to do some magic maneuvers, especially when they ended up on the edge of a residential neighborhood. There was minimal traffic to hide behind and he was afraid that if he cut over to another street, he'd lose them.

What to do. What to do.

Fuck! Where the hell could they be going, anyway? These streets dead-ended at La Jungla. Was that where the Kane woman was hiding? If so, she must have a lot of guts, because it wasn't exactly a friendly place. The SUV reached the end of the street and stopped. Were they really going into that overgrown hellhole? Were they walking? Driving an impossible route?

He had to do this very carefully. But one thing he seemed to be good at was being invisible. Hardly anyone ever paid attention to him. Today that was going to pay off, if only he could figure out how to follow them. Just in case, he pulled out his cell and took a picture of the vehicle.

Then, as if in answer to a prayer, a landscaping truck pulled in front of him and parked in front of the next-to-last house. Bruno parked behind them and got out, walking up to the men as they climbed out and greeting them as if they were friends.

The man who appeared in charge stopped and studied him.

"Can we help you?"

"*Por favor.* I was driving around looking for work because I am a good at this kind of stuff. I thought, maybe mow a lawn or something. Then I saw your truck and I wonder, are you looking for more workers? I work hard and do a good job."

The other man shook his head. "No. Sorry. Full up right now. Lots of people looking for work, you know."

"*Si. Si.*" He heaved a sigh, still keeping an eye on the SUV. It had pulled onto a dirt turnaround at the edge of the jungle. "Maybe I will walk around some more and see if anyone's house looks like it needs some loving care."

The man snorted. "Good luck with that. We have to scrounge for these jobs as it is."

Bruno nodded but hung around for a few more seconds, waiting to see what the SUV did. It sat there for a moment. Then—he could hardly believe it—it drove slowly into the thick overgrowth.

Hijo de perra!

He stood there watching for a few more seconds, doing his best not to be obvious. Good thing the landscapers had started their work and were not paying attention to him. He'd expected the people in the SUV to get out and start heading into the thick undergrowth and trees, so he was shocked when the vehicle just kept going into the jungle.

Well, damn. He certainly couldn't follow it, not that he wanted to. That hellhole was too dangerous. But it was certainly a good place for the woman to hide. Who the fuck would go in there looking for her? Who would even think she was there?

He would have to report all this to *El Presidente*. But what if he was wrong? Maybe he should wait until the raid tonight on the Albado house. When it produced no results, he could end up being the hero. The woman would still be in La Jungla. Even if someone was helping her, how the hell would they get her out of there, anyway?

He headed back to his car, prepared to do some heavy thinking. He wasn't going to put his foot in his mouth and get it chopped off.

Chapter Twelve

*...like the feel of a soft leaf dusting the skin on his face.
Then, as if picked up by a slow breeze, it slipped down his
chest, danced over his nipples and skated down between his
thighs. His cock twitched at the gentle touch of it, throbbing
with need as the sensation spread through his body.*

*He slid his hand down his thigh, fingers curled, reaching
for his swollen dick, ready to grasp it and pump it to
completion. Except there was already...*

Rocket's eyes flew open and Mallory's soft laugh
filled his ears like music, and he realized what was
happening. They'd eaten lunch, protected from the hot
midday sun by the thatched roof of the hut, then
stretched out on the pallet to try to rest.

They'd talked about her books and he'd told her
how Galaxy had come to be. It was obvious they were
talking around their crisis, waiting for Rocket's sat
phone to ring with updates from Blaze or one of his
other partners.

"I don't know what kind of extraction the guys have planned," Rocket told her, "but we need to be rested when they give us the signal."

Eventually they'd fallen asleep, where he'd dreamed of a naked Mallory, stroking his body, teasing his cock.

And woken up to discover the touch was real.

He dropped his hands to his sides and reached for his control. This was too good to have it end before he could blink. He loved the soft stroke of her fingers and the feel of them curled around his hot, aching dick.

"You been doing that long?" He had to work to steady his voice.

"Not really." She grinned and slowly ran her tongue over her lower lip. "But I figured it was a good way to wake you up."

He barked a hoarse laugh. "No kidding. I'm awake now. Don't stop."

"Don't worry. I wasn't planning to."

It was late afternoon, and the sun that managed to penetrate the thick canopy of branches and leaves cast soft shadows in the hut. If not for the situation they were in, he'd have believed they were on vacation at a resort, spending the day in the most enjoyable manner possible.

Her fingers were soft and firm at the same time. As she moved them up and down in a gentle rhythm, his cock swelled even more. When she slipped her other hand between his thighs and lightly squeezed his balls, heat speared through him.

"Jesus!"

He clenched his fists, seeking control, as Mallory's hand continued to stroke up and down and her fingers continue to manipulate his balls in the same rhythm.

He coasted his hand down her back to the sweet curve of her ass, realizing she was wearing only her thong. As if it was the most natural thing, he slipped his fingers into the hot crease, tugging the little bit of fabric aside and stroking the wet opening there.

Her fingers tightened reflexively on his cock and a tiny moan slipped from her throat.

"Like that?" he asked in a husky voice.

"Mmmm."

"One of these days, when we're in a real bed and have all the stuff we need, I'm going to fuck you there until you scream with pleasure."

"I can't wait." She whispered the words.

The mental image of him with his cock inside her ass sent a jolt of pleasure straight to his balls. He closed his eyes to give himself over to it, but then he felt the soft sweep of her tongue over the velvet head and *shit!* He reached a hand to her head, threading his fingers through the silk of her hair and winding it around his fingers. When she slid her mouth along the length of his shaft, he used his grip to move her head up and down, setting a steady rhythm.

This was more than just sex. He didn't have a name for it, but he wanted this connection to go on forever. Everything else faded except for Mallory's strong fingers, her soft mouth, her magic tongue., His balls tightened even more and he clenched his hand in her hair as he held her head in place. He tried to urge her to move her mouth faster, but she was just as determined as he was to make it last. Her soft lips slid up and down, her teeth grazing the sensitive skin and sending heat to every part of his body.

As if she could tell when he was close to the edge, she sped up the movement of her mouth and her hands, pushing him higher and higher, the explosion curling inside him and finally bursting forth. The orgasm gripped him, shaking him, sending his pulse into orbit. With his fingers still wound in her hair, holding her head in place, she swallowed each pulse of cum as it hit her tongue, until finally he was depleted. His heart hammered, seeking to slow its pace from its frenetic beating.

Mallory kept her mouth on him, swallowing every last drop, licking the sensitive head of his dick, stroking up and down its length and gently squeezing his balls. Finally, finally, finally, his heartbeat returned to normal, his dick softened and his body relaxed. He eased his grip on Mallory's hair and brought her head close to his face.

"How did I ever stay away from you for five years?"

"Let's not discuss that. Let's talk about the next five, and all the years beyond that."

"Sounds good to me." She brushed her mouth over his. "But first we have to—"

Whatever she would have said was cut off by the sound of Rocket's sat phone indicating an incoming call.

"Hand me that, would you, honey?" He hoped he had the strength left to hold it.

She grabbed the phone from where he'd set it on the counter and brought it over to him.

"Here you go. Maybe they figured out how to get us away from here."

He pressed the button that connected to Blaze's phone. "You got us a ticket out of here?"

"Yeah, we do." Blaze's voice was harsh, not a good sign. "In fact, it's a ticket for all of us. We need to split, and fast."

"Well, let's have 'em. Whatever it is, we'll make it work. Better than hanging out here, that's for sure."

"Anyway, we're about three minutes away from you. We just wanted to give you a heads-up we were coming."

And so was I, just seconds ago. Good thing you called before storming in here.

"The guys are on their way here," he told Mallory. "In fact, almost at our door."

"Good thing they didn't show up five minutes earlier," she teased.

"No shit. I'd better put some clothes on."

Mallory was already on her feet, smoothing out her shorts and T-shirt. They hadn't been able to bring any luggage with them, obviously, and she certainly hoped before long she'd be able to weather wash these clothes or throw them out for fresh ones. Rocket pieced himself back together and checked to make sure the hut was respectable, then stood in the doorway watching for the SUV. It wasn't too long before he caught the sound of the engine as the vehicle slowly made its way through the jungle. Moments later, it crunched over dead leaves and other botanical debris and came to a stop right by the ladder.

Everyone piled out then walked around to the rear of the vehicle. He looked on in astonishment—although why he should be surprised was a good question—and followed Ed to the rear of the vehicle. Ed lifted the tailgate, fiddled with something to push the rear seat forward and twisted something else to removed what looked like flooring. Then he began handing out weapons to everyone, keeping two for himself, and went for the ladder.

Eagle looked up at him and grinned. "Do I know how to pick my friends or do I know how?"

Rocket just shook his head and stepped back as they all headed for the ladder.

Blaze looked up at him before he stepped on the first rung. "Will that thing hold all of us?"

Ed, right behind him, laughed. "Count on it. I watched it being built. Anyway, it's better than sitting on the ground with the zillion bugs crawling around here. Come on, guys."

As soon as they were all inside, Ed passed one of his weapons to Rocket, who studied it with curiosity.

"Looks like a miniature AK47."

Ed nodded. "That's exactly what it is. It's a Draco AK 47 pistol. The Glocks you guys like pack a big punch, but I keep these just in case. And tonight might be one of those 'in case'."

"Because?"

"Because if somehow Barrera gets wind of what we're doing, he might bring his patrol boats into that area, and handguns aren't going to be a lot of good against their weapons."

"Okay, then. Let's have it. Getting out of here is good, but I'm guessing by these weapons, the rest of it is bad."

Blaze nodded. "It's not pretty, that's for sure. Ed, you want to fill him in?"

"Barrera set up a checkpoint at every exit road from the city, originally to make sure Mallory hadn't found a way to sneak out," Ed told him. "Oh, no one's lined up with guns, or anything like that. But every car that approaches a checkpoint gets a looksee. Mallory, Barrera pulled your picture off the internet and all his men have a copy of it. If they see anyone in a vehicle who even resembles you, they have orders to pull it over and bring the people in."

Mallory frowned at him. "How did you get this information?"

"You can easily see the checkpoints, plus I have a line into Barrera's goings-on."

Rocket snickered. "Of course you do."

"Anyway, we had to be careful not to approach the setups too closely or be too obvious when we turned away from them. They also had guards at the marina and the access road to where we landed is blocked off. So getting you to anyplace where a boat could pick you up is out. Period."

"And Ed has resources he taps into," Eagle added. "Like the guy whose house we brought you through when we got you out of the Albados. He's the one who's getting feedback for us on the checkpoints."

"Speaking of the Albados." Mallory took a step forward. "Where are they? I thought Barrera was planning to raid their house. And where's Inez?"

Blaze held up a hand. "All taken care of. They're both on their way to a little place in Baja California, where there are people who will give them a place to hide out until we can make them legal. Rocket, we need you to call Senator Kane and tell her part of the fee for fetching her sister is to take care of this situation with Inez and her family."

"Inez is okay," Mallory told them. "She was in the United States for so long between college and her work that she was able to become a citizen. It's her parents who need the help."

"I'll take care of it just as soon as we're finished here," Rocket assured them. It was certainly the least he could do. "Okay, let's have the rest of the bad news."

"Since water access is cut off," Blaze told him, "we're going with option two."

"The helo," Viper added. "Trouble is, it's a long walk from here to the cliff where Saint will pick us up. Ed figures about four hours. Can you handle that, Mallory?"

"I can handle anything," she told him, "except not getting out of here."

"She did fine in Afghanistan," Rocket put in. "She's a trooper."

"There's a possibility Saint might not be able to land. He might only be able to hover and you'd have to be hauled in?"

"Like I said, she's fine with whatever," Rocket confirmed.

"*She* is right here," Mallory snapped, "and *she* can do whatever it takes to get the hell out of here. Let's move along, okay?"

Rocket had to smother a grin.

"We just leaving the car here?" Viper wanted to know. "Isn't that a giveaway?"

"It's outlived its usefulness. So has this hut. And we won't be coming back here, anyway."

"So where is the chopper picking us up?" he asked. "La Jungla is thicker and more overgrown than most jungles. Is Saint good with this?"

"He's on board," Blaze assured them. "Where the jungle ends, there's a strip of rocky land that ends at a steep cliff. That's where he'll extract us."

"We called him," Viper added, "and he's ready to rock the second we give the go-ahead. So let's get going here. But the rest of this hellhole is too overgrown to drive the SUV through it. We'd need some kind of ATV, which we don't have. That's why the exfil is at the rocky area at the top of a steep cliff. Which, as I say, is about a four-hour walk from here. So." He looked around. "Everyone ready for a stroll through the jungle?"

* * * *

"I want to hit that house right now."

Barrera was pacing back and forth in his office at the presidential palace. When none of his men had turned up any of the Albados anywhere in town, his anger reached the boiling point. Where the fuck had that bitch nurse and her parents disappeared to?

"I thought you wanted to wait until nighttime," Ruben reminded him. "You said the dark was more effective."

"I've changed my mind. It's Saturday. People will be home and they will see the shame."

Ruben sighed. "*Jefe*. What if they aren't there? What if somehow they've managed to disappear? We haven't been able to find these people. You don't want people to see you raid an empty house. Do you still want to do this?"

What he wanted was to line up everyone who had given him a hard time and shoot them. *Painfully.*

He should have done this the night before. He knew it. But he couldn't do it while entertaining Gerard Moreau. All because he wanted to run the show himself. To receive the glory for frightening and punishing people who had challenged him by bringing a destructive influence into his country. He had trouble admitting that his own vanity was at fault here.

But now he had a decision to make.

"*Jefe*, what are your thoughts?"

Maybe if he put on a show, someone would come forward with the information he needed about where the woman was hiding.

He turned to Ruben. "Here's what I want to do."

At seven o'clock that evening, when people were returning from the open market and getting ready for Saturday night festivities, six Santa Marita Army vehicles, lights flashing, pulled up in front of the house where the Albado family lived. Five uniforms headed to the rear of the building while the rest marched up to the front door. One of the men knocked three times. Hard. When the door did not open, a man in uniform and carrying a battering ram climbed the three steps and smacked the ram into the door. One more try and it slammed open.

The soldiers moved into the house, guns drawn as if they were seeking a criminal.

Barrera watched from his vehicle until they'd moved inside and one of them motioned him forward. As he moved from his vehicle to the house, he took in the crowd beginning to gather in the street and on the sidewalk. He pulled himself up to his full six-foot-four height and looked around.

"You neighbors, the Albados, have committed crimes against the state. In addition, they have smuggled an enemy agent into the country, who is attempting to do us much harm. We will search every inch of this house, but as you can see, most likely they have fled. However, every exit from the island is controlled by our well-trained army and they will not escape. When the search is finished, we will confiscate all their possessions."

Preening, he strode into the house and followed Ruben as the man moved from room to room.

The house was much the same as others in this area of Santa Marita, constructed of adobe with arched doorways. The furnishings were a combination of old and new, the decorations very colorful, much like the ones in the home where he'd grown up in Mexico.

But as he moved through the house and it became obvious there was no one here, his simmering anger grew hotter and hotter. Then Ruben called him to come into one of the bedrooms and what he saw made that anger erupt.

"Look at the ceiling." Ruben pointed to a carefully painted Mayan sun.

"A painting." Barrera shrugged. "So what?"

"Watch."

There was a small wooden chair in the room that someone had dragged close to the bed. Ruben stood up on it and pressed one of the black dots in the painting. A large square of the ceiling in the center of the painting dropped down, hanging on its hinges. Ruben reached into it and pulled down a little four-rung ladder.

"God damn it." Barrera exploded. "That bitch was hiding here all this time."

Ruben nodded. "So it seems. I'm going to hoist myself up there and take a look."

Barrera paced, grinding his teeth as he struggled to get a grip on his temper while he waited for Vidal to finish his exploration. Three of his soldiers stood silently in the small room with him, rigidly at attention. He knew they wouldn't say or do anything to turn the heat of his wrath on them. They watched as he paced the floor, cursing steadily under his breath.

What the fuck was taking Ruben so long? How big could a crawl space be? And what was that stomping that he suddenly heard overhead?

At the point his temper was ready to boil over, Ruben's feet appeared and he lowered himself to the chair, then the bed.

"We've been scammed," he told Barrera. "You will not like this one bit."

Barrera clenched his fists. "What did you find?"

"This is more than just a crawl space. It's a little bigger and it has a sleeping bag, some other items scattered around, and even a little window, which is open. But that's not the worst of it."

"What more could there be?" he demanded.

"There's another trap door, this one in the ceiling of this little attic, that leads to the roof, so I went up there. I'm guessing Mallory Kane spent time up there those last couple of days. I'm pretty sure it's also the way she got out of this house without being seen. This roof has a short lip all the way around and one side has the marks of some kind of rope ladder. All she had to do was climb down and take off with whoever was helping her."

"And who the fuck would that be? Certainly not any of the Albados, including that bitch nurse, Inez. They took enough chances hiding her. No, someone's helping her and I want to know who the fuck it is." He glared at Ruben. "Understood?"

"*Si, mi general.* I will put someone on it at once."

"And while you're at it, arrange for a truck and have some of the men clear out this house. If the Albados do return, I want them to find nothing but bare walls. They have forfeited all their possessions."

"Consider it done." Vidal hurried out to the front of the house where the rest of the men were awaiting orders.

Barrera headed after him, the men left in the room following behind him. Outside he saw there were still some official vehicles, although a few had left to carry out Ruben's orders. But neighbors were crowded in front of every house, watching, fear etched on their faces.

"Your neighbors have broken the laws of Santa Marita," he told them. "They will be punished accordingly. Keep this in mind if you are ever tempted to do the same thing."

His driver held open the door to his official vehicle and he climbed into the back seat. He needed a drink. Badly. Suddenly there were cracks in his carefully constructed existence, in his own little kingdom. He could not allow that to happen. He would ferret out every single soul who had a hand in this and punish them accordingly, especially that bitch Mallory Kane. It was the only way to maintain his control of the country and the level of fear he had created.

And he had to do it soon.

Chapter Thirteen

The best thing about walking through the jungle, Rocket thought, was the canopy of trees overhead, which shielded them from the sun. The worst thing about walking through the jungle was the canopy of trees overhead, which locked in the heat. It was like strolling through a steam oven. Good thing he'd had plenty of practice during his years as a SEAL.

He scanned the others as they made their way slowly over the exposed tree roots, pushing aside the thick leaves of the dense bushes, doing their best to scratch themselves as little as possible. The men all wore long pants and running shoes of some type. They had, after all, dressed to pretend they were fishermen. But Mallory wore what she'd had on at the Albados'. Shorts and a T-shirt weren't much protection, and nor were the leather sandals on her feet. But she soldiered on without complaining once.

Again, he made a mental note to himself to arrange some special pampering if they got out of this. No, not if. *When*. Because their life together wasn't going to end before it even got started.

The thick silence was broken occasionally by the song of one of the many species of birds that flitted from tree to tree. The bright hues of their feathers were pops of color against the unremitting green of the flora. Rocket checked every time there was a rustling of leaves to make sure it wasn't a snake slithering toward them or one of the small aninals looking to take a bite out of someone's body.

Then of course there were the predators, although the larger ones like the jaguar had long since become extinct. He wasn't as much worried about lizards and tree frogs as he was about snakes. Ed had pulled out his many-bladed pocketknife when they started out, broken thick branches over some of the bushes and whittled handles on them. Now they each had an instrument that doubled as both a walking stick and a weapon.

Ed had also taken the lead, since it was agreed he had a better idea of where they were going than anyone else. The watches the Galaxy men wore all had compass functions in them, but nothing beat familiarity with an area. Rocket knew they were all worried about Ed's ability and endurance with the prosthetic. It had to be killing him, but he showed no outward signs of stress. And he kept up a steady rhythm both walking and striking at the bushes to dislodge small predators and beat off snakes.

The man also seemed to have an endless supply of whatever was needed. From the cabinet under the little counter, he'd produced a handful of thin, flat backpacks.

"*Not ideal,*" he'd told them, "*but they were only meant to carry a few things if someone was stashed here and had to vacate in a hurry. They'll do for this. It shouldn't take us more than four hours to reach the cliff. It's about five miles.*" He'd looked at Mallory. "*Think you can handle this?*"

Four hours?

She'd managed a smile. "*If the only other alternative is Barrera, I can definitely make it. I work out at home to stay in shape.*"

"*Good deal. Okay. Load up, everyone.*"

They'd divvied up bottles of water and power bars, and the small flashlights Ed also distributed. Then they'd pulled on the backpacks and headed out. Now they were following Ed as he led them on a twisting route. There wasn't even a real path to walk, so they had to be extremely careful.

It was impossible to tell how much daylight was left because the thick canopy of leaves and branches overhead blocked so much of it out. Dead leaves rustled beneath their feet and the notes of songbirds broke the silence now and then. Ed was still using his stick to make sure no snakes crawled up their legs.

After about an hour, Ed held up his hand and called a stop.

"Ten-minute rest break."

"We're good to keep going," Rocket assured him.

"You won't be if you don't take a break. Forget your training already? I'm guessing you guys haven't done any forty-mile hikes in full battle rattle since you became civilians, right?"

"We keep in shape," Blaze assured him. "But yeah, a ten-minute stop to hydrate is a good idea."

Ed pulled a bottle of water from his pack, drank greedily then turned to them.

"I hope you guys aren't worried about me. I can do as far on my fake leg as you all can do on both of yours. No lie."

"Don't worry about me, either," Mallory told them. "Like I said before, I work out all the time. I won't hold anyone up."

Rocket swallowed a smile. She was just as gutsy as she'd been five years ago and he was exceptionally proud of her.

Blaze pulled his sat phone out of his backpack. "I'm going to touch base with Saint. Tell him about where we are. I'd guesstimate we're about three hours from pickup. Is that about right, Ed?"

"Yup. Check in, then let's get moving again. We've got extra daylight because it's summer, but there isn't that much of it left."

Blaze finished his call and turned back to the others.

"Saint said he did a flyover after he got the first call from us. Although the strip between the edge of the jungle and the edge of the cliff is very rocky, he spotted a couple of smooth places large enough to set down for a few minutes. He also said because of the geography, it's very windy there, so the minute he lands, we need to be ready to board."

"I think we can all agree none of us wants to hang around," Ed agreed. "All right. Let's get moving again, folks."

They adjusted their packs and started forward again. Without being too obvious, Rocket positioned himself behind Mallory.

"You watching my rear?" she teased.

"I'd like to do a lot more with your rear than watch it," he told her in a low voice. "So make sure you don't put it in the line of fire."

She grinned. "Yes, boss."

* * * *

It was Saturday night as usual in Santa Marita. Parties were in full swing on many of the boats in the marina. The streets were crowded with people looking for a little fun, a little joy in their lives. Those who chose to get off the water for a while, as well as the residents who liked to let it out on the weekend, filled the more upscale restaurants and bars. At many of the places frequented by the natives, local musicians played familiar salsa music. At others, loudspeakers poured the sound out into the streets.

There was no music or celebration at the presidential palace, however, after the aborted raid. Felix Barrera had retreated to his office after the failure at the Albados. He poured a shot of brandy into a cut-crystal glass and tossed it back with one swallow. Then he poured another and carried it with him to his desk.

Instead of sitting, he paced his office, consumed with anger and the hunger for revenge. In all his years in this business, first with the Sinaloa cartel then running his own in a country he owned, he didn't recall ever being in a rage as intense as this.

It was that fucking bitch, Mallory Kane. Everything was fine until she had come to Santa Marita, sticking her nose into his business. Why hadn't his men given him earlier warning that this stranger seemed to be overly interested in what was going on in his country?

"Where in the hell could the Albados be hiding?" he demanded of Ruben, who stood in front of the desk. "You've had men watching every form of exit."

"I have, and there's been no sighting of them."

"Even at the marina? It's hard to be inconspicuous there. The docks are all under guard so someone would have spotted them. Could they have disguised themselves so well without anyone noticing it? And where did this transformation take place, if there was one?"

"Whoever is helping these people is no novice," Ruben pointed out. "I'm not saying they got the Albados onto a boat or boats, but if they did, it was done so cleverly no one tipped to it. That takes people with experience and connections."

"I want a list of every single boat that was docked yesterday," he demanded, "along with the name of the owner and-or the captain. And I want it now."

He was annoyed when Ruben shook his head.

"I will do anything you ask, you know that, but I have to say this is a waste of time. Any boats they might be on are long gone and we don't even know where. It would be a useless waste of our resources."

"Fuck." Barrera pounded his fist on the desk. "*Mierde!* All right, then. I want to turn this country upside down looking for Mallory Kane. Check every place of business, every home, every shack. And I want regular updates."

Ruben nodded. "Let me get the men working on it. I'll be right back."

Barrera lit a cigar and took a long, slow draw on it. He seemed to be smoking a lot of them lately, but he supposed it was better than drugs. He'd seen what his merchandise could do to people. He trusted Ruben to give all the men their marching orders, and to monitor things so every area was covered. He'd been kept up to date on the reports from the checkpoints. That was an ongoing process since there were so many of them.

And yet, somehow, the bitch had managed to escape them.

He was still doing his best to control his temper when Ruben returned, followed by a very ordinary little man in a wrinkled uniform who looked very nervous. Barrera frowned, annoyed at the lack of respect for the official clothing and wondering what the hell Ruben was doing bring the man here.

"What's going on?" He snapped the words at Ruben. "You know I don't allow the lowest rank of soldiers in my office. Send him back where he came from."

"Meet Bruno Elizondo, *Presidente*. He is a private in the Santa Marita military. I think you will find what he has to say very interesting and perhaps even wish to reward him."

"It better be damn fucking important," Barrera spat. "We have too much going on right now for me to take time to listen to gossip."

"Not gossip," Ruben assured him and turned to the soldier. "All right, Bruno. Tell him what you told me."

Bruno licked his lips, a nervous gesture. "I have been making the coffee runs to the checkpoints," he began. "An assignment, I assure you, that I have been honored to fulfill." He paused, and Barrera frowned.

"That's it?" He looked at Ruben. "You waste my time with this?"

Ruben shook his head. "Listen to it all. Go ahead, Ruben."

"I was at a coffee bar late last night filling an order. It was very crowded but I particularly noticed four men who looked as if they did not belong there. I could tell they weren't citizens or soldiers or part of any activities of Santa Marita."

He paused and Ruben gestured for him to continue.

"I managed to overhear them. I am unremarkable, *Senor Presidente*, so people pay little attention to me. They were discussing the checkpoints and the Mallory Kane woman that everyone is looking for."

Barrera sat up straight in his chair, a tiny thrill skittering through him.

"You heard the name?"

Bruno nodded. "I did. I got the impression they know where she is and were planning to get her off the island. They were discussing how to avoid the checkpoints."

Barrera stared at him. For a moment he wanted to choke the life out of the man, but he managed to control himself.

"And you didn't think that was important enough to bring to me?"

The man turned pale. "I wanted to make sure. I took a picture of their car and intended to look for it, to get more proof before bringing this to you."

So much time lost, wasted because this little turd was afraid to bring him false information. Better to prove it wrong than not to have something to act on at all.

"Show me the picture."

Ruben pulled his cell phone out of his pocket, scrolled through to the picture and handed it to Ruben. He in turn passed it to Barrera.

The general studied the shot. It was a beat-up SUV, a few years old. Barrera vaguely remembered seeing it as he was driven around Santa Marita but he'd paid no attention to it, dismissing it as just another junker clunker. He looked at his lieutenant.

"Have this checked at once. There is someone on duty, yes?"

"There is. The electronics room is on duty at all times. But you'd better hear the rest of this first. Go on, Bruno."

"As I was finishing a coffee run, I spotted the same vehicle zigzagging through the streets, away from the center of town. I managed to follow without being seen. I—"

"How do you know that?" Barrera demanded.

"Because they didn't stop or turn back, just kept heading in a certain direction."

"So where did they end up? Ruben, we needed to get people there this moment."

If these men knew where the Kane woman was, he'd torture them until they told him.

"They are in La Jungla." The man shifted nervously. "I could not follow them in there."

Barrera stared at both men. "The jungle? They went into the jungle? What the hell? That place is a death trap."

A tiny smile tipped up one corner of Ruben's mouth.

"But what better place to hide someone from us?"

Barrera was trying to contain his excitement. Even if the Kane woman were being hidden in that dangerous place, he still had to put a big search party together of men who could be coerced into going into that overgrown death trap.

"Agreed," he said at last. Then he turned to the man standing in front of him. "Bruno, you will be generously rewarded for this. Ruben, be sure this is taken care of. Find out what this man wants and see if we can give it to him."

"If I may, *Presidente.*"

"Yes? Go ahead."

The least he could do, even though he was impatient to begin, was see what the man wanted.

"I would like to be assigned to your personal detail."

Barrera looked at Ruben who nodded.

"I think we can accommodate that. Ruben, make a note and see that it happens."

He waited impatiently while Ruben escorted the man out of the office and turned him over to one of the guards.

"I will get the search process started," Ruben told him when he returned. "They have no place to go if that's where they are. There are no landing spots for a boat to pick them up and it's a very steep drop from the cliff at the edge of La Jungla. We can locate them and surround them."

"Who are these men who have hidden her?"

Ruben shrugged. "I have no idea, but I promise you, we'll find out."

Barrera pushed himself away from the desk and stood. "Good. Let's get moving. I can't just sit here and wait."

"*Si, mi president.* I am driving you myself."

Barrera sometimes wondered what, if anything, it took to shake Ruben Vidal's ever-present calm. He actually hoped he'd never find out, because from what he knew about the man, it would take something pretty drastic.

He rode down in the elevator with Ruben and the other two guards who had been waiting outside his office. His car, as usual, was waiting in its special parking space outside the side entrance. It was a specially constructed SUV with three rows of seats and every type of armoring protection that could be purchased. It would take mortar rounds to do it any damage.

Barrera climbed into the middle row of seats, while Ruben sat behind the wheel, a guard riding shotgun beside him and two more in the rear seats, facing through the back window to watch for any kind of approaching trouble. They headed down the side driveway and entered the stream of traffic in the street. Even at this late hour, there was still a significant number of vehicles filling the roads.

Barrera watched through the side window as they drove through town, automatically looking for any sign of trouble or disturbing activity, but it was just the usual scene. Soon they left the commercial area and headed into a residential district. Streetlights provided plenty of illumination, but once they hit the edge of the jungle that changed. The minute they bumped off the pavement and into the thick growth of trees and bushes, the only light source available was their headlights.

"Be careful, Ruben," Barrera warned. "This is a dangerous place to be in. And there are no designated roads."

"*Si*." Ruben dipped his head, but that was all he said.

Barrera clenched his fists as they moved along at a snail's pace. After what seemed like an interminable amount of time, they came into a small clearing with a hut on stilts in its center.

"This is where they've been hiding her." Barrera spat the words out. "Practically under our noses, because they knew we'd never look for her in here. *Mierda*. Which is exactly why we should have."

He was glad no one pointed out that he had been driving the search and had never directed them toward La Jungla. If they lost this woman, it would be on his shoulders, and that he could not abide.

"All right, let's look around."

He climbed out of the vehicle and leaned against the door. He would oversee the search while the others crawled around, climbed the ladder to the hut and did whatever else was needed to see if they could find a trace of where Mallory Kane was now.

They covered every inch of the area slowly and methodically, until he wanted to scream and tell them to get their fucking asses in gear. But he also knew that they had to take enough time to make sure they didn't miss any clues. At the end, they at least had bits and pieces for him.

"She was definitely here," Ruben told him. "and someone was with her. There is a pallet on the floor of the hut that's obviously been used. A good part of the bottles of water beneath a small counter are gone and there are only a few empties in a trash bag. There's also some debris from food that's been sealed up and added to the bag."

"So she's been here and gone."

"*Si.* But someone's with her."

"It can't be one of the men from the SUV. They were seen all together every time they were spotted. So there's someone else that's also part of this equation."

Barrera wanted to strike something. Or someone. All of this made him realize that Mallory Kane wasn't just a writer snooping around to write some kind of exposure piece. She had friends who weren't everyday people. *Military? Former military? Former police?*

Whatever they were, they spelled big trouble for him unless he could eliminate all of them.

"We can't follow them on foot." He looked at Ruben. "It would take too long and I'm not sure we're all in shape to do so."

Well, at least he wasn't, but he didn't want to single himself out.

"I don't know what they'll do when they reach the cliff," Ruben mused. "Even if there's a boat waiting for them, that's a hell of a dive to the water. And it's nighttime, although it could be close to dawn by the time they reach that place."

"It is," Barrera agreed. "But they have to have something planned and we have to find out what it is."

"We need to get back to the palace," Ruben suggested, "and move from there."

"A boat," Barrera told him. "Not for them, but for us. Whatever they've arranged, we need to be there and ready for them. I want two boats loaded with military and fully armed."

In seconds, they were all back in their vehicle.

"Benno will drive," Ruben told him, "so that I can make any necessary phone calls."

"Good, good."

"We need to make sure to take Mallory Kane alive," Ruben told him once they were moving. "We have to find out if she's reported any information to anyone or sent notes to someone. If she's made any arrangements for publication of that information if anything should happen to her. And who she's made arrangements with. There has to be a way to get that information."

"Look into it." Barrera's mouth curved in a humorless smile. "I have discovered you have contacts and outreach almost everywhere. A very valuable talent to have. Once we have resolved this, I see a big promotion in your future. Perhaps a new title."

"If it pleases you. I am just happy to serve."

But Barrera had caught a fine edge of excitement in his voice. *Good.* Ruben Vidal was a valuable asset to him and would continue to be.

"And find Bruno Whatever his name is," he went on. "We would not have found this place if not for him. He should have a place on one of the boats, no?"

"I agree. Meanwhile, let me call the patrol boat office at the marina and tell them we will need two fully staffed gun boats readied right now. Take us directly to the harbor. And turn on lights and sirens so no one gets in our way."

He listened while Ruben made the call and gave the orders, his blood churning at the thought of eliminating people who dared to try and undermine him. He had planned for too long and worked too hard to get to this point. He was not about to let some idiot female and a bunch of what he was sure were hired thugs tear it all down.

"Bruno Elizondo will be waiting for us at the harbor," Ruben reported. "The patrol captain will take care of it."

"Good, good, good."

What else did he need to do? If any word of this got out, his entire empire would be destroyed. If his cartel customers found out, he would lose the trust he had worked so hard to build. The people of Santa Marita who he had under his control, who were afraid to oppose him, might suddenly rise against him. They were not the size of, say, Sinaloa. They just had this small island which he had entirely under his thumb — and he planned to keep it that way.

Tonight would be about more than just disposing of what he considered an enemy. It would be about asserting his authority and letting people know what happened to anyone who tried to bring him down.

He drew a breath as they pulled into the harbor patrol marina. *Time to flex my muscles.*

Chapter Fourteen

It felt to Mallory as if they'd been walking forever. She was close to the point of exhaustion, but she still managed to put one foot in front of the other. There was no way she was going to wimp out, not when these men had put their lives on the line to rescue her and get her out of a situation of her own making. She hated to admit it, but she hadn't done the research for this project the way she usually did. That was her own stupidity.

Inez had called her and begged her to come to Santa Marita and see for herself what was going on. Usually, she dug into the internet for everything she could find, turning up articles that would give her background. But this time she'd been in a hurry and done a hasty job, and had also made a stupid assumption. She'd thought because this was a tiny island run by a cartel reject, there wouldn't be much to write about.

How wrong she'd been.

She was still processing the destruction of the agriculture economy to grow drugs, and how that money had never had the trickledown effect on the people.

Because she was so busy letting her brain run wild and because it had gotten so dark, she stubbed her toe on a tree root and bumped into Blaze, who was walking ahead of her.

"Whoa." Rocket grabbed her from behind and steadied her on her feet. "You okay?"

Everyone had instantly come to a stop and shone their flashlights in her direction.

"I'm okay." She righted herself, embarrassment heating her cheeks. "I just need to pay better attention to where I'm going."

"Just walking can be dangerous out here." Ed's calm voice settled her nerves. "Especially in the dark like this."

"Thank you for saying that, and I promise to be less clumsy."

Rocket put his arms around her and pulled her close to his chest, which surprised her.

"Not to worry. I've got your back."

She could have stayed there forever like that, warmed by the heat of his body, assured by the strength of his arms, but that wouldn't solve anything. She took a step back.

"I'm good." She looked at the others, just black forms in the darkness highlighted by the tiny flashlights. "Let's do it."

They had barely started forward when Blaze's cell phone chirped and Mallory heard him answer.

"Everything still a go?" he asked. "Yeah. Yeah. Okay. We're probably about a half hour out. Okay. I'll give you a heads-up with a ten-minute warning. Thanks."

"He all set?" Rocket wanted to know.

"Good as ever. You know Saint."

Ed shifted his pack. "Let's hydrate again, then move. We're almost there."

Mallory thought the last half hour of this march was the longest walk she'd ever taken. Her legs ached to the point they were numb and her feet felt as if they were on fire. But they were doing this for her, so there was no way she was going to complain or hold them back. When she got home, she could lie in a hot tub for a week and recover.

Hopefully with Rocket.

At last, they were there. The sudden egress from the jungle was so startling, she almost stumbled again. One minute they were walking beneath a thick canopy of greenery, the next they were in wide-open space beneath a black sky dotted with silver stars. Mallory had to blink to get her bearings.

Rocket put his hand at the small of her back to guide her.

"Careful where you step."

"Got it."

And careful was indeed the word. The land beneath her feet was all rocks and pebbles, lumpy and bumpy and difficult to walk on. This time, because she was so tired and her balance wasn't the best, she allowed herself to hold on to Rocket's arm to steady herself. They all moved slowly, carefully feeling their way as they approached the edge of the cliff. Falling on these rocks could mean broken bones or multiple fractures.

"Here." Blaze had moved ahead of them all when his flashlight illuminated a large plateau created by four enormous flat rocks.

"Is that big enough for the helo to set down?" Ed asked.

"Saint could set down on the head of a pin. We need to use our flashlights to guide him. He didn't want to hover and call too much attention to himself, but he should be here any minute now. So everyone get ready."

Mallory took her Glock from her backpack and checked the magazine to make sure there was a bullet in the chamber. Just as she did so, she heard the sound of a motor, but it didn't sound like any helicopter she'd ever heard.

* * * *

Because Ruben had called ahead, they were waiting for Barrera and his party when they arrived. Two patrol boats were set to go, each with a full crew and the mounted guns loaded and set.

"Whatever we can do for you, *mi general*," Captain Emilio Suarez told him, shaking his hand.

"Your men understand that this is a critical mission? That we are chasing criminals who have committed crimes against the state and who cannot be permitted to leave this jurisdiction?"

Captain Suarez nodded.

"They are well aware that the safety of the state must be protected at all costs."

The two men exchanged a meaningful look. Suarez had been a part of Barrera's team from the very beginning. Even a man as respected as President Alcante practiced a little nepotism now and then. Suarez had been relegated to a low position in Alcante's administration while his younger son ran the harbor patrol. When Barrera had made his move on Santa Marita, Suarez had managed to get an audience with him, a deal had been struck and now Suarez ruled the harbor police from top to bottom. People who violated Suarez's orders fell on unhappy times.

Like the Mexican navy patrol boats, these boats were armed with a single Melara 76 mm naval gun and a pair of turret guns. They could take down any boat with ease, but he wasn't too sure about their range firing upward. However, he was going to do the best he could because he owed so much to this man.

"Private Elizondo is on the second boat," Suarez told him. "We have him set up with one of the gunners. Come. Let's get ready to move."

Barrera followed the captain onto the lead boat, moving to a place where he'd be out of the way but could see all the action. Ruben was escorted to the other boat, then they were ready to shove off.

The night air had cooled slightly, and on the water, it was almost cold. The breeze coming in off the Pacific Ocean was pretty stiff at this time of night and Barrera was glad he'd thought to bring his jacket. They moved slowly away from the dock, one boat in line behind the other, and when they had cleared the harbor, they began to increase their speed.

"I know exactly the spot you are looking for," Suarez told Barrera "A very dangerous place. We call it *buceo mortal*. Death Dive."

"There has to be a reason for that."

"Before you came here, for many years young and foolish people would try to dive off that cliff. But the water below is not deep enough to absorb them and they can't dive out far enough."

Barrera lifted an eyebrow. "I'm assuming people have gotten a lot smarter since then?"

Suarez shrugged. "It is to be hoped. Surely these people you are after aren't stupid enough to think they can escape this way."

"I don't know what they're thinking, but by heading for the cliff out of the jungle, they've left themselves with no options."

"Perhaps they plan to scale down on ropes and meet a boat that will pick them up."

Barrera made a derisive noise. "If they know anything about Santa Marita, they should know that's impossible." He grinned at Suarez. "Our incomparable harbor patrol would put an end to that."

"We are most definitely ready," Suarez assured him.

"How long a ride is it to get there? The island isn't that big."

"There are dangerous reefs and shoals that can't be seen from the surface. You need an underwater map. We provide them for divers, but not everyone asks for them. Some people are stupid enough to think they can just spot them visually and bypass them."

Barrera frowned. "But if you don't know the location, you can rip the bottom out of your boat."

"Sad but true," Suarez agreed. "But that's the simple explanation for the wide detour."

The further they got away from the shoreline, the faster the boat moved, until finally it turned and headed toward that far side of the island. They were moving towards the face of the tall cliff when another sound attracted their attention. Barrera looked up, tracking the sound. When a searchlight hit their faces, they both blinked.

And Barrera cursed.

* * * *

The sound of the helo's blades — *whump, whump, whump* — cut into the night and the movement stirred the air like a wind off the water. The six of them — the four Galaxy men, Ed and Mallory — were all gathered together near the landing spot for the chopper at the edge of the cliff. They held up their flashlights, even as weak as they were, so Saint could see them and the spot to set the helo down.

Rocket was focused on getting Mallory to the chopper and inside so she wasn't in anyone's line of fire. They had all moved into position to get ready when another sound came. *Motors. Loud ones.* He shaded his eyes and looked out toward the water, the direction from which the sounds had come.

"Goddamn."

"Fucking shit." Ed spat the words out. "It's the goddamn harbor patrol. How in the fuck did they even know we'd be here?"

"First question," Rocket growled, "is how did they even find out we were in the jungle, because that's the only way to get to the cliff. Something's wrong here."

"My guess?" Ed snapped. "They shut us off from every other exit and this was all that was left. Or some asshole somehow found out what was going on and ran to Barrera. I don't know how, but you know as well as I do that kind of shit always happens."

"FUBAR." Viper looked like he wanted to pound something. *Fucked Up Beyond All Repair.*

A sound split the air, one they were all familiar with that upped the critical nature of the situation. Bullets. Lots of them.

"Wrong?" Eagle backpedaled. "What's wrong is that those boats are shooting at us."

"None of them are reaching the surface up here, though," Viper noted, as bullets bounced off the face of the cliff.

"Yet," Ed pointed out.

"I think they're short-range guns, but that doesn't mean they can't adjust them to a certain extent."

The words had hardly left his mouth before chunks of rocks at the edge of the cliff flew into the air.

"Not that short range," Viper contradicted. "You're right about adjusting. We need to get the fuck out of here."

With the rotors kicking up the air around them, the helo lowered, barely touching the surface of its landing spot.

"We better load in a hurry," Ed told them, "before any of those bullets hit somebody. Come on. Mallory first."

He yanked out his Draco, snapped the handle in place and began spray bullets toward the boats. More bullets were flying as the others added their own firepower.

Rocket nearly had a heart attack when Mallory pulled her own gun from her backpack, crouched down beside him and aimed toward the boats.

"Are you crazy?" Rocket tried to pull her away and toward the helicopter.

"I can shoot, too," she insisted.

"But not against these guns."

He had his own weapon out now, firing toward the water with one hand and tugging Mallory toward the chopper with the other. But the damn woman was still shooting toward the water.

"Mal." Rocket kept dragging her. "That won't hardly reach them and the guys are on top of it. Come on."

"But at least it's more metal coming their way," she protested, digging in her heels.

Before they could move again, more bullets kicked up rocks around the helo's runners.

"I don't know if we can hit them from up here," Blaze shouted, "but at least we can give them something to think about."

He pulled out the Draco, set the lever, pointed the gun and pulled the trigger. Immediately bullets hit the water near the boats, kicking up tiny waves.

"Get Mal inside," Blaze hollered. "We'll handle this."

Rocket swore, just hefted Mallory over his shoulder and ran toward the chopper while the others laid down cover fire. But before he had moved more than three steps, another spray of bullets hit the rocks and sent debris flying, some of it stinging against his skin. He didn't know if it was the chips of rock or the bullets that hit them. He had nearly made it to the helo when he felt her jerk in his arms and cry out. Immediately he felt the warmth of blood on his arm where it pressed against her ribs.

Fuck.

He wanted to stop and look, but he knew it was more important to get to the safety of the chopper. He just raced the last couple of steps, fear welling in his throat as he felt the blood spreading, while the others returned more fire to the boats. He was barely aware of everyone backing toward the helo, still firing, doing their best to avoid the bullets hitting the rocks.

Rocket had placed Mallory carefully across two of the chopper's seats, grateful that this was one of the larger birds, and was frantically trying to stem the flow of blood from her side.

"There's a first aid kit under the other seat in the cockpit," Saint hollered at them, "if someone can grab it. My hands are a little full right now."

Blaze dug it out, opened it and began handing stuff to Rocket.

"The bullet hit a rib and burrowed inside," he said. "We gotta get her to a hospital."

"Pack it good," Blaze told him, "so you can slow the bleeding."

"I know that, damn it. Saint, is there a hospital in Manzanillo that has a helipad on its roof?"

"The Navy Hospital does," Ed told them. "Making contact with them."

"Okay. Checking right now," Saint yelled back. "Everyone in?"

"We are now," Eagle yelled as he hauled Ed into the cabin. He slammed the cabin door closed as the chopper lifted off the ground and away from the cliff. "Goose it."

With bullets still flying around them, Saint lifted the chopper off the cliff and sidestepped away from the danger zone. Seconds later, they were in the air and headed toward Manzanillo.

Rocket's hands were shaking so badly he was having trouble making a pressure bandage for Mallory's side.

Blaze crowded in beside him. "Let me. Come on, Rocket. I'll take care of it."

Rocket watched as Blaze efficiently pressed material into place against the wound and wound tape around it to hold it in place.

"That's the best I can do," he said. "But it'll hold until we get to the hospital. It's not that far."

He'd have to call Alicia Kane and tell her that her sister was safe, but not until they were out of here and at the hospital. For now, he stayed in position as the chopper swept through the night. The others had moved into empty seats with their backpacks, but everyone's focus was on Mallory. Even Ed, who rolled up his pantleg to temporarily remove his prosthesis. Rocket barely noticed the redness and irritation on the stump of the leg. He'd worry about Ed later. Right now, all he could think about was Mallory.

And pray.

Chapter Fifteen

Their arrival at the Navy Hospital had prompted a flurry of activity. Three people in scrubs were waiting with a gurney. As soon as Saint touched down, they lifted Mallory from the chopper, strapped her carefully onto the gurney and raced into the hospital.

"There's a surgical waiting room," one of them hollered back. "We'll look for you there."

The rotors on the chopper finally stopped spinning, but Rocket hadn't waited for that. He'd raced after the gurney and followed it down the hallway to an elevator. The medical personnel with Mallory started to tell him he'd have to wait, but one look at his face and they managed to crowd in and make room for him.

He followed them all the way from the elevator to a set of double doors with *Surgical Suite* painted on them.

"You can wait in there." A man in scrubs pointed to a room to their left. "There's coffee and magazines. We'll get a report to you as soon as we can."

It killed him that he couldn't follow them all the way to the operating room, but he knew making a fuss would only delay things. There were some chairs against the walls, but he was too on edge to sit. He thought about coffee, but caffeine was the last thing he needed. He was pacing the floor when the others arrived.

"I'd tell you to take it easy," Blaze told him, "but I know my words would fall on deaf ears. I'll just say pacing doesn't make the time go faster. And Mallory is in good hands."

"I know." Rocket nodded. "But I don't think I can sit still."

All the missions he'd been on where he'd often had to sit still for hours, all the hours of training where he'd been unable to move, still hadn't prepared him for this. He'd never pictured himself falling in love. He'd never felt that kind of connection with any woman, although he hadn't been looking for it, but Mallory was different. Whatever was between them had been simmering since Afghanistan, and now he couldn't imagine his life without her. Their time together in the hut had reinforced that. Now he just wanted all this shit over with.

Saint strode into the room, stopped and looked around.

"Any news?"

Rocket shook his head. "Not yet. Praying hard."

"Chopper's okay for now on the helipad," Saint told them, "but I told the guard I'd move it in a few. I can take it back to vacation rentals, catch a ride to where we parked the rental car and drive back here if someone gives me the keys."

"Here you go." Blaze dug into his pocket and tossed the key ring to him.

"So." Saint stuffed the keys in his pocket. "When I pulled away from the cliff, I got a good look at the decks of both boats, and guess what I saw? A couple of bodies."

"Bodies?" Viper echoed.

"Uh-huh. At least two, so you guys did some damage even from that distance."

"I think we just kept firing and praying," Blaze told him. "We just wanted to spray enough bullets to spoil their aim or distract them."

"Well, you definitely hit at least two people."

"Be nice to find out if Barrera was one of them," Eagle mused.

Ed had been sitting quietly in a corner chair, massaging his leg that now had the prosthesis attached again.

"I can find out. Elias will know. He's been pissed at being left out of the action, but we needed a final backup if all else failed. Let me give him a call."

He limped out into the hallway, pulling his cell from his pocket as he went.

"Okay." Saint jingled the keys in his hand. "Let me go return the helo and pick up our car. And maybe I can pick up some gossip at the same time. Blaze, I'll ring you when I'm on my way back."

"Grab the pouches with all our identification, too," Blaze told him. They always left them with Saint when they went incognito like this trip to Santa Marita. If they got caught, they didn't want the enemy to be able to identify them. "And we'll need at least one credit card for Mallory's expenses here. No way is this getting charged to her."

"Got it."

He left and silence dropped over the room again.

"I hope one of those bodies really is that bastard Barrera," Rocket blurted out. "If it isn't, I might have to go back and kill him with my bare hands."

"Nobody's going anywhere," Blaze told him. "Your first priority is Mallory. Let's see what the situation actually is before we go flexing our muscles."

Rocket sat back in his chair, doing his best to keep himself under control. Blaze was right. Mallory came first. But if he had a chance to make Barrera and his rotten people pay...

"I have updates." Ed limped back into the room. "And you're gonna like them."

"Don't keep it to yourself," Eagle urged. "Share."

"Elias says at least two dead bodies on the boats and a load of shit is going on."

"Who's dead?" Viper demanded. "That's the first question."

"You'll like the answer." Ed managed a little smile. "Both Barrera and his right-hand man, Ruben Valdez, bought the big one. They —"

"Let's allow ourselves one moment for a cheer," Viper interjected. "That's like hitting the big jackpot."

"But there's a big landslide effect from that," Ed pointed out. "The head of the harbor patrol wanted to take the bodies to the palace so they could lie in state."

"But?" Eagle made a gesturing motion. "There has to be a but."

"But...there are too many people waiting for this to happen. There was a battle at the harbor patrol office and those left over from Alcante apparently won. They've got the two bodies locked up in a freezer until they can all figure out what's going on. It's mayhem there right now."

"You don't think his army will find someone to take charge?" Viper asked.

"Without Barrera, they're in chaos. And I don't think one of the cartels will step in. Not enough money in their scheme of things to make it worth all the hassle."

"So what's going to happen?"

"In case you forgot or didn't know, the son of the late President Alcante is in the United States, looking for the opportunity to restore his father's government."

Blaze smiled. "I bet we step in and help him. Off the books, off course."

"Elias promised to keep me up to date. Meanwhile, we should be glad we aren't there, because it is holy chaos."

"Damn it," Rocket swore. "Fucking damn it."

"You upset about the situation on Santa Marita?" Eagle asked. "I'd think you'd be delighted."

"I'm upset because we haven't heard one fucking word about Mallory. I'm ready to barge into that operating room right now."

"Calm down." Blaze's voice was low and even. "It hasn't even been an hour. You know how tricky bullet wounds can be. And I understand the staff here is top notch. I know how hard the waiting is, but I truly believe she's going to be fine. If we don't hear anything soon, I'll see if I have any contacts who can help us. That work?"

"I guess it has to." Rocket leaned back in his chair and closed his eyes.

And silently prayed.

* * * *

Chaos would have been a mild term to describe the situation on Santa Marita. Emilio Suarez was torn between wanting to shoot everyone and getting the hell out of there. The moment Barrera fell to the deck, the crimson pool rapidly spreading on his chest telling the story of his situation, Suarez could feel the threads of the regime beginning to fray.

"Help him," he shouted at his crew.

Already one of the crewmen had a first aid kit out and was crouching over the body of their leader.

Suarez was battling a surge of panic. Only those who directly benefitted from Barrera or who wanted to would be anxious to see this resolved, to have the man still alive and things to remain in place. Everyone else in Santa Marita had been a victim in some way and had prayed for deliverance. That was a known fact.

He had to bring down the people who had done that. Maybe that would help.

"Shoot at the helicopter," he ordered the gunner next to him. A glance to the left showed him that the man in charge of the other boat was also in an argument with the gunner.

"*Capitan*, there is no way the bullets from this gun will reach that high. That's not what it's meant for."

"Idiot." He yanked the man's arm and pulled him aside. "Let me at it."

Suarez grabbed the controls of the gun, aimed it skyward and pulled back on the trigger. The *rat-tat-tat* of the continuous feed of ammunition split the air, but even he could see the helicopter was already too far away for them to hit.

"Idiot." He curled his hands into fists so he didn't give in to temptation and punch the lights out of the gunner.

"*Capitan.*" The gunner cowered next to him. "We must attend to *El Presidente.*"

Suarez alternated between wanting to smash something and wanting to throw up. The moment word of this got out, there would be utter madness. Perhaps Ruben Valdez could help him pull this together. Coordinate things at the presidential palace. Keep a lid on everything.

He made his way to the radio in the cockpit and pressed the mic button.

"Ruben Valdez, come in. Come in please. Now."

After a few seconds of static, he heard the voice of the captain of the other boat.

"Sir, we have a problem here. Lieutenant Valdez has been shot and we cannot revive him."

Suarez wanted to vomit.

"Did you check for a pulse? Breathing? Anything?"

"*Si.* There is no question that he is dead. *Finito.*"

God fucking damn.

"Is anyone else hurt?"

"One of the men took a bullet in the arm and another in the thigh. They were spraying the boat continuously with—"

"I know!" Suarez shouted. Then he hauled in a breath. It would not do for him to fall apart, not in the middle of this. Maybe he could still hold on to his position if he played this right. "Just make sure they are attended to. I will radio the harbor patrol office and prepare them."

But to do what? Who would even be in charge of the country to give orders? Barrera had held the reins in his hands with a tight grip, sharing only with Ruben Valdez. *Shit.* What a fucking disaster. He had to find a way to create order out of chaos, but at the moment, he did not have a clue.

"Return to port," he ordered. "We will see what happens after that."

* * * *

At the moment that Rocket was ready to tear someone's head off, a man in hospital scrubs with a surgical mask hanging from his neck.

"I'm Dr. Moreno. Family of Mallery Kane?"

"Here." They all stood and spoke at the same time.

The man looked from one to the other. "All of you?"

Rocket stepped forward. "I'm John Hardin, her fiancé." At least he fully intended to be, the moment she woke up. "Please tell me she's going to be all right."

"It's been touch and go," Moreno said. "There was a substantial amount of ricochet damage, plus the bullet nicked an artery."

"But she'll be okay." Rocket wanted to shake the man.

Moreno nodded. "Yes. She'll require a lot of care and rest, but with time and care she'll recover fully. It's just going to be a long process."

Rocket felt a sudden weakness in his body. He didn't know if he was going to throw up or pass out. He tried to say something, but his brain seemed to have stopped functioning.

Blaze was beside him in a hot minute, gripping his arm and infusing him with strength.

"Thank you, Dr. Moreno," he told the surgeon. "When can we see her?"

"She'll be in recovery for an hour. After that, if all her vitals are good, we'll move her to a room—"

"Private room," Rocket snapped. "I want her in a private room. One like you reserve for VIPs."

Moreno looked at each of the men, an eyebrow raised.

"We're good," Rocket insisted. "As soon as my friend brings my documents, I'll take care of it. We don't usually carry anything with us when we go fishing."

Moreno's mouth quirked up in a hint of a grin.

"That must have been some fishing trip you were on. But..."

"Okay, just hold on." Blaze held up a hand. "Rocket, get Senator Kane on the phone. She's been waiting for a call, anyway."

"You're right. I just wanted to wait until we were away from Santa Marita."

Rocket was amazed at how quickly his call was put through.

"You have her?" Alicia Kane asked the moment she answered.

"We do. But she's —"

"She's alive?" There was a touch of fear in the words.

"Yes, but —"

"That's what's important. When can I speak to her?"

Rocket walked into the hallway as he gave the senator a brief but detailed report, assuring her that as soon as Mallory woke up, she would call. Then he explained the current situation.

"Hand him the phone," she ordered.

Rocket walked back into the waiting room and held the phone out to Dr. Moreno.

"Senator Alicia Kane would like to speak to you. She's on the Senate Armed Services Committee."

Moreno gave him a weird look as he took the phone from him.

"Garth Moreno here."

Rocket watched as the expression on the doctor's face changed from irritated to perplexed to awed to accepting.

"No problem," he said at last. "I'll take care of it."

"All set?" Rocket asked taking the phone back.

"It's done," Alicia confirmed. "Just be sure she calls me. And, Rocket? Thank you very, very much."

"I did it for me, too," he told her, and disconnected the call.

"I'll make all the arrangements," Moreno assured him. "In fact, let me go take care of them right now so her room will be ready when we move her out of Post Op."

He hurried from the room as if his ass were on fire.

Blaze laughed. "Nice to have friends in high places."

The next hour, to Rocket, seemed to drag. Elias arrived to collect Ed, bringing a little news.

"Santa Marita is a mess," he told them. "The way Barrera had it set up, everyone was under his thumb except for Vidal. With both of them dead, it's turning out a free-for-all. All the hate and resentment that built up is spilling over."

"So what's going to happen?" Blaze asked.

"Even as we speak, Benito Alcante is gathering his troops and making plans. He's reaching out to his allies for support. I have an idea that before long things will settle back to the way they were on Santa Marita."

"Good. Those people deserve it."

Fifteen minutes after Ed and Elias left, a nurse knocked on the door jamb of the waiting room.

"Family of Mallory Kane, I take it?"

"Yes." Rocket stepped forward. "I'm her fiancé."

"Then come along with me."

"What's the room number?" Blaze asked. "Rocket, you need some alone time with her first. We have phone calls to make and arrangements to see to. We'll be up in a while."

He thanked them and followed the nurse. An elevator ride took them up two floors, then she led him down a long, wide corridor to a corner room that he was sure was big enough for four people. He hurried to the bed but stopped short at its side, his eyes focused on Mallory.

She lay still and white, surrounded by beeping machines. Only one arm was in the hospital gown she wore, exposing the heavy bandages wrapped around her chest. She was almost as pale as the sheets and heavy circles darkened the skin below her eyes. How had he not been able to protect her from this? How had it happened that she was the only one who had been shot?

"I'd be gentle," the nurse told him in a soft voice, "but you can hold her hand. She'll be able to sense you being here."

"Are you sure?"

"I am. I've been doing this for a long time. Go on. Get close to her."

Rocket pulled the chair close to the bed, lowered himself into it and reached through the siderails to take Mallery's hand. It was cold, but when he pressed the tips of his fingers to her pulse, he could feel the slow, steady beat of her heart. He wasn't ready to relax, but he felt a little better.

He was definitely taking Mallory home with him. She'd told him she was a nomad. Both parents were dead and it was just her and Alicia. She'd lived in a lot of different places. Now she could make Tampa her home.

They could talk about her plans after she was on the mend, but he'd already made up his mind. He was taking her home with him and putting a ring on her finger the first chance he had. And whatever she had planned for her future, it would be with him. He could hardly wait to see her settled in his house.

Life was looking good and the future was bright.

At least once they got out of here and could plan for it.

Chapter Sixteen

Mallory muted the television and picked up the mug of coffee.

"Santa Marita is still all over the news." She looked at Rocket, who was intently reading on his tablet. "Find something interesting there?"

"An interview with Benito Alcante. He's really got his act together."

"He's been back in Santa Marita for a month now. I'm gathering from your comment things are going the way he wants them to?"

"To say the least. He gathered most of the people who were on his father's staff as well the top officials in the military. It took a week or so, but they're all back in place and cleaning up the mess Barrera made."

"Inez and her parents are back on the island and picking up the pieces of their lives." Mallory sipped her coffee. "I owe my sister big time for that. From what I understand through Inez and from what you've told me, Barrera just quite literally stormed the island, killed

President Alcante and took over, bringing in his drug business and killing the rest of the agriculture."

"That's true." Rocket set his tablet to the side and turned to Mallory. "The population is damned glad to have gotten rid of him. I understand they gave Alcante an impromptu parade the day he flew in with his people as well as the army officers Barrera had tried to have killed."

"I hate to see people celebrating someone's death, but in this case, I might make an exception." She set her mug back on the coffee table. "What happened to all the cartel customers? Did they get the word or did they just show up, demanding to know what was up with their business?"

Rocket laughed. "I'm sure you know the US Drug Enforcement Agency is able to work internationally as long as they have an arrangement with a country's police."

"I do. In fact, I plan to do a lot of reading up on it."

"So Benito Alcante resurrected Santa Marita's police force and assigned four of the top men to work with our DEA. The drug dealers Barrera cultivated arrangements with are either looking for new suppliers or spending time in someone's jail. In fact, the United States has sent people from a number of different agencies to not only help put Santa Marita back in business and better than ever, but we've offered ongoing help."

"President Alcante must be thrilled."

"To say the least." He grinned. "Your sister twisted a few arms for this, too."

"I think my sister would have thrown herself at you and kissed you all over the day we came home and she arrived here to see me for herself."

Rocket laughed. "I should be kissing her. If not for her, I might never have reconnected with you, stupid idiot that I was."

They had talked about that many times since they'd arrived in Tampa. Mallory had settled very comfortably into Rocket's home. As soon as she was really on her feet, they were going to do some shopping to make it a 'them' house instead of a 'him' house. There was no argument about the fact that they'd be living together from now on. And if she wanted a more solid arrangement, well, she was sure they'd get there when the time was right.

She'd sold her condo in Houston, including all the furnishings. Rocket refused to let her travel and go through the effort of packing her stuff while she was still healing.

However, Peyton West and Hannah Modell, who were engaged to two of the Galaxy partners, had both visited a few times. The three women had connected immediately and had volunteered to take care of Houston for her, despite her protests. They'd handled it very well and all her personal belongings had been shipped. Little by little, she was opening the boxes and putting things away.

Rocket had taken himself out of the action for the duration, despite her protests.

"I'm doing fine," she kept telling him.

"And I want to make sure nothing changes that."

This whole week she'd actually felt more like herself and begun some light exercise. And started compiling notes on her laptop.

"What did your agent say about your proposal?" Rocket asked.

"Considering the headlines plastered everywhere about Santa Marita and the fact that it leads almost every newscast with the latest events, she's pretty excited. She wants the outline and the first three Chapters by the end of the month."

"She's savvy," Rocket pointed out, "and wants to move on this while it's still current news."

"I think she's looking at the long haul. It will be a year before the book comes out. But by the time I finish it, I can add more details about Santa Marita's current situation. I think this story will be hot news for quite a while."

She took the last sip from her coffee and curled up in a corner of the couch.

"I think you're right," he agreed.

"So what's on the agenda today? I feel better every day and I'd love to see more of the Tampa area, since I'm going to be living here."

"Well." He slid over and placed her legs on his lap, gently massaging her feet. "I thought maybe we'd do some jewelry shopping."

The look in his eyes was very intent and filled with emotion. A tiny thrill wriggled its way through her.

"Oh? Need some trinkets, do you?"

He slid a hand up one leg and eased it beneath her sleepshirt.

"I have a particular trinket in mind, since you asked."

"Such as?" she teased, watching his face very carefully.

"I was thinking along the line of matching engagement and wedding rings. What do you think about that?"

The look in his eyes was so intent it burned into her. His hand had crept up to the tiny thong she wore to bed and eased the fabric aside.

"I think—" She gasped as a finger slid between the slick lips of her sex and began a slow rubbing motion. "I think it's a great idea. Ohhhhh."

"I've never said the words," he told her, keeping up the steady rubbing motion. "But I can't imagine my life now without you. I love you, Mal, more than I ever thought I could love a woman. I want you with me. Always."

"I feel the same," she whispered, using her hips to press against the touch of his hand. "Oh, god, Rocket. Don't stop."

"Didn't plan to." He pinched her clit, sending sharp arrows of heat coursing through her.

"We'll have to coordinate with Peyton and Hannah. They were here first, after all."

"Logistics. That's easy. You ladies can work it out."

Now he'd eased two fingers inside her wet heat.

"Oh, god."

She dug her fists into the couch cushion for leverage as she pressed her body into his touch. When she tried to move, to get into position to straddle his lap, he used his other hand to hold her in place.

"Uh-uh. Just like this. In case I haven't told you, finger fucking you is one of my great pleasures in life."

"Oh, good." She could hardly catch her breath. "Because having you do it is one of mine."

She pressed against his touch again, riding his hand. More tremors rippled through the walls of her sex and she did her best to ride his hand, even as he held her in place. But when she was so close to the edge that she was sure she'd explode, he suddenly removed his hand, stood up and pulled off the sweatpants he'd thrown on earlier.

She took a moment to drink in the sight of his body, all hard muscle and a dusting of black hair making his chest even sexier.

"Don't stop," she begged. "Come back."

"I'm here," he murmured, a rough edge defining his voice. "Right here."

He knelt between her spread-wide legs, lifting them over his shoulders so every bit of her sex was exposed. Holding his shaft in one hand and separating the lips of her sex with his other, he poised for a moment at her entrance then, with a hard thrust, buried himself inside her.

"Oh, god!"

The feel of him was just as incredible as the first time. Rocket braced his hands on either side of her, drew in a breath and began to thrust in and out, hard then harder, more then more. Mallory dug her heels into the small of his back to lock them together and gave herself over to the storm. It went on and on, heavy spasms that shook both of them. Nothing existed but the two of them. Together.

Finally, the spasms subsided, leaving her weak and spent, her heart thudding so loud she wondered he didn't hear it.

Slowly he eased her legs down and braced himself with his hands on either side of her body.

"I love you, Mal." His voice was thick with emotion. "More than I can even express."

"I love you, too." She smiled. "And I'd say that was a pretty good expression."

"We'll have a lot more of those for a very long time."

He brushed a soft kiss over her lips. She gave silent thanks for the Fate that had brought him back into her life. She could hardly wait for the rest of their future to begin.

Want to see more from this author? Here's a taster for you to enjoy!

Galaxy: Absolute Zero
Desiree Holt

Excerpt

Sierra Hunt pried her eyes open and looked around. Where was she? Her hotel room? No, not hers, but one like it. Then whose?

She scrunched her forehead, trying to remember that and how she got here.

Her brother Jeremy's attorney had told her their last appeal had been exhausted. The prosecutor had told her there was nothing else she could do because the case was closed. She had tried three other attorneys who'd all told her they saw nothing to indicate there were grounds for yet another appeal. And the governor's office would not take her call.

She'd flown to New Orleans to meet with a high-profile attorney who she'd been told was a champion of difficult cases like this. She'd waited all day in his office, only to have him tell her she should accept the fact her brother was guilty and prepare herself for his execution. She'd left his office depressed and discouraged. She had one option left but she couldn't exercise it until the morning, damn it.

Exhausted, she'd been paying no attention to anything as she made her way through the lobby. Hot tea, she told herself. That was what she needed to soothe her nerves. The drink wagon was still open in the lobby and the scent of the various brews tantalized her senses. Then, as she turned away to head toward the elevators, she bumped smack into a solid wall of masculinity, spilling her hot tea all over the shirt of the man standing in front of her.

"Oh, my god! I am so sorry."

She grabbed napkins from the drink wagon and tried to blot his shirt dry, but he grabbed her hand.

"I'll handle it. Don't worry." But he was pulling the damp material away from his chest and shaking it slightly.

His voice was rich and deep. Thick brown hair was distinguished by a shocking strip of white that ran from forehead to nape. His sharply defined jaw and high cheekbones were softened by chocolate eyes and thick lashes. His lips, curved into a hint of a smile, looked as they were usually set in a grim line. She wondered what created that.

"No, no, I am so sorry."

Flustered, she made things worse because she was still holding the now half-empty cup of tea and more splashed out of it. When she turned to toss it into the trash, her hand bumped the metal edge of the counter. She dropped her purse, which fell open, scattering her things on the floor.

If she could have melted into the floor, she would have. She crouched down, doing her best to gather items and stuff them back into her purse. And of course the stranger insisted on helping her.

She grabbed her key card from her purse, and in the process scattered some of the contents again. God. If only the floor would open up and swallow her.

"You going to your room? Come on, I'll make sure you get there."

Let a strange man escort her up to her room? Was she crazy?

"No, thanks. I—"

"You're bleeding." The stranger took her hand and lifted it. "You must have hit it pretty hard on the counter."

She glanced at it, shocked to see blood welling form a long cut and running down over her fingers. *Holy god. What next?*

The stranger grabbed more napkins and pressed them against the cut.

"You can't let that go like that. I can get you to a walk in clinic—"

"No. Please." That was all she needed. "I just want to get to my room."

"Do you have bandages? Antiseptic? If not, you could be courting an infection. I can fix it, at least temporarily."

She was so rattled that she didn't even have the brains to refuse. Instead she let him lead her across the lobby to the elevators. Inside the car, he punched the button for the tenth floor.

"I'm on nine," she protested.

"But first aid's on the tenth, in my room."

He was taking her to his room? What if he…?

"Don't worry." He grinned at her. "I'm not planning to attack. That is, unless you want me to. Ah, here we are."

Still in a daze, she let him lead her down the hall and into his hotel room. She had to admit he was very efficient in cleaning and bandaging her cut.

"Are you a doctor?"

He shook his head. "Former SEAL. We learn how to field dress wounds. Okay, there you are." He frowned. "You're still trembling. What can I get for you?"

"Can you just hold me for a minute? I've had the day from hell and this hasn't helped."

For a moment he looked as if he were about to refuse. But then, just as she was on the point of getting, up, he put his arm around her and pulled her against him.

"We should at least introduce ourselves. I'm Vic Bodine but people call me Eagle. That was my call sign."

She figured the streak in his hair had something to do with that.

When she didn't respond, he shrugged. "Okay, No problem."

And still he held her.

His touch was gentle for a man his size, and that was what probably broke the dam of her emotions. One minute she was sitting there and the next she was crying all over his shirt, tears she'd been holding back since this whole nightmare started.

Everything after that was a blur. From blubbering on his shoulder, she was hugging him.

"I'm going to kiss you," he said slowly. "If you don't want it, just say so. That's okay. I'm not in the habit of forcing myself on women."

But there was no force involved, except maybe for her clutching him so desperately and kissing him so hungrily, as if that could erase this whole nightmare. It seemed her body's needs had awakened after dozing for months. Awakened by a man who could best be described as sex on a stick. As their kisses grew hotter so did her body. And then it was as if someone had flipped a switch.

Their kisses were hot and demanding and involved a whole lot of tongue. Their clothes somehow disappeared. Hands coasted over naked skin, touching and squeezing and stroking. While he cupped her breasts in his palms, brushing the nipples with his thumbs, she reached between them to wrap her fingers around his hard, thick cock.

They tumbled onto the bed, barely taking time to strip back the covers.

Heat blazed in his eyes as he raked them over her naked body while he touched her everywhere. At each stroke of his hands another fire ignited, until she was squirming with need. She tried to reach between them to find his hard shaft again but he brushed her hand away.

"Too close," he rasped.

He swirled his tongue around her nipples, grazing them with his teeth before trailing his tongue down her body to her shockingly heated sex. She hadn't been with anyone in so long that she'd almost forgotten what it was like, but apparently her body woke up in a hurry.

Nudging her thighs apart, he settled himself between them and bent to lap greedily at the wet folds of her sex. Each stroke of his tongue lit more flames, awoke more nerves. Her inner walls fluttered, seeking something to fill her greedy channel…seeking his cock that was hot as it brushed against her skin.

"I can't wait," he panted. "I have to be inside you right now. Next time will be slower, I promise."

He grabbed one of the condoms he'd dumped on the nightstand and rolled it on with hands that shook slightly. Then bending her legs back so he was wide open to him he drove into her, filling every inch of her. She was grateful she was so wet that she took him easily.

He stared hard into her eyes, hunger blazing in his, setting a rhythm that was hard and fast. But she was ready. Oh, more than ready, a shock after going for so long without. He pounded hard, his movement almost desperate.

"Look at me," he growled, desperation in his voice.

She lifted her gaze to lock with his, mesmerized by the heat blazing in those deep chocolate eyes.

"I can't hold off much longer."

"Don't…hold back," sha gasped, the orgasm already rolling up from deep inside her.

"Let go," he told her.

And she did.

They exploded together, an upsurge of volcanic proportions, her inner walls quaking with spasms as they gripped his shaft, milking him again and again.

And then they were done.

He collapsed forward on his elbows, doing his best to catch his breath while studying her face as if memorizing every inch of it.

Sierra had no ide how long they lay there like that, too weak, she was sure, to even move. Finally, he eased himself from her body, pinching the condom closed, and moved into the bathroom to dispose of it. Then he crawled into bed next to her, pulling her body against his and…

And this morning her body hummed pleasantly with intense satisfaction one got from hours of great sex, even as her face flushed with embarrassment.

Oh, my god! Oh, my god!

This is not me. I don't do things like this.

But apparently she did.

My god, I've never even met the man before. I must have been out of my mind.

She'd chalk it up to severe emotional stress combined with exhaustion and depression. Lifting the sheet and blanker covering her, she peeked at her body. *Oh, god!* Just as she suspected. She was completely naked. *Crap!* What in hell had she done?

She closed her eyes…and it all came slamming back into her.

Oh, dear sweet lord.

They'd had sex so many different ways that she was surprised they'd gotten any sleep. And why wasn't she more tired this morning?

Morning!

Holy hell, she had to get out of here. She had urgent business to take care of. Looking around the room in desperation, she saw her clothes draped over the back of a chair with her purse on the table next to it. He must have folded her clothes, because she'd ripped them off so fast last night and tossed them so that they'd looked like refugees from a windstorm. Heat crept up her entire body as she remembered her reaction to him and the things they'd done.

Where was he, the stranger who she'd fucked her brains out with?

No, not really a stranger, not after the things they'd done together. And she knew his name, right? A duffel bag sat beside the chair where her clothes lay and a laptop sat on the desk. But where was he? Then, from behind the closed bathroom door, she heard the sound of the shower running.

Good. Maybe she could get out of here before she had to face him.

Wriggling out of bed, she dragged the sheet so she was at least partially covered while she grabbed her clothes from the chair. She forced herself to check her purse before she did anything else. There was no reason to think he'd robbed her. He certainly hadn't looked like he needed money, but then, what the hell did she know? She'd spent the night having imaginative sex with a man and didn't even know his name.

She wanted to stick her head in the toilet and flush it.

Okay, money and keys still there.

Dropping the purse, she began pulling on her clothes, not paying much attention to how well she did it, just yanking them on as fast as she could. She'd worry about showering and taking care of her hair later. Right now, all she wanted was out of here.

She had just stepped into her second shoe when the door to the bathroom opened and her "date" walked out, wearing nothing but glowing skin and a towel knotted at the waist.

Kill me now, please.

"Leaving?" He cocked an eyebrow. "Ï was planning on offering you breakfast."

"What? Oh, um. No. I have to…" She hurried toward the door. "I have to leave."

"Wait. I want to buy your breakfast." He grinned. "I'd offer to shake hands but…" He gestured at the towel knotted at his waist "I want to make sure this stays in place."

She shook her head and moved toward the door again.

"I can't. Sorry."

She had business to take care of today. Jeremy's execution was a black cloud enveloping her.

"Hey, wait." Eagle started toward her.

She yanked the door open. "Gotta go."

"But I didn't even get your name! I want to buy you breakfast. Talk to you. Get your phone number."

She didn't know what to say to that so she dashed out of the room and hurried down the corridor, losing one of her shoes in her haste. She picked it up and ran, one foot unshod, to the elevator. She glanced at the room numbers and gave thanks her room was on a different floor.

She jabbed the elevator button a dozen times, silently urging it to get here fast.

"Hey!"

Don't look. Don't look.

So of course she looked. He was standing just outside the open door to his room, wearing nothing but the towel and watching her. Thank the lord the elevator arrived just then. She leaped into it, bumping into three people who looked at her as if she had the measles or had just escaped an asylum. After last night's stupidity, maybe she needed one.

The doors slid shut and she punched the button for her floor. The moment the doors opened, she leaped out and hurried down to her room. Inside, she collapsed on the bed, throwing her arm over her eyes.

What in god's name had she done?

She certainly enjoyed sex as much as the next person—at least she had until Jeremy had been arrested and her whole life had focused on his situation. But she had never been one for sex with strangers, and certainly not a stranger she'd met in a hotel lobby bar and whose name she didn't even know. What had she been thinking?

I wasn't, and that's the problem. I just wanted a little time to blot out the disaster ruling my life.

She finally managed to push herself off the bed, strip off her clothes and step into a steaming hot shower. She remembered to keep her hand out of the water so the bandage didn't get wet. And she'd have to do something about that today. The smart thing would have been to scrub her body so there was no memory of the sexy stranger with the streak in his hair. But it seemed these days she wasn't smart, because all she could think of as she lathered herself was what it would feel like if it were his hands doing this.

Just the memory of his electric touch, his ability to know just how and where to stroke her, set her hormones racing again. The pulse between her legs began to throb and her nipples ached.

Stop it!

She had to wipe this whole episode from her mind. She had important things to take care of today and thinking about Mr. Sex God wasn't one of them. She turned the shower to icy cold and stood under it until every hormone in her body ran for cover. Then she dried off and wrapped herself in the hotel robe hanging on the back of the door.

Thankful for the coffee setup in the room, she fixed herself a cup then dug into her purse for the slip of paper with the name and phone number on it. She sat at the desk, gathered her shit together and dialed the number.

"Senator Kane's office."

"Uh, yes, my name is Sierra Hunt. I was given this number by a mutual friend. He said he would call the senator ahead of time to clear the way for me."

"Oh, yes, Miss Hunt. Apparently he called the senator at home last night. She said to put you right through."

"Thank you."

Okay, one hurdle conquered.

"Hold one minute, please."

And then another voice came on the phone. "Good morning Miss Hunt. This is Senator Kane. I understand you have a problem that I might help with?"

"Yes." Sierra swallowed. "I was told to ask you about something called Galaxy and for their unlisted cell phone number. That they'd really helped you with your sister."

Silence hung thick for a moment. Was the woman just going to hang up?

"I'm going to give you the name and number of the man who helped my sister. Tell him I referred you and you want one of their flights to nowhere."

Sierra had no idea what that meant but she wrote it down. When she hung up, she'd program it into her cell. But what was so mysterious about something called Galaxy that they didn't even have an office or a listed phone number?

Oh, well, here I go.

"Yes?" The male voice barked the greeting.

Well, this didn't sound very friendly.

"Is this John 'Rocket' Hardin?"

"Who wants to know?"

"I was referred by Senator Alicia Kane. I was told I could call this number and book a flight to nowhere."

A minute later, she had an address where a plane would be waiting for her at five o'clock. In Tampa, of all places, where she and her brother lived and where the crime had taken place. Which meant she had to hustle her ass and get on a flight right now. A plane? This was the weirdest meeting she'd ever had, but if they could help Jeremy, she didn't care.

Time to get dressed and get moving.

* * * *

Vic "Eagle" Bodine closed the door to his condo and headed for his bedroom to unload his duffel. He had volunteered to stay behind at the location of Galaxy's last assignment after successfully closing it. It had been his turn to do the wrap-up with the client and that was fine, but he was glad to be home. Rather than bother Saint, their pilot, to come fetch him, he'd booked an early commercial flight back to Tampa. Now he was finally home and looking forward to a day doing nothing.

Until the phone call this morning...

"I'm passing this along to you," Rocket had said. "We just finished that case in Houston and Mallory and I are still trying to get back to normal after Santa Clarita. Plus we're arranging to get her moved here. The woman's name is Sierra Hunt.. The woman's set for a five o'clock flight to nowhere on the Gulfstream. She has directions to the hangar. Meet her. See what her story is. If it's worth taking on, then give us a call."

"What's her story? Did you get a hint of it?"

"Her brother is about to be executed in two weeks for a murder he did not commit. His lawyer has given up, the prosecutor won't talk to her and she can't get in to see the governor and plead his case herself. Eagle, she sounds desperate."

"I've heard a lot of people say they're innocent," Eagle had pointed out.

"Yeah, me, too," Rocket agreed. "But Eagle? There's something in the sound of her voice that makes me believe her."

"Okay. I'll let you know how it goes."

"Good enough. Just make sure if we take this, whatever it is we're done before the end of the month. Peyton will kill you if I have to postpone the wedding."

"No sweat." Eagle had laughed. "That would be certain death."

"Well, thanks again, man."

At four o'clock, he changed out of his jeans to what he called his client outfit — slacks and a soft-collared shirt. He considered suits and ties to be for executions and weddings. He avoided the one and dreaded the other.

Since he was driving against the flow of traffic to get to the outskirts of Tampa where they hangered the plane, he made good time getting there. The plane was already out on the tarmac. Saint's car was parked in the turnoff area as well as a silver rental sedan. He slid into line next to the sedan and headed toward the plane.

Where the hell's the client?

Saint came to the cabin entrance, saw him looking around and jerked his head toward the interior of the plane.

"She's inside. She got here about twenty minutes ago. I didn't see any sense in letting her just sit out there in her car, so I brought her in and gave her a cup of coffee."

"Well, aren't you the great host."

Saint glared at him. "Be nice. She's a messy wreck."

Eagle sighed. Weren't they all?

He locked his car and trudged up the stairway into the plane.

"She's in the seating area in the middle of the cabin." Saint inclined his head. "She's got her coffee but she's so nervous I worried she might spill it."

"Okay, thanks. I've got it from here."

The woman was looking out of the window when Eagle approached. Her thick blonde hair was pulled back in a tight ponytail and she was so nervous she practically vibrated.

"Hello," he began. "Welcome to Galaxy I'm—"

He stopped, his jaw practically hitting the floor. Sierra Hunt was so shaken she dropped her cup, spilling coffee on the floor and shattering the ceramic.

Eagle found his voice first as he stared at his hot date from the night before.

Then they both spoke at the same time.

"Eagle?"

"*You're* Sierra Hunt?"

What the fuck?

Home of Erotic Romance

Sign up for our newsletter and find out about all our romance book releases, eBook sales and promotions, sneak peeks and FREE romance books!

About the Author

A multi-published, award winning, Amazon and USA Today best-selling author, Desiree Holt has produced more than 200 titles and won many awards. She has received an EPIC E-Book Award, the Holt Medallion and many others including Author After Dark's Author of the Year. She has been featured on CBS Sunday Morning and in The Village Voice, The Daily Beast, USA Today, The Wall Street Journal, The London Daily Mail. She lives in Florida with her cats who insist they help her write her books, and is addicted to football.

Desiree loves to hear from readers. You can find her contact information, website details and author profile page at https://www.totallybound.com